CAT TRICKS?

"Hercules," I called. "C'mon, puss. Where are you?"

There was silence and then a faint "meow" from the other side of the closed door.

He was in there. Somehow he was in there. I grabbed the doorknob. Locked. I twisted the knob in frustration. Of course it was locked. The room was part of a murder investigation. And I'd just been trying to get inside. I yanked my hand away from the door like it was suddenly on fire.

Now my fingerprints were all over the door. I used the hem of my T-shirt to rub the doorknob. Then I dropped to my knees and polished the bottom section of the door where I'd looked for some kind of hidden access panel.

I caught a bit of my reflection in the brass kick panel and realized what I was doing. "You're nuts," I said aloud, sitting back on my heels.

I shouldn't have touched the door at all. I took a couple of deep breaths. I should call the police, I realized. How else was I going to get Hercules out? Then I thought, *Oh, sure, call Detective Gordon and tell him my cat just walked through the door into the room. No, that wouldn't make me look like a nutcase.*

Was that what was wrong? Was I crazy? I remembered a psych prof in first year telling the class that if you could ask the question, then you weren't. Of course, three-quarters of the time he came to class in his pajama bottoms.

Then I remembered how Owen had seemed to just materialize on Gregor Easton's head, just the way he'd suddenly seemed to appear in midleap, chasing that bird in the backyard.

I couldn't breathe. Was it possible? Did my cats have some kind of magical ability?

CURIOSITY THRILLED THE CAT

A MAGICAL CATS MYSTERY

SOFIE KELLY

AN OBSIDIAN MYSTERY

OBSIDIAN
Published by New American Library, a division of
Penguin Group (USA) Inc., 375 Hudson Street,
New York, New York 10014, USA
Penguin Group (Canada), 90 Eglinton Avenue East, Suite 700, Toronto,
Ontario M4P 2Y3, Canada (a division of Pearson Penguin Canada Inc.)
Penguin Books Ltd., 80 Strand, London WC2R 0RL, England
Penguin Ireland, 25 St. Stephen's Green, Dublin 2,
Ireland (a division of Penguin Books Ltd.)
Penguin Group (Australia), 250 Camberwell Road, Camberwell, Victoria 3124,
Australia (a division of Pearson Australia Group Pty. Ltd.)
Penguin Books India Pvt. Ltd., 11 Community Centre, Panchsheel Park,
New Delhi - 110 017, India
Penguin Group (NZ), 67 Apollo Drive, Rosedale, North Shore 0632,
New Zealand (a division of Pearson New Zealand Ltd.)
Penguin Books (South Africa) (Pty.) Ltd., 24 Sturdee Avenue,
Rosebank, Johannesburg 2196, South Africa

Penguin Books Ltd., Registered Offices:
80 Strand, London WC2R 0RL, England

First published by Obsidian, an imprint of New American Library,
a division of Penguin Group (USA) Inc.

First Printing, February 2011
10 9 8 7 6 5 4 3 2 1

ACKNOWLEDGMENTS

There are many people who have helped take the Magical Cats from an idea to a completed book, and I owe them all my thanks. Thank you to my agent, Kim Lionetti, for answering endless questions and never losing her patience, and to Jacky Sach for making everything happen. Thank you to my editor, Jessica Wade, whose editorial skills make me look good.

Thanks also go to Lorraine Bartlett, who urged me to write this story, and to Judy Gorham, Susan Evans, and Janet Koch, who have always been terrific cheerleaders.

A special thank-you to the Guppies; a more supportive group of writers doesn't exist.

And a big thank-you to Dr. Jennifer Brown, veterinarian, who answered all my questions about cats. Any errors or out-of-character cat behavior in these pages is due to my playing with the facts.

And last, thanks to Patrick and Lauren, who make it all worthwhile. Always.

1

Slant Flying

The body was smack in the middle of my freshly scrubbed kitchen floor. Fred the Funky Chicken, minus his head.

"Owen!" I said, sharply.

Nothing.

"Owen, you little fur ball, I know you did this. Where are you?"

There was a muffled "meow" from the back door. I leaned around the cupboards. Owen was sprawled on his back in front of the screen door, a neon yellow feather sticking out of his mouth. He rolled over onto his side and looked at me with the same goofy expression I used to get from stoned students coming into the BU library.

I crouched down next to the gray-and-white tabby. "Owen, you killed Fred," I said. "That's the third chicken this week."

The cat sat up slowly and stretched. He padded over to me and put one paw on my knee. Tipping his head to one side he looked up at me with his golden eyes. I sat back against the end of the cupboard. Owen climbed onto my lap and put his two front paws on my chest. The feather was still sticking out of his mouth.

I held out my right hand. "Give me Fred's head," I said. The cat looked at me unblinkingly. "C'mon, Owen. Spit it out."

He turned his head sideways and dropped what was left of Fred the Funky Chicken's head into my hand. It was a soggy lump of cotton with that lone yellow feather stuck on the end.

"You have a problem, Owen," I told the cat. "You have a monkey on your back." I dropped what was left of the toy's head onto the floor and wiped my hand on my gray yoga pants. "Or maybe I should say you have a chicken on your back."

The cat nuzzled my chin, then laid his head against my T-shirt, closed his eyes and started to purr.

I stroked the top of his head. "That's what they all say," I told him. "You're addicted, you little fur ball, and Rebecca is your dealer."

Owen just kept on purring and ignored me. Hercules came around the corner then. "Your brother is a catnip junkie," I said to the little tuxedo cat.

Hercules climbed over my legs and sniffed the remains of Fred the Funky Chicken's head. Then he looked at Owen, rumbling like a diesel engine as I scratched the side of his head. I swear there was disdain on Hercules' furry face. Stick catnip in, on or near anything and Owen squirmed with joy. Hercules, on the other hand, was indifferent.

The stocky black-and-white cat climbed onto my lap, too. He put one white paw on my shoulder and swatted at my hair.

"Behind the ear?" I asked.

"Meow," the cat said.

I took that as a yes, and tucked the strands back behind my ear. I was used to long hair, but I'd cut mine several months ago. I was still adjusting to the change in style. At least I hadn't given in to the impulse to dye my dark brown hair blond.

"Maybe I'll ask Rebecca if she has any ideas for my hair," I said. "She's supposed to be back tonight." At the sound of Rebecca's name Owen lifted his head. He'd taken to Rebecca from the first moment he'd seen her, about two weeks after I'd brought the cats home.

Both Owen and Hercules had been feral kittens. I'd found them, or more truthfully they'd found me, about a month after I'd arrived in town. I had no idea how old they were. They were affectionate with me, but wouldn't allow anyone else to come near them, let alone touch them. That hadn't stopped Rebecca, my backyard neighbor, from trying. She'd been buying both cats little catnip toys for weeks now, but all she'd done was turn Owen into a chicken-decapitating catnip junkie. She was on vacation right now, but Owen had clearly managed to unearth a chicken from a secret stash somewhere.

I stroked the top of his head again. "Go back to sleep," I said. "You're going cold turkey . . . or maybe I should say cold chicken. I'm telling Rebecca no more catnip toys for you. You're getting lazy."

Owen put his head down again, while Hercules used his to butt my free hand. "You want some attention, too?" I asked. I scratched the spot, almost at the top of his head, where the white fur around his mouth and up the bridge of his nose gave way to black. His green eyes narrowed to slits and he began to purr, as well. The rumbling was kind of like being in the service bay of a Volkswagen dealership.

I glanced up at the clock. "Okay, you two. Let me up. It's almost time for me to go and I have to take care of the dearly departed before I do."

I'd sold my car when I'd moved to Minnesota from

Boston, and because I could walk everywhere in May-ville Heights, I still hadn't bought a new one. Since I had no car, I'd spent my first few weeks in town wandering around exploring, which is how I'd stumbled on Wisteria Hill, the abandoned Henderson estate. Everett Hender-son had hired me at the library.

Owen and Hercules had peered out at me from a tumble of raspberry canes and then followed me around while I explored the overgrown English country garden behind the house. I'd seen several other full-grown cats, but they'd all disappeared as soon as I got anywhere close to them. When I left, Owen and Hercules followed me down the rutted gravel driveway. Twice I'd picked them up and carried them back to the empty house, but that didn't deter them. I looked everywhere, but I couldn't find their mother. They were so small and so determined to come with me that in the end I'd brought them home.

There were whispers around town about Wisteria Hill and the feral cats. But that didn't mean there was anything unusual about my cats. Oh no, nothing un-usual at all. It didn't matter that I'd heard rumors about strange lights and ghosts. No one had lived at the estate for quite a while, but Everett refused to sell it or do any-thing with the property. I'd heard that he'd grown up at Wisteria Hill. Maybe that was why he didn't want to change anything.

Speaking of not wanting change, Hercules was not eager to relinquish his prime spot on my lap. But after some gentle prodding, he shook himself and got off. Owen yawned a couple of times, stretched and took twice as long to move.

I got the broom and dustpan from the porch and swept up the remains of Fred the Funky Chicken.

Owen and Hercules sat in front of the refrigerator and watched. Owen made a move toward the dustpan, like he was toying with the idea of grabbing the body and making a run for it.

I glared at him. "Don't even think about it."

He sat back down, making low, grumbling meows in his throat.

I flipped open the lid of the garbage can and held the pan over the top. "Fred was a good chicken," I said solemnly. "He was a funky chicken and we'll miss him."

"Meow," Owen yowled.

I flipped what was left of the catnip toy into the garbage. "Rest in peace, Fred," I said as the lid closed.

I put the broom away, brushed the cat hair off my shirt and washed my hands. I looked in the bathroom mirror. Hercules was right. My hair did look better tucked behind my ear.

My messenger bag with a towel and canvas shoes for tai chi class was in the front closet. I set it by the door and went back through the house to make sure the cats had fresh water.

"I'm leaving," I said. But both cats had disappeared and I didn't get any answer.

I stopped to grab my keys and pick up my bag. Locking the door behind me, I headed out, down Mountain Road.

The sun was yellow-orange, low on the sky over Lake Pepin. It was a warm Minnesota evening, without the sticky humidity of Boston in late July. I shifted my bag from one shoulder to the other. I wasn't going to think about Boston. Minnesota was home now—at least for the next eighteen months or so.

The street curved in toward the center of town as I headed down the hill, and the roof of the library building came into view below. It sat on the midpoint of a curve of shoreline, protected from the water by a rock wall. The brick building had a stained-glass window that dominated one end and a copper-roofed cupola, complete with its original wrought-iron weather vane.

The Mayville Heights Free Public Library was a Carnegie library, built in 1912 with money donated by the industrialist and philanthropist Andrew Carnegie. Now it was being restored and updated to celebrate its centenary. That was why I had been in town for the last several months. And why I'd be here for the next year and a half. I was supervising the restoration—which was almost finished—as well as updating the collections, computerizing the card catalogue and setting up free Internet access for the library patrons. I was slowly learning the reading history of everyone in town. It made me feel like I knew the people a little, as well.

I paused at the bottom of the hill, looked both ways and crossed over to the same side of the street as the library.

Old Main Street followed the shore from the Stratton Theater, past the James Hotel to the marina. *Main* Street continued from the marina to the edge of town, where it merged with the highway. Having two Main Streets made getting directions very confusing if you hadn't lived in Mayville Heights very long.

The streets that ran from one end of town to the other all followed the curve of the shoreline. The cross streets mostly ran straight up and down the hill, all the way to Wild Rose Bluff. The bluff, I'd discovered, had provided much of the stone for the foundations of the gorgeous old buildings in the downtown.

For me the best part of Mayville Heights was the riverfront, with all the big elm and black walnut trees that lined the shore, and the trail that wound its way from the old warehouses at the point, past the downtown shops and businesses, all the way out beyond the marina. Mayville was still a pretty busy Mississippi River town, but it was mostly tourists coming and going now. From the porch of the James Hotel you could watch the barges and boats go by on the water the way they had a hundred years ago.

I stopped at the bottom of the library steps. Oren Kenyon had installed the new railing. The wrought-iron spindles look like fat licorice twists. The center spindle on each side seemed to split apart into a perfect oval about the size of both my hands and then reform into a twist again. The letters M, H, F, P and L, for Mayville Heights Free Public Library, were intertwined and seemed suspended in the middle of the circles.

I climbed the stairs, stepped inside and turned to look up above the entrance. A carved and pieced wooden sun, easily three feet across, hung above the wide maple trim. Above it were stenciled the words "Let there be light." It was beautiful.

Oren had brought the sun to the library last week. He was tall and lean, in his midfifties, I guessed, with sun-bleached sandy hair, like a farm-boy version of Clint Eastwood. He'd stood silently by the temporary checkout desk for who knows how long until I'd looked up.

"Could you look at something? If you have time. Please?" he'd asked.

After I'd asked him to call me Kathleen he'd stopped calling me Miss Paulson, but he hadn't started using my first name. I'd followed him out to his ancient pickup. The sun had been lying in the truck bed, braced in a frame padded with an old wool blanket and covered with a tarp. Oren pulled back the canvas and my breath caught in my chest. I reached out to touch the wood and then stopped, as I realized the significance of the carving.

I looked at Oren. "For over the entrance?" I asked.

A carving of the sun and the words "Let there be light" were over the entrance of the first Carnegie library in Scotland. I knew that, but I had been surprised Oren did. Carefully I ran my finger along one of the sun's rays. The wood was smooth and hard.

He nodded.

"Thank you," I whispered, my voice suddenly husky with the sting of tears. I'd wanted to hug Oren, but somehow I knew that would be wrong.

Looking up above the doorway I felt the prickle of tears again. Oren was quiet and gentle and wonderfully talented. Everything the library had needed done that the general contractor couldn't do, Oren had done. He'd made the new railing. He'd hand-turned trim identical to the original. He'd done the painting, carefully matching the colors to the original 1912 paint.

He never said very much, and watching him over the past several months I had the feeling that Oren had been broken somehow. He made me think of a shattered vase or cup. You carefully glue the pieces back together, so carefully that none of the cracks show. It looks beautiful again and it holds tea or water and roses from the garden, but somehow it's not quite the same. Something, somehow, is different.

I heard voices then, coming from the back of the library where the new digital card catalogue and computers were going to be located. Voices too loud for the library. Now that the major work on the building was finished we were open to the public again, but it was usually quiet in the early evening.

I walked past the new shelving units, ready for books. Susan, one of my staff members, stood with her back to me, next to the boxes of computers waiting for the new electrical outlets to be installed so they could be set up and connected.

"—do understand how frustrating this is," I heard her say in her patient-mom voice. Susan had two preschoolers at home and nothing rattled her.

"My dear, there is no conceivable way that you could fathom the depth of my frustration," the man standing opposite her said. He made a sweeping gesture with both hands. Since he was well over six feet tall the movement looked very theatrical, and maybe that was what he'd intended. "How am I supposed to work under these insufferable conditions?"

I came out from the row of bookshelves and moved to stand next to Susan. There were two pencils poking out of her Pebbles Flintstone updo. She gave a small sigh and an even smaller smile.

"Susan, is there a problem?" I asked.

"Mr. Easton was hoping to use one of our computers to send some e-mail," she said. "His BlackBerry isn't working."

Easton. Of course. Gregor Easton. The well-known composer and conductor was the guest artist for the Wild Rose Summer Music Festival at the Stratton Theater. He'd been in town practicing for about a week.

"Mr. Easton, I'm sorry," I said. "As you can see, our computer system isn't ready yet."

"Yes, I can see that," he said, making another flamboyant gesture with his arm. "And you would be?" He looked me over, taking in my plain white T-shirt, cropped yoga pants and messenger bag. I slipped the bag off my shoulder and reached up to set it on top of the metal cabinet we were using to hold most of the old card files. "I'm Kathleen Paulson," I said, offering my hand. "I'm the head librarian."

I probably didn't look like I should be in charge. I've always looked younger than my age, and my mother promised that once I was over thirty I'd be happy about that. Sometimes I was. This time I would have liked to look older and a little more imposing—hard to do when you're only five and a half feet tall with a half-grown-out pixie haircut that sticks out in all the wrong places.

Easton had to be in his early seventies, but his grip was strong and his hand was smooth and uncallused. A lot smoother than mine.

"Miss Paulson, I'm sorry to say your library is in chaos."

I couldn't help a glance around. The end wall with the stained-glass window had been reinforced and the window itself repaired and cleaned. Most of the new shelves were filled with books. The walls had been plastered and painted. The circulation desk was almost finished, and Oren's sun seemed to shine over everything. So many people had spent so many hours on this building. It looked wonderful.

I swallowed to hide my annoyance.

He continued. "According to the guidebook in my hotel suite the library is supposed to provide Internet service."

"I apologize for that," I said. "The guide arrived early and our computers arrived late."

"But your computers are here now," he said. "Why couldn't one of them be connected?"

Connected? To what? Did he really expect us to unpack one of the computers right now and magically get it up and running so he could check his schedule?

Susan and I exchanged looks. Her mouth was a

straight, serious line, but the eyes behind her glasses were laughing.

Easton gave me a practiced celebrity-greeting-the-little-people smile. Unpack one of those computers just for him? *When pigs fly,* I thought.

Unfortunately, it wasn't a pig that suddenly launched itself onto the conductor's head. It was a cat.

My cat. Owen.

2

Carry Tiger to Mountain

For a moment Owen perched on top of Easton's head, tail twitching, like some sort of kitty Davy Crockett hat. Before any of us could move, he leaped over to the top of one of the bookshelves, shook himself and gave us a wide-eyed stare. What was he doing at the library? How the heck had he gotten into my bag with my noticing?

Easton bellowed a word I'd heard before but never in a library, and swiped at his head. "Miss Paulson, your library is infested by vermin! I have been attacked by a rodent!"

"That's not a rodent. That's a cat," Susan pointed out, oh, so not helpfully.

"Mr. Easton, I'm so sorry," I began. I wasn't sure whether to check his head for claw marks or rescue Owen from the shelf and stash him in my office.

"A cat?" Easton roared. He glared at Owen. "No wonder this building has vermin. If you believe that mangy, unkempt creature is capable of controlling an infestation of rodents, well, look at that—that thing!" He jabbed his finger in Owen's direction.

Big mistake. Owen let out a loud yowl of indignation.

He hissed at Easton and spat for good measure. Then he jumped to the floor, flicked his tail at the conductor—what I guessed was the kitty version of giving the finger—and stalked away. I needed to get him back in the bag and into my office as quickly as possible, but first I needed to deal with Gregor Easton.

I glanced at Susan, who wouldn't meet my look. Her lips were twitching. *Oh, Susan, please don't laugh,* I thought. It was going to take a lot to soothe Easton's ruffled feathers without Susan giggling and making things worse. His face was an alarming shade of red and his thick hair was standing on end. I couldn't see any scratches, so I hoped that meant Owen had kept his claws sheathed.

"Miss Paulson!" Easton's voice boomed around the small space. "This library is woefully inadequate. Your service is simply not acceptable. There is no Internet connection, despite its being promised. And your selection of major newspapers is lamentable."

Our newspaper selection? Where had that come from?

He continued. "And you have a vermin problem that you have tried—unsuccessfully, I must point out—to conceal by bringing in an obviously inbred alley cat, which probably spends most of its time rutting with the town population of female felines."

I took a deep breath. Owen didn't spend his time chasing female cats. He spent most of his time chasing the birds in the backyard and chewing the head off Fred the Funky Chicken. Information I probably shouldn't share with Easton. I thought of what my mother's advice would be in this situation: "Act it, darling. Act it."

I stepped forward. "Mr. Easton, you have my profound apologies." He wasn't the only one who could sound pretentious. "Owen is my cat and he must have climbed into my bag before I left the house. I had no idea. I assure you he wasn't chasing anything. We don't have a vermin problem here at the library." Well, not anymore, we didn't.

I looked past Easton's shoulder. There was a blur of movement over by the windows. *Please let that be Owen,* I prayed silently. Behind me Susan made a sputtering sound like someone trying to siphon gas from a car. So she'd seen it, too.

The conductor let out an exasperated breath. "Be that as it may, Miss Paulson, in the short time I have been at your library I've been denied basic service and attacked by an out-of-control animal. This was not what I was expecting when I agreed to rearrange my schedule and step in to help your little music festival at the eleventh hour." He smoothed a hand back over his hair, but one clump continued to stand at attention.

He really was a condescending old goat. An old goat I needed to placate. "And the entire town is grateful that you agreed to step in at the last minute," I said. Just saying the words made my teeth hurt. I took a step backward, lowering my heel slowly onto the toe of Susan's right shoe, easing some of my weight down as a warning to her not to say anything, and especially not to laugh at my blatant sucking up. "Again, Mr. Easton, I'm so sorry for what's happened here." Susan wiggled her shoe under my foot. I pressed down a little harder. "Please allow me to send breakfast to your suite in the morning to make amends for this evening."

He twisted a gold pinkie ring around his finger. The upright piece of hair bobbed at me. I kept the pressure on Susan's foot. "Please, Mr. Easton. It's the least I can do." Well, that part was honest.

"Very well, Miss Paulson," he said, "but it doesn't excuse what happened here."

"No, it doesn't," I said, trying not to look at his hair, which seemed to have a life of its own now and was waving merrily at me.

I moved forward again and took Easton's hand, sandwiching it between mine. "Thank you for your understanding." I walked him toward the entrance as I talked.

He paused at the doors. "Miss Paulson, most people would make an issue of this. I, however, am not most people."

"I appreciate your graciousness," I said, smiling sweetly at him.

He pushed through the doors and disappeared down the stairs.

I sagged against the wall. I hated this kind of thing, charming and flattering people to defuse their anger.

"'I appreciate your graciousness?'" Susan laughed behind me. "I'm going to use that on the preschool teacher the next time the twins glue themselves to the top of the monkey bars."

"Okay," I said. "Easton may be a bit of a pompous . . ." I hesitated.

"Windbag? Twit? Horse's rear?" Susan asked.

"Person," I said. "But he is right about the computer room. It should be ready by now." I straightened and walked to the back of the library. "And he didn't deserve to have my cat pounce on him. Where is that fur ball, by the way?"

"Did you see the man's hair?" Susan asked. "It was like a little flag up there, waving in the breeze."

I rubbed the space between my eyebrows with the heel of my hand. "That reminds me. Would you call Eric and ask him to send breakfast to Easton's room tomorrow?" Susan's husband, Eric, owned Eric's Place, a café near the marina. He used local fruits and vegetables, and made everything in the café's kitchen. "Ask him to send the bill to me, please. Not the library board. And could you ask him to make it . . ." I waved my hands in the air. "Make it elegant, please."

"Will do," Susan said. "Why did you bring the cat with you, anyway? Were you going to ask me to babysit—I mean cat sit?"

"No," I said. "I didn't bring him on purpose. He just somehow snuck into my bag. I don't know how," I finished lamely.

"Owen? Where are you?" I called, walking back to the computer area. I looked behind a stack of boxes. A low *murp* came from the wall of windows. I pushed my way around a stack of chairs. Owen sat on the window ledge, seemingly looking out at a sailboat passing on the lake. He was chewing something. I looked around for a head or a corpse of some ill-fated rodent, but found nothing. I wasn't sure if that was good or bad.

"You are in so much trouble," I told the cat as I picked him up. He gave my chin a gentle head butt, his way of pointing out to both of us that he really wasn't in that deep. "Do you realize who that was?"

Owen yawned.

"I think he does," Susan said. "Hey! I have half a tuna sandwich left. Would he like it?"

Owen's ears twitched at the word "tuna."

"Are you sure you don't mind?" I said. "Maybe he'd stay in my office if he had something to eat, and I could still get to tai chi."

I carried Owen upstairs, and Susan got the leftover sandwich from the refrigerator up in the staff room. Inside my office, with the door firmly closed, she unwrapped the waxed paper and set the half sandwich on the floor behind my desk. Owen sniffed the bread, then carefully licked the filling. His back end did a little wiggly dance of joy. "Thanks," I said to Susan.

"Oh, that's okay," she said. "I like cats." She watched Owen hold the bread with a paw so he could lick out more of the tuna filling. "I thought your cats didn't let anyone but you touch them. So how come this one jumped on the maestro?"

"They don't," I said. "But I don't think Owen meant to land on Mr. Easton's head. I think maybe he was startled. He jumped and he just miscalculated." I grinned at her. "Or, heck, maybe from his vantage point on the top of the cabinet, Easton's head looked like the back end of a squirrel."

Susan snickered. "You know, I didn't even notice the cat," she said. "Suddenly there he was on the maestro's head. It was almost like one second he was invisible and the next he wasn't."

I felt my face getting warm. Before Susan could notice, the phone began to ring down at the circulation desk.

"I'll get that," she said.

I dropped into my desk chair as the door closed behind her. "Saved by the bell," I said to Owen, who had managed to pull the bread apart so he could get at the rest of the tuna, pickle, and mayonnaise. My cheeks were burning. Because the thing was, for a moment, just a moment, I thought Owen *had* been invisible.

Which wasn't possible.

I leaned down closer to him. "You have to stop doing whatever it is you're doing," I said. "Someone's going to see you. Or not see you."

The cat didn't even waste the energy it would have

taken to look up at me. I wondered what Susan would
have said if I'd told her I thought maybe the cat actually
had vanished for a moment. Probably looked to see if I
was lining the inside of my sun hat with aluminum foil.

Okay, so, here was the thing: This wasn't the first time
I'd thought I'd seen the cat disappear. The first time had
been about six weeks ago. I'd been in the swing in the
backyard. Owen had been at my feet, watching the birds.
And then he wasn't. I'd looked for him, certain he'd
darted away to stalk some unsuspecting robin. Then
he'd appeared again, about ten feet away and in midair,
in midleap over a tiny black-and-yellow finch.

"Owen!" I'd shrieked. Startled, the finch had flown
away, I'd fallen out of the swing and the cat landed on
the grass, legs splayed, looking very undignified. He'd
shaken himself and come across the lawn, making
pissed-off cat sounds in his throat.

I'd gotten in the swing again and he'd jumped up beside
me. We'd swayed slowly back and forth and I'd decided I
hadn't really seen him disappear and then reappear. The
sun had been in my eyes. My mind had been wandering.

Okay, I didn't drink. And this was not one of the signs
of a stroke they'd been talking about during the commercial breaks of *Gotta Dance* last night on TV. Was I having a breakdown or maybe a very freaky hallucination?

"Owen, do that again," I'd said. He'd stared at me.
"C'mon. Disappear." I had slid my hand up and down in
front of my face. I'm not sure what I had been expecting; maybe some sort of slow fade-out, the way Alice's
Cheshire Cat had disappeared in Wonderland, until only
its smile was left. The cat had looked at me like I'd lost
my mind. And then he'd disappeared.

Of course, he'd only disappeared behind the red
chokeberry bush.

Cats could not become invisible. It was that simple. Right? Right. Still, I'd been watching him since then. Afraid—or excited?—that something unusual would happen again, no matter how often I told myself what I'd seen was impossible.

Owen had finished eating his tuna and was licking the waxed paper. So I thought I'd seen him disappear again. (So much for those multivitamins.) I was still tired and stressed and there were still problems with the work on the library. So what if once in a while my eyes played tricks on me and it seemed like my cat could make himself invisible? Back in Boston there had been a very nice man on the bus with an invisible friend.

I could still make class if I left right now, I realized. "Okay, you," I said. "I'm going to tai chi and I'm going to lock you in. Stay here." The cat started chewing at something stuck to his paw. "No yowling at the door. No disappearing and no jumping on people's heads. I'll be back in an hour."

I got Owen a dish of water from the staff room and locked the office door. "I'm going to tai chi," I told Susan as I passed the desk. "Owen's in my office. Please, *please* don't let him out."

"Okay," Susan said. "See you later."

It was Rebecca who had originally invited me to come to tai chi. In the few months I'd been in town I'd spent almost all of my time at the library. I'd decided to try the class because I was afraid I was going to turn into one of those crazy cat ladies who spent her evenings watching TV with her kitties and acted like they were people. Okay, so technically I was already doing that.

Classes were on the second floor of the artists' co-op building, downtown across from the river walk. The main floor of the co-op was a craft store. On the second floor were two rooms used for yoga, meditation and tai chi.

Maggie, the instructor, was a mixed-media artist and potter—jugs, mugs and vases all shaped like zaftig naked women. Maggie herself was tall and slender, with green cat eyes and close-cropped blond hair. We've been friends since the evening I arrived early for class and found her online at the *Gotta Dance* Web site, voting for Matt Lauer.

The class was just beginning the warm-up. I changed my shoes and took my place in the circle next to Rebecca. She wore a sea-green scarf with her white T-shirt. The color looked good with her silver hair and fair skin. "Welcome home," I whispered. Rebecca, who had retired from hairdressing a couple of years ago, had been out of town for the last week. I'd been taking in her mail and watering the plants. Knowing her, she'd probably gotten Owen another Fred the Funky Chicken.

"Thank you," she whispered back.

"Kathleen, bend your knees," Maggie called.

I blew my bangs out of my eyes and bent my knees a little more. Across the circle Violet smiled at me. Her form always looked so smooth and fluid. Like Rebecca she was in her midsixties. She was tall and slim and the only time she didn't wear heels was in class.

Next to me Roma Davidson was already starting to sweat. I envied her dark hair cut in a smooth bob that never seemed to fall in her face. She gave me a sly smile and mouthed, *Bend your knees* just as Maggie said it again. Roma was the only vet in Mayville Heights. It struck me that I should ask her about Owen's catnip addiction, just to be sure he wasn't going to turn into a little kitty junkie. As far as his hypothetically invisible antics, I'd keep those to myself.

By the time class was over Maggie had told me to bend my knees at least half a dozen times. I was more awkward than usual and my hair kept flopping in my face. At one point Maggie had passed behind me and touched the back of my head with two fingers. "Empty your mind, Kath," she'd whispered.

Easy for her to say. If I emptied my mind where was I going to put everything?

We always ended with the complete form. Only Maggie and Ruby can do all 108 movements. One by one the rest of us moved to the side to watch them. When they were finished Maggie gave a slight bow and said, "See you all on Thursday. Practice."

Ruby stretched both arms out to her sides. She painted huge abstracts and she was the most flexible person I've ever seen. She had more piercings than anyone I've ever seen, either.

Ruby always had a couple of historical romances among her books on organic gardening and back issues of *Mother Earth News*. A woman of eclectic interests. She was also in the festival choir. "How's practice for the final concert going?" I asked.

"Okay, considering the world-famous conductor is a creepy old perv," she said. She stretched her arms up over her head, then bent forward and put both hands on the floor. "And he's not that great a conductor," she added, turning her head sideways to look at me. "I've had twelve years of voice and I know the difference between an okay conductor and one who can really feel the music." She walked her hands out away from her feet, the tips of her spiky hair just brushing the floor. It was blue this week.

I couldn't help thinking that if I were in that position it would sound a lot like someone deboning a turkey.

"And worst of all, he's a feelie."

"A what?" I said, pulling at the neck of my T-shirt. I was sweating.

"A feelie. You know, he has to put his hands on your shoulders to fix your posture. He has to put his hands on your diaphragm to check your breathing. A feelie." Ruby laughed, which sounded more like a snort because she was upside down. "I had to put my elbow in his diaphragm a couple of times. To check *his* breathing, of course." She began walking her hands back to her feet again. "If I were Ami Lester . . . boy."

Ami Lester? Right. A pretty strawberry blonde who'd borrowed all of Diana Gabaldon's books from the library. She was one of the summer interns at the Stratton. "What do you mean?" I asked.

"Ami has two solos," Ruby said. She pulled her head in against her tanned legs, and her voice was slightly muffled. "Easton likes her. I don't mean holy-crap-can-she-sing likes her. And yeah, she can. I mean, he's-a-dirty-old-man likes her."

She slowly unrolled so she was standing up again. "I told her if it were me, he wouldn't be a baritone anymore. He'd be singing soprano." She grinned, shrugged and then walked over to the table in the corner where Maggie kept the cups and tea.

There was a noise at the door. Rebecca was standing there. She bent to pick up the shoe she'd dropped. I walked over to her. She watched Ruby choose a mug and take a chamomile tea bag from the box before she turned to me. She looked tired.

"Thanks for taking care of the house for me, Kathleen," she said.

"Anytime." I pushed my hair back and sighed in frustration. Why had I cut it? Oh, right. Because I'd changed; new place, new job, new life, so new hair.

Rebecca reached over and ran her fingers through my straggly layers, lifting the hair and letting it drop. Her hand trembled a little and her scarf brushed my cheek. "You have lovely hair, dear," she said. "It's grown down over your ears now, which is the hardest part. Come over this weekend and I'll shape it up a little."

I smiled. "Thank you. I will." She went out to the bench to change her shoes.

Maggie walked over to me, carrying a mug of tea. "Matt's ahead in the voting," she said with a grin.

"There's no way you can know that," I told her.

"He is going to win the coveted crystal-globe statue," she said.

"Never going to happen."

"I suppose you think that would-be superhero in a loincloth is going to win," Maggie said.

"*Mr.* Kevin Sorbo is not a would-be superhero. He was the very yummy Hercules, and he can dance Matt Lauer under the table."

She just rolled her eyes and shook her head at me.

"I have to get back to the library," I said. I looked around and lowered my voice. "Owen's in my office."

"Was today Bring Your Cat to Work Day?" Maggie said. "I thought that was next week."

"Very funny," I said. "He climbed into my bag. I didn't know until we got to the library and he jumped out."

"Not on the checkout desk, I hope."

I tugged at the hem of my T-shirt. "No," I said. "That would have been all right. He jumped onto someone's head."

She really did try not to laugh. "Owen jumped onto someone's head. I wish I'd been there."

"No, you don't. The someone was Gregor Easton."

Maggie almost choked on her tea. "You're kidding." Then she saw my face. "You're not kidding."

I shook my head. "I'm sending breakfast over to his suite. I hope that's enough."

"Poor Owen," Maggie said. "He's probably traumatized."

"I'm traumatized," I said. "I better go. I'll see you tomorrow night." I started down the stairs, then stopped half a dozen steps down and turned back to Maggie. "Veggie sticks or brownies?" I asked.

"Brownies," she said.

Of course.

"And don't try to sneak any pureed prunes in these, either," she called after me.

I walked back to the library as fast my achy legs could move. Susan was at the desk. "How's everything?" I asked.

"Not a meow out of anyone," she said with a grin.

I hurried upstairs and unlocked the office door, wondering what I was going to find. Owen was sitting on my desk chair. "Hey, fur ball," I said. "I didn't figure you'd stay on the floor."

I opened my bag and pulled out my shoes. "C'mon," I said, offering him the empty case. Owen jumped onto the desk and walked across to peer inside. He looked up at me as if to say, *What—you expect me to get in there?*

"You came down here that way and that's how you're going home." I gave his backside a gentle nudge. He meowed what I was fairly sure was a swear word in cat and climbed in. I left the zipper partway open.

It was almost dark by the time we'd walked up the hill to the house. Now that it was August I could see the days getting shorter. I turned on the lamp in the living room and let Owen out of the bag. He glanced at me, shook himself and sauntered in to the kitchen. I sat on the edge of the black leather chair and picked up the phone. I knew the number for Will Redfern, the contractor on the library renovation, by heart. The call went to voice mail. Calls to Will always went to voice mail. I couldn't decide if the man was avoiding me or the job, or if he was just a totally disorganized person. I left my name and number and wondered what excuse he'd use for not getting back to me. He'd already used Dead Grandmother twice.

Hercules twisted around my legs. I picked him up and went out to the kitchen. "Do you know what your brother did?" I asked him. Herc tipped his head to one side and looked at me quizzically. I told him what had happened with Owen, and he made sympathetic meows every time I paused.

I put him down on the floor and he watched while I poured a glass of milk and made toast with peanut butter. Then I sat at the table, feeding bits to Hercules and Owen, who had appeared the second the toaster popped.

"I need that computer room set up," I told them. "If the rest of the carrels and the chairs were put together I could at least unpack one computer and get it up and running." I broke off another couple of bites of toast, one for Owen, who immediately dropped it on the floor, and one for Hercules, who licked off the peanut butter while I held the bread.

"Redfern's not going to call me back, is he? He'll say a raccoon stole his phone or his tools fell off the back of his truck." I slumped in my chair. "Should I call Everett?" Everett Henderson had hired me to supervise the library renovation. He was financing the entire project. His gift to the town for the library's centennial.

"Merow!" Owen didn't even stop chewing.

"You're right," I said. "I'm supposed to deal with this kind of thing, not Everett."

Hercules pulled the soggy bit of toast he'd been licking from my fingers and dropped it on the floor. Owen looked at him, whiskers twitching. Herc nudged the bread toward his brother, then went around the table and sat in front of the refrigerator.

"What? You don't like peanut butter anymore?" I asked.

"Merow!" Owen yowled, louder than the last time, again without even bothering to stop eating.

Hercules looked over his shoulder at the other cat. Why did I have the feeling they were talking about me?

Then suddenly Herc jumped, swiping his paw at the *Gotta Dance* magnet on the refrigerator door. The magnet went skittering across the tile in one direction and the scrap of paper it had been holding floated to the floor at my feet.

"Hercules!" I shouted. "What did you do that for?" The paper had Oren's address. I bent to pick it up.

Oren. Of course.

"Oren could get everything put together," I said. I swear I saw the cats exchange a look. I'd started talking to them just to have someone to talk to, but pretty quickly I'd realized that they seemed to be listening. Not that I told anyone that. "He's working on the stage setup at the Stratton. He'll be there early in the morning. You know Oren."

Herc looked up at me. "Is that what you were trying to tell me?" I said. He had a dab of peanut butter on the end of his nose. I reached down to wipe it off. He batted my finger away with a paw.

"That's what I'll do," I said. "I'll go see Oren first thing. And I think I'll take him some of those banana muffins."

The toast was gone. Owen yawned and so did I. Hercules began to wash his face. Nine thirty on a Tuesday night and here I was, sitting with my cats, ready to go to bed. I definitely was the crazy cat lady.

Owen woke me up at quarter to six the next morning, just before the alarm went off. He put one paw on the edge of the mattress and his face about an inch away from mine. He had a very bad case of morning breath. I wondered if Listerine made a version for cats.

By six thirty I was on my way to the Stratton with four banana muffins in a brown paper bag. I didn't see Oren's truck in the staff parking lot at the back of the building. Maybe he was in the main lot on the other side. I tried the stage door. It was unlocked. I stepped inside and followed the hall to the side stage entrance. Something was spilled on the wooden floor. Paint, maybe?

"Oren!" I called. "Are you here?" I pushed through the heavy red curtains and came out onto the stage proper. There was a tiny charm on the floor in front of me, a musical note hanging from a circle of silver. I picked it up and caught sight of someone at the piano, upstage. "Oren, are you all right?" I called again. "It's Kathleen."

I crossed the stage to the piano. The person slumped over the keyboard wasn't Oren. It was Gregor Easton. And he wasn't okay.

He was dead.

3

Grasp Bird's Tail

I've seen a lot of stage bodies. From a distance makeup and fake blood can be pretty convincing, but up close it's impossible to hide the fact that Colonel Mustard, who was hit with a candlestick in the library, is really a living, breathing person.

Gregor Easton wasn't living or breathing. His skin had a waxy paleness and there was a gash on the side of his head, an ugly red-and-purple wound that stood out in stark relief almost as though it had been painted on by some makeup artist. But there was no blood. I touched his wrist to feel for a pulse and jerked my hand away. His arm was stiff and cool.

My hands shook as I fumbled for my cell phone. Then it hit me that I was in an empty theater with a body at quarter to seven in the morning. I backed across the stage, felt for the opening in the curtain and all but ran down the corridor. Outside I sat on the step and called 911.

The paramedics arrived first—a man and a woman. Him I didn't know, but I'd seen her at the library. Jane. No, Jaime—Sandra Boynton board books, and several on potty training.

"He's at the piano onstage," I told them. "Go down the hall and through the curtain."

A police car arrived next, lights flashing. The officer got out of the car and walked over to me. "Ms. Paulson?" he asked.

"Yes."

"You reported finding a body?"

"Inside. At the piano onstage." I said, pointing. "The paramedics are in there."

"Ma'am, what are you doing here?" he asked. "Are you involved with the festival?"

I explained that I was looking for Oren. A car and an SUV pulled into the small lot, followed by a police van. The woman in the car and the man driving the truck had to be police officers, I decided as they got out of their vehicles. They were both dressed in cop shoes—sturdy, heavy-soled black footwear. My father always said shoes are the key to a character. "Nail the footwear and you'll nail the man."

The woman had gotten out of her car, holding a stainless steel coffee mug. She took a couple of mouthfuls and bent to set it back in the car. The man said something to her and grinned. She made a face at him and took one more drink.

The patrol officer walked over to them.

There was a wood and wrought-iron bench at the end of the parking lot. I sat down and waited. No one had told me not to leave, but I figured I shouldn't until someone told me I could. I couldn't hear what the three police officers were saying, but at one point they all turned and looked at me. I tried to look innocent and not mess with my hair.

I was still holding the bag of muffins. What was I going to do with them? And where was Oren? Along with the work he was doing at the library, the festival committee had hired him to paint and make some repairs at the theater. He was always on the job by seven.

The male paramedic came out the stage door, pulling off a pair of purple disposable gloves. He stopped to talk to the three officers. The two new ones had gloves of their own in their pockets. They pulled them on and went inside. More police vehicles pulled into the lot.

I probably sat on the bench for another ten minutes or so before the officer who had driven the SUV came out of the theater. He walked over to me, pulling off his gloves. He was tall, with dark wavy hair about two weeks overdue for a trim. He had the tanned skin of someone who was outside a lot, which was probably why I'd never seen him in the library.

"Ms. Paulson?" he said.

"Yes." I stood up.

"I'm Detective Gordon. You found the body?"

I nodded and tried not to shiver. It was cloudy and not as warm as it had been the past few days.

"What were you doing here so early?"

"I was looking for Oren Kenyon," I said. All of a sudden I felt embarrassed, clutching my paper bag of muffins. "He's been doing some of the renovation work at the library. I'm the head librarian and I needed to talk to him."

"This early?" he asked.

What did he mean by "this early?" It wasn't as though I'd wandered down in my nightgown and slippers before the sun was up. "Oren starts work by seven at the latest. I wanted to talk to him before he got involved in something here." Did he nod, ever so slightly?

"What's in the bag?"

"Muffins." I handed the detective the bag so he could see for himself. He unrolled the top and looked inside. Then he looked at me again.

"Ms. Paulson, were you and Mr. Easton involved? Were you two meeting here at the theater?"

"Involved?" I said, and my voice actually squeaked, I was so surprised. "No. I told you, I came here looking for Oren."

Detective Gordon looked around the small parking lot. "Was his truck here?"

I pulled my hand back through my hair, which probably only made it messier. "Well, no. But I thought maybe he was parked on the other side. The door was unlocked so I went in to see if he was working."

Why wasn't he writing any of this down? I looked at his hands. They were twice the size of mine and callused. He did more than not write down what people told him. No wonder I'd never seen him in the library. "I saw someone at the piano," I told him. "I thought it might be Oren. I went over and realized it was Mr. Easton."

"So you did know him?" the detective said.

I shook my head. "I only met him last night. He came into the library looking to use a computer. But the computer room wasn't ready. That's why I was looking for Oren this morning."

The detective stared intently at me. Did he think maybe I'd break and admit that I'd been having a torrid affair with Gregor Easton and that he'd died while we were having wild monkey sex on the piano?

"When I realized he was dead, I came back outside and called nine-one-one," I said.

He glanced back at the theater. "Did you touch anything?" he asked. He'd missed a tiny patch of stubble on the left side of his jawline when he'd shaved.

I thought for a moment. "The stage door," I said. "The curtain. And I touched Mr. Easton's arm."

"That's it?"

"I think so," I said. The silver charm was in my pocket. I pulled it out and handed it to him. "I almost stepped on this," I said. "And there was something spilled on the floor in the hallway. I think I may have gotten it on my shoes."

I grabbed the back of the bench and held up my right foot. He leaned over to look at the sole of my shoe.

"I'm going to need your shoes, Ms. Paulson."

I put my foot down carefully. "I have a pair at my office at the library. May I go get them?"

"I'm also going to need your fingerprints," he said. "Officer Craig will take you to your office and then he'll take you to the station to be fingerprinted—if that's all right with you?"

It was the kind of question you didn't say no to. So I didn't.

Officer Craig was the patrolman. He looked to be about twenty, with his close-cropped boot-camp haircut. He drove to the library and stayed with me while I got my tai chi shoes from my office. He took a bag out of his trunk, sealed my running shoes inside and actually gave me a receipt for them. Then we drove to the police station, where I had my fingerprints taken.

Officer Craig drove me back to the library. I went into the staff room and put on a pot of coffee. Even though I'd already washed my hands with some sort of industrial-strength Day-Glo orange cleaner at the police station, I washed them again.

I was worried about Oren. He didn't have a cell

phone. If something had happened to him . . . I'd just poured a cup of coffee when I heard a tapping on the main doors. I could see Detective Gordon through the glass. I unlatched the metal gate and unlocked the door.

"Ms. Paulson, I'm sorry to bother you," he said. "I have a few more questions."

I opened the door wider. "Come in," I said. Maybe I could get him to look for Oren. I locked the door behind him but left the gate open.

"You don't have an alarm system?" he asked, eyeing the metal barricade with its spiderweb design. The gates were almost as old as the building.

I smiled. "No. Up till now the only thing in this building has been books. It's not like someone was going to break in to read."

He smiled at that. He had a nice smile, with even white teeth and a strong jawline.

"We can talk in the staff room," I said, leading the way up to the second level.

My coffee cup was on the table. I saw him look at it.

"Detective Gordon, would you like a cup of coffee?" I asked. "I just made it."

"Thank you. I would," he said. "Black with two sugars, if you have it."

I did. I handed him a steaming mug. He wrapped both hands around it and drank, then looked at me. "It's good. Thanks."

I remembered the muffins then. I'd carried them around for a while, but they were wrapped in wax paper inside the bag and they hadn't been dropped or sat on. The bag was by the sink. I put two muffins on a plate and set it and a napkin in front of him.

My palms were sweaty. I wiped them on my capris

and sat down opposite the detective. This time he pulled out a small notebook and a pen.

"Ms. Paulson, you said you were looking for Oren Kenyon this morning. Did you have an appointment?"

"No. But as I told you at the theater, I know he starts work early and I wanted to talk to him."

"What about?"

"The computer room here at the library. The contractor is behind schedule. I was hoping Oren could get some of the chairs and carrels put together so I could at least get one computer set up and connected." It didn't seem like a good idea to tell him my cats had suggested it.

He scribbled something on his pad.

"Did Oren show up?" I asked.

"I'm not sure," Detective Gordon said. He put down his pen and took one of the muffins from the plate. "Ms. Paulson, you said you met Mr. Easton for the first time yesterday?" He broke the muffin in half and took a bite.

I nodded. "He came in to the library. There was something wrong with his BlackBerry and he needed Internet access."

"But your computer room isn't set up."

"No, it's not." I traced the inside of the mug handle with my finger. "But according to the visitors' guide Mr. Easton had, it was."

The detective broke the remaining half of muffin into three pieces and immediately ate one piece. "How did Mr. Easton react?"

"He wasn't happy."

He leaned back in his chair and tented his fingers. Not only were his hands large, but he also had long fingers, what my mother would call piano-player fingers.

"So you didn't arrange to meet Mr. Easton this morning?"

I let out a frustrated breath. "No. I didn't arrange to meet Mr. Easton. I wasn't having an affair with Mr. Easton. He was older than my father. Before last night I'd never even met the man." Before he could say anything I held up my hand. "I did order breakfast to be sent to his suite this morning—from Eric's Place—as an apology. Breakfast for one." I wondered if it was too late to call Eric and cancel.

"Do you buy breakfast for everyone who comes in to the library, looking for an Internet connection?"

I resisted the impulse to point out that I was basically giving *him* breakfast right now. "Of course I don't," I said. I took a sip of coffee. It was cold. I got up and moved behind him to get to the coffeemaker, poured another cup and leaned against the counter. How was I going to explain this?

He turned to look at me.

"My, uh, cat had accidentally ended up here at the library yesterday. And . . . he—the cat—jumped on Mr. Easton . . . Mr. Easton's head."

The detective's lips twitched. "His head?"

I nodded. He looked at me without saying anything. I felt myself flush.

He drained his cup and stood up. "Ms. Paulson, do you mind if I look around?"

I wondered what he thought he'd find. "It's a public building, Detective," I said, setting my own mug on the counter. "You don't need my permission to look around. But it's all right with me."

I smiled to show I was a good sport; then I led him across to my office and stood in the doorway while he poked around. After that, I took him to the main part of the library. He walked through the stacks and around the magazine shelves without saying anything. I showed him the temporary circulation desk and the area where the permanent desk would be.

"Where is the computer area?" he asked.

I took him to the back section of the library. The sky was gray and cloudy outside the bank of windows.

He pointed to the stacks of cartons. "What's in the boxes?"

"Computers, monitors, a printer. Would you like me to open one?" I asked.

He shook his head and bent to look at a couple of shrink-wrapped chairs. "That's not necessary," he said. He straightened, looked around and then gestured across the library. "What's over there?" I had to walk around a couple of shelving units to see where he was pointing. A huge sheet of plastic was draped over one corner of the wall.

"Oh, that's where the meeting room will be," I said. "Right now it's where the contractor is keeping his tools and things."

"Can I see it?"

"Sure." I led the way and pulled the plastic aside. Since the library was locked at night, the door wasn't even closed.

We both saw the splotches at the same time, dark blotches on the brown paper protecting the tile floor.

My mouth went dry. "Is that dried blood?" I said, taking a step forward.

The detective's arm shot out, stopping me from going any farther into the room. "Wait outside please, Ms. Paulson," he said, pulling another pair of disposable gloves from his pocket.

I moved back to the edge of the plastic. "Is that blood?" I asked again.

"Outside, Ms. Paulson," he snapped, pulling on a glove. "Please wait outside the building."

The detective bent forward and picked something up as I stepped back and let the plastic drop. That was blood on the floor. What was it doing in my library?

4

Repulse Monkey

Blood in the library and Gregor Easton's body at the Stratton. It wasn't a coincidence. I wanted it to be, but it wasn't.

I could see Detective Gordon's blurry shape moving on the other side of the heavy plastic. Any minute now he was going to come out and tell me again that I had to leave the building. I hurried up to my office and collected my bag, sweater and laptop, because it seemed pretty clear I wouldn't be getting any work done there, and locked the door.

I headed for the front entrance. The sky had darkened and spits of rain hit the glass. Now what? I didn't want to walk home in the rain. I had an umbrella in my office. Then I remembered. No, I didn't. I'd used it the last time I'd been caught at the library in the rain.

I stood in the entryway and looked through the wavy glass in the old wooden doors. The wind was pushing heavy gray clouds across the sky. It was probably only going to be a shower. I could wait here, out of Detective Gordon's way, until the rain stopped, and then go.

I heard the murmur of his voice then. I leaned sideways, just far enough to look through the ironwork gate.

He was standing by the temporary circulation desk, back to me, talking on his cell phone. His voice seemed to bounce off the library's high ceiling all the way across to where I was standing.

I couldn't help hearing what he was saying. Well, maybe I could have, but I would have had to stuff my fingers in my ears and start humming the "Battle Hymn of the Republic" to do it, and I was trying to stay unobtrusive. After all, Detective Gordon had asked me to leave the building and he already seemed to think I was mixed up in all of this. It was better if I just waited quietly until the rain stopped, and then left.

". . . found the primary crime scene," I heard him say into his phone. He listened. "No. Now would be better . . . Fine." He snapped his cell shut, and I stepped back out of his line of sight.

Which didn't do me any good, because instead of going back to his "primary crime scene" he walked across to the entrance. I stood to one side of the heavy doors and tried to look as though I wasn't doing anything wrong. Which, really, I wasn't.

"Ms. Paulson, why are you still here?" he said.

I gestured at the glass. "It's raining."

"I see that. You can't make it from here to the parking lot?"

"I don't have a car." And this was the first time I'd regretted that since I'd arrived in Mayville. "I don't have an umbrella, either," I added.

Just then a young man came dashing across the grass, holding a giant golf umbrella—alternating red, green, and blue sections—and a large black case. Detective Gordon unlocked the door for him. The man shook his umbrella, stepped inside and handed it to the detective, who immediately handed it to me.

"Now you have an umbrella," he said.

It looked like a circus umbrella, or, more accurately, like a circus tent. There was a logo for spiced Jamaican rum on one panel. The other police officer opened his mouth, looked from me to Detective Gordon and closed it again. "I'll make sure you get this back," I told him. I pulled my key ring out of my pocket and unsnapped the library keys from the rest. "Silver one is for this door," I said, holding them out to the detective. "Brass one is for the security gate. The other key is the master for all the inside locks."

"Thank you," he said. He leaned in front of me to open the door.

I ducked under his arm, then turned on the top step. "There are two more muffins and half a pot of coffee in the staff room. Please help yourself." I popped open the umbrella and headed down the steps, waggling it at the bottom to let him know that I'd heard his surprised thank-you.

The rain stopped about halfway up Mountain Road, and by the time I was walking up the driveway I could see a patch of blue sky over the left corner of Rebecca's house. I left my wet shoes and socks and the dripping umbrella on the porch and stepped into the kitchen.

Owen was sprawled on one side by the table, chewing on something. He looked up, startled, with a *What are you doing home?* expression on his furry gray face.

"What are you eating?" I asked, and I swear he put both paws on top of whatever it was he'd been gnawing on. "Oh, like that's going to work," I said, crossing the kitchen floor. "Let me see."

The cat looked up at me with big golden eyes. "Let me see," I said again.

He dropped his head and lifted one paw. A mangled

piece of what had to be part of a Fred the Funky Chicken carcass lay on the floor.

"Owen! Where did you get that?" I said.

He made a rumbling *merow* sound.

"Do you have Fred the Funky Chicken parts stashed all over the house?"

Nothing.

I crouched down next to the cat. "Owen, look at me," I said.

He slowly lifted his head. If a cat could look guilty, he did.

He leaned forward and gave me a head butt. Sighing, I scratched behind his left ear and Owen began to purr. "You are such a suck-up," I told him.

Hercules came in from the living room and stopped when he saw us. He tipped his head to one side and looked up at me.

"Yes, I know I'm not supposed to be home." I gave Owen one last scratch. "I need more coffee," I told the cats. "And I have to make a couple of phone calls."

I started the coffeemaker, and while it did its thing I called Mary, who was one of my full-time staff members, to tell her not to come to work. Luckily, her husband answered the phone, so I didn't have to get into any details on the why. I left a message for Jason, our summer student, on his voice mail. Then I called Everett Henderson's office and briefly explained what was going on to his secretary, Lita.

When the coffee was made I poured a cup and padded, barefoot, out to the porch, with the cats trailing behind me. The stretch of blue sky above the roofline of Rebecca's house was getting bigger. I slid my feet into a pair of rubber clogs and went out into the yard.

Rebecca waved from her back step. I set my mug on

the landing by the screen door and headed across the grass toward the gap in the lilac hedge. Owen moved ahead of me, stalking like some sleek jungle cat on the prowl—probably hoping Rebecca had a treat for him.

I glanced back over my shoulder. Hercules was coming, too, stopping every few steps to shake the damp from his feet. Herc was a bit of a fussbudget, a cat version of Goldilocks. He didn't like anything to be too hot, too cold, or wet at all.

He gave me his *I am such a poor pathetic kitty* look.

"It's a little rain on the grass, you wuss," I said. "I'm not carrying you." He shook his right front paw and gave me the look again. "I have a blister on my foot from walking up the hill in those canvas flats, and you don't hear me complaining," I said. Herc just stood there, paw in the air. He didn't move, didn't blink. I waited another twenty seconds or so to save face before going back to pick him up.

Ahead of us, Owen had climbed onto the railing of Rebecca's gazebo, pointedly ignoring Rebecca, who was calling to him and holding out her hand. I set Hercules on the gazebo steps and walked over to Rebecca. Like me, she was wearing rubber clogs. She had a gardening glove on one hand and she was holding a bouquet of lavender mums. *Should I tell her about finding Gregor Easton's body?* I wondered. No. I didn't want to be one of those people who couldn't wait to spread bad news, and it wasn't as though Rebecca would have known Easton.

"Good morning, Kathleen," she said. "How are the cats?"

"Hi, Rebecca," I said. "The cats are fine."

"Do you think Owen would like another catnip chicken?"

"If he has any more catnip he's going to end up with

the munchies and an overwhelming urge to rent *2001: A Space Odyssey*."

Rebecca looked puzzled.

"He's addicted to catnip. He's decapitated four chickens and hidden pieces all over the house. He's a kitty junkie."

"Maybe he's stressed," Rebecca said. "Maybe it just helps him relax a little."

I looked over at the gazebo. Hercules sat on the railing like an ancient Egyptian cat statue guarding the tomb of the pharaoh. Owen, on the other hand, was stretched out on his belly on the same railing, eyes closed, legs hanging down on either side.

"Thank you for caring about the cats," I said. "But Owen doesn't need any more catnip."

"All right," Rebecca said, but I saw her glance over at the cats and I knew she'd try to sneak Owen another fix, and who knew what to Hercules.

"Your flowers are beautiful," I said, to change the subject.

"Would you like them?" Rebecca asked. "I already have two vases in the house."

"Are you sure?"

"Of course." She handed me the flowers, and as she did her sleeve slipped back and I saw that her right wrist was bandaged. "Rebecca, is your arthritis acting up again?" I asked. Rebecca used herbal poultices for her arthritis. Her wrists were often wrapped with unbleached cotton strips to hold the poultice in place.

She nodded and smoothed the pale blue sleeve down over the bandage and kept her hand there. "Yes," she said. She looked a little uncomfortable. "I suppose I sound like an old lady, but I'd rather use something natural than take a lot of drugs."

"You don't sound like an old lady," I said. "There's a lot of interest these days in natural medicine. At the library where I worked in Boston we had an entire section on alternative medicine—dozens of books on using plants to treat and heal everything from a scrape to serious illnesses. The books were out a lot."

"Do you miss Boston?" Rebecca asked.

"Sometimes." I ran my fingers over the rosy-purple flower petals. "My parents are actors, so I've lived all over the place. But Boston is where I lived the longest, so it feels like home."

"Your parents act?" Rebecca said. "Theater?"

I nodded. "And my dad has done various commercials over the years. Other than that they've been onstage."

"Would I have seen your father in anything?" she asked.

Should I tell her he was the middle-aged man shaking it like James Brown in a commercial for medication to treat erectile dysfunction? Or that he was also the golfer telling his friends he could play eighteen holes again, thanks to his disposable undergarments?

"Do you remember the ad for the cereal Flakies— oat bran flakes and plump raisins?" I said, finally. "The leading competitor had the shriveled-up raisins."

"I do remember that," Rebecca said, pulling off her glove. "In fact, I've eaten the cereal. The announcer had a wonderful deep voice. Was that your father?"

I felt my cheeks getting red. "No, he was one of the shriveled-up raisins."

Rebecca struggled to keep from smiling, but couldn't help it. "The raisins were good, too," she said.

Just then we heard footsteps coming up Rebecca's gravel driveway. "That's probably Ami, back from the store," Rebecca said. "Have you met her? She's interning at the theater and she's also one of the lead voices in the festival choir. I've known her since she was a little girl." She smiled. "She has an apartment near the Stratton, but you'll see her here quite a bit. I'm teaching her to cook before she leaves for college."

"She's been in the library a few times," I said, as Ami Lester came around the side of the house.

She had a canvas bag slung over one shoulder. A loaf of bread wrapped in brown paper and the dark green leaves of a head of romaine poked out of the top of the bag. Her red-blond hair was pulled into a high ponytail and she wore a gray T-shirt with a bust of Mozart silk-screened on the front. Mozart was wearing headphones, and I think his eyes were crossed.

Ami's eyes were troubled and her face was pale. She stopped beside us and Rebecca touched her shoulder. "Is everything all right, dear?"

Ami swallowed a couple of times. "I, uh . . . I can't believe it, but Mr. Easton is dead."

Rebecca's mouth moved, but at first no sound came out. She dropped the glove she'd been holding. "Dead?" she finally whispered. Her color was worse than Ami's. I took her arm. "Here. Sit," I said, easing her down on to the top step.

"I'm sorry," Ami said. "I didn't mean to upset you." She looked at me. "You're the librarian, aren't you?"

"Yes. I'm Kathleen." I pointed at my house. "I just live right there."

Rebecca reached for Ami's hand. "You didn't upset me, dear. You just caught me by surprise," she said. "It's not as though I knew Mr. Easton. I just knew of his reputation." She rubbed her wrist. "Are you sure he's . . . dead?" Her voice wavered a little.

Ami swung the bag off her shoulder and set it on top

of her feet. "Uh-huh. Someone found his—him—early this morning at the theater."

"I, uh, did," I said.

They both stared at me.

"You found him—at the Stratton? At the theater?" Rebecca asked weakly. She let go of Ami's hand. "Oh, Kathleen, I'm so sorry. Are you all right?"

"I'm fine," I said, giving her hand a gentle squeeze.

"What were you doing at the Stratton?" she asked.

"I was looking for Oren." I picked up the dropped glove and handed it to her.

"But why was he at the theater so early?" Ami said. "We never had early practice, because he said he only worked at a civilized hour."

"Do the police know what happened?" Rebecca asked.

"I don't think so," I said.

"He was old," Ami said. "I bet he had a heart attack."

I remembered the injury to Easton's head. I wasn't so sure it was a heart attack that had killed him. I felt a brush of fur against my leg. Owen. He sat beside me and looked intently at Rebecca.

"Did you come to check on me?" Rebecca asked him. Owen meowed softly.

"He's beautiful," Ami said. She leaned forward and held out her hand to Owen, who ignored her. He took a few steps closer to Rebecca and meowed softly again.

"I'm fine, Owen," Rebecca said. "At my age I should be a little more accustomed to people dying." She stood up and managed a smile for Ami. "Let's make brunch." She looked at me. "Kathleen, would you like to join us?"

"Thank you," I said. "But I have a pile of paperwork I need to start on." I turned to Ami. "It was nice to see you again."

"You, too," she said.

Rebecca took a couple of steps toward me, reached up and laid a hand on my cheek. "My dear, I'm so sorry that you had to be involved in that man's death." She was still very pale.

"It's all right," I told her. "Take care of your arthritis, and call me if you need anything. And thank you for the flowers."

"You're welcome," she said.

I started across the yard to the house. Hercules had disappeared from his perch on the gazebo railing. Behind me Owen meowed. I stopped and turned back to him, tucking Rebecca's flowers under my arm. He looked at me and then at Rebecca's house.

"She's fine," I said. Owen took a step toward Rebecca's and stopped. "She's fine," I said again. "Ami is with her."

He started back across the grass toward the small white house. I followed, scooped him up and started for home again.

Owen squirmed until he was turned around and could look over my shoulder. I opened the porch door, set the cat down inside and grabbed my cup from the railing. There was a fat, green-and-black-shelled bug doing the backstroke in my coffee. I picked it up and dropped it down into the grass. Three cups of coffee today, and I'd barely had one sip.

In the kitchen I put the flowers in water, got another cup of coffee, then almost dumped it on my bare feet when Hercules came up behind me and licked my ankle.

"Don't sneak up on me like that," I said. He rubbed his face against my leg in apology. "How did you get in? Did I not close the screen door?" I padded out to the porch again. Herc followed. The screen door was closed.

Somehow he'd come in behind Owen and me and I hadn't noticed.

I was trying really hard to distract myself, to not think about Gregor Easton's body slumped at the piano at the Stratton. Or about the detective's questions. He didn't really think I'd done something to the conductor, did he?

In Rebecca's backyard Ami was spreading a yellow-flowered tablecloth on the table in the gazebo. Rebecca came out the back door, carrying a tray. Ami scurried to take it from her. I watched the two of them set the table, and I felt a sudden ache of homesickness settle in the middle of my chest like a lumpy blob of cold potatoes.

I went back into the kitchen and sat at the table with my coffee. Boston suddenly seemed a long way from Minnesota. My mother and father were doing Shakespeare in the Park again this summer. This year it was *A Midsummer Night's Dream.* My mother was directing, with my father in the role of Nick Bottom.

On any given day, if they weren't rehearsing or performing, they were reading a play to each other. So they might be completely in sync, grinning at each other like a couple of love-struck teenagers, or they might be going through "artistic differences" where they'd only speak to each other through other people. I wasn't sure which version of their marriage was worse.

My parents had married each other twice. My younger brother and sister, Ethan and Sara—twins—were the result of their reconciliation. I was fifteen and mortified by the undeniable proof that my mother and father, whom I thought weren't even speaking to each other, were instead having sex, and unprotected sex at that.

They were crazy . . . and I missed them. They drove me crazy . . . and I missed them. I felt the ache in my chest press up into my throat. I had eighteen more months in the contract I'd signed with Everett. Eighteen more months in Minnesota.

Hercules went to the living room door, stopped and looked back at me, then disappeared. After a minute, when I didn't follow him, he came back to the door, stared at me and went back into the living room. "What?" I said. I set my cup down and went into the next room to see what the cat was up to.

He was sitting next to the cabinet that held the CD player and CDs. He swatted the door with a paw.

"Okay, I get it," I said, reaching inside for a CD. "But it's going to make Owen crazy."

I picked up Herc as the first notes of "Copacabana" came through the speakers. About a week after I'd adopted the cats I'd discovered Hercules shared my love for Barry Manilow. When I'd put on a Manilow CD he would sit blissfully in front of the CD player, eyes closed to slits, bobbing his head to the music. Owen, on the other hand . . .

At that moment there was a loud yowl of cat outrage as a gray streak flashed by us and dove into the closet by the front door.

Herc and I looked at each other. I shrugged. Mr. Barry Manilow is not everyone's taste.

Herc and I followed "Copacabana" with our kick-line version of "Can't Smile Without You." By the time that song was over I felt a little better. I kissed the top of Hercules' furry black head and set him on the floor, turned down the CD player and went to make lunch.

I worked all afternoon at the kitchen table. By suppertime I had made up the staff schedule through the end of September, ordered the books I wanted for the children's section, and arranged to have several crates of reference material brought back to the library from one of Everett Henderson's warehouses, where they'd been stored during the messiest part of the renovation. Plus, there was a pan of double-chocolate brownies cooling on the counter for when Maggie arrived to watch *Gotta Dance*.

She tapped on my back door at quarter to eight. "I heard what happened," she said, kicking off her shoes. "Are you okay?"

I nodded. "I'm fine."

"I hope Mr. Easton will be welcomed by the light," she said, bending down to look for something in her backpack. "But if what I've heard about him was true, I think he has a few more lessons to learn." She pulled out a bottle of wine and stood up.

"Ruby's latest vintage," she said with a grin. "I volunteered us as taste testers."

She followed me into the kitchen. I got a plate from the cupboard for the brownies, while Maggie got the corkscrew from the drawer by the sink and set to work opening the wine.

"What is this wine made from?" I asked.

"I'm not sure," Maggie said. "Maybe rhubarb. Maybe dandelions."

"Do brownies go with rhubarb wine?" I said as she popped the cork.

Maggie's grin got wider. "Brownies go with everything." She swiped one from the plate as she passed behind me to get the wineglasses. "How long will the library be closed?" she asked as she poured.

"I don't know." I said. I picked up the brownies and headed for the living room. "I just assumed we'd be able to open tomorrow." For the first time it dawned on me that the police could keep the library closed for days, putting the renovations even further behind schedule.

Maggie followed with the glasses. The TV was already on and Owen and Hercules were waiting by the footstool. "Hi, guys," she said to the cats. She knew better than to try to pet them.

I set the brownies on the footstool and sat down, tucking my legs underneath me.

Maggie handed me my glass and curled up in one corner of the sofa. "What were the police doing at the library, anyway?" she asked.

I took a sip of my wine. It was light and fruity. "They—or at least the detective in charge—seem to think Easton and I were involved."

She set her glass on the floor by the arm of the sofa and reached for a brownie. "Involved? You mean?" She waggled her eyebrows at me.

"Uh-huh. Apparently, onstage at the theater at six thirty in the morning."

"They have to ask questions like that," Maggie said, picking chocolate crumbs off the front of her T-shirt. "It doesn't mean they think you actually did anything . . . or anyone."

"They found blood at the library," I blurted.

She sat up straighter. "Blood? Where?"

"In the part of the library that's not finished, where the meeting room is going to be." I took another sip of my wine.

Maggie relaxed against the cushions again. "So? With all the work that's been going on and all the things that have gone wrong, I'm surprised they didn't find part of an ear and a couple of fingers. Anyway, you said Easton was in the computer room."

She was right. Gregor Easton hadn't been anywhere near the space still being renovated, as far as I knew. I felt my stomach unknot.

Owen had been quietly moving across the floor toward Maggie's glass. Now he stuck his nose in the top, sniffed and jumped back at the aroma. "Back off, furry face," she said, picking up the glass.

Owen made low, grumpy sounds in his throat and moved back in front of the TV.

Maggie shifted position on the couch. "Kath," she said, "Gregor Easton wasn't a young man. He probably had a heart attack. There's no way anyone would seriously believe you had anything to do with his death. And as for the blood at the library—assuming it is blood and not paint—it's more likely one of the workmen cut himself." She gestured at Owen, sprawled on his side now in front of the television, intently watching a talking dog sell baked beans. "And no one is going to believe you set your attack cat on Easton or that you two were . . ." She paused, looking for the right word. ". . . Getting funky with each other. C'mon!"

I thought about the gash on the side of Easton's head. Of course, just because he'd hit his head didn't mean that was what had killed him. He still could have had a heart attack. I leaned into the sofa cushions and stretched out my legs onto the footstool. "Why are you always so sensible and logical?" I asked.

"You forgot my winning personality and stunning good looks," Maggie said with a grin. The grin faded to a smile. "Seriously, Kath, this will be over in another day or two. Don't worry about it."

The opening music for *Gotta Dance* began and Maggie turned to the TV. In the recap of the previous episodes there was a shot of rocker Pat Benatar with a gash on one side of her forehead from a fall when a lift went wrong. I pictured the wound I'd seen on the side of Gregor Easton's head. There had been no blood around the injury or in his hair. Had someone cleaned it? And what had Detective Gordon picked up off the library floor as he'd moved me out of the way? And why had a police car driven by my house at least three times in the last few hours? It was hard to concentrate on the TV.

I wanted to believe Maggie was right. I wanted to believe that this would all be over in a day or two. But I couldn't shake the feeling that things were just getting started.

5

White Crane Spreads Wings

Hercules woke me up. Unlike Owen, who just lurked and breathed on me, Herc preferred a more direct approach. He'd stand on his back legs by the side of the bed and swat my face with a paw, no claws. If that didn't work he'd lean over and meow loudly in my ear. He'd never needed to do anything beyond that.

I got up, made coffee and fed Hercules. There was no sign of Owen. I took my coffee cup and stood by the front door, looking down the hill.

The sun, climbing in the sky, sparkled on the river. It was so quiet, so peaceful. It was another one of the things—to my surprise—that I'd discovered I liked about being in Mayville Heights. Hercules came to sit at my feet and started washing his face. A glass and a half of Ruby's wine—which was a lot more potent than its light, sweet taste suggested—had had me yawning by the time *Gotta Dance* ended. Matt Lauer and his partner were still, inexplicably, in first place, but the talented Kevin Sorbo and his partner were safe in second.

"Would it be wrong to get a couple hundred different e-mail addresses so I could vote more than once?" I asked Hercules. He meowed loudly once, and went back to washing behind an ear without even looking up.

A glass and a half of wine had also made Maggie's belief that Detective Gordon's suggestion that I'd been involved with Gregor Easton was just a routine question seem perfectly logical. It didn't seem so logical now.

Owen yowled from the kitchen. "Your brother's up," I said to Hercules, who continued to wash his face.

In the kitchen I found the tabby sitting by his dish. The fur on the top of his head was standing on end, and there were a couple of dust bunnies stuck to his tail. I filled his dish and gave him fresh water. After yesterday it was pretty clear Owen had parts of more than one Fred the Funky Chicken hidden somewhere. Which made sense. The cat knew every inch of the little farmhouse. How many times had he appeared out of nowhere and scared me half to death?

I leaned against the counter and watched Owen eat. No matter what Maggie had said, I couldn't stop thinking about Gregor Easton. Detective Gordon hadn't said I was a suspect or told me not to leave town, but the police car that kept driving by my house since yesterday afternoon didn't do it because Easton had died of a heart attack.

There was nothing I could do about that, no matter how unsettled it left me. But I did need to do something about the library renovation. I'd committed to seeing it finished on schedule. Probably not a good idea, in retrospect. I couldn't let things get any more behind.

Owen finished eating and nudged his bowl aside. He twisted sideways, trying to get at the dust bunnies stuck to his tail. "Step one: See if I can get into the library today," I told him.

I went back to the living room, sat on the footstool

and pulled out the phone book. I was transferred to three different people at the police station before I got an answer: Yes, the library could reopen today. An officer would meet me there to return my keys. The meeting-room area would remain closed off for at least another day.

I let the cats out, let them back in again, got dressed, sighed at my hair in the bathroom mirror, packed lunch and set out down the hill in plenty of time to meet the officer to get my keys. I glanced back at Rebecca's house and made a mental note to check on her later.

Oren's truck was in the library parking lot. He got out and walked across the grass to meet me. I felt the tension ease out of me.

"Oren, I'm so glad to see you," I said.

"Good morning, Kathleen," he said. "How are you?"

"I'm fine." We walked the rest of the way across the grass and turned up the stone walkway to the main entrance.

A branch had blown onto the path. Oren bent and moved it onto the grass. Then he straightened and looked at me. "I heard what happened. I'm sorry you had to find Mr. Easton," he said. "I should have been there."

"I was worried something might have happened to you."

"I had some personal business in Minneapolis." We stopped at the bottom of the steps. "You were looking for me yesterday."

I nodded. "I was hoping you'd have time to put the chairs and the computer carrels together. I'd like to get at least one computer working."

"I can do that for you." He looked up at the library. "Are we allowed in the building?"

"Yes. But the meeting-room area is off-limits for now."

Oren swiped his hand over the back of his neck. "Then I can't finish the painting. That's where all the paint is stored." He thought for a moment. "Do you mind if I work at the Stratton today? That building's open. I could come about four thirty to put those things together for you."

Below us a patrol car pulled into the library parking lot.

"Go ahead," I said. "Four thirty is fine." My shoulders relaxed. "Thank you."

The young police officer who'd driven me to and from the police station the day before got out of the car and started toward us.

Oren pulled his keys out of his pocket. "Kathleen, Will Redfern is a good builder," he said, quietly. "He's also really good with excuses."

"I'll keep that in mind," I said.

He headed back to his truck, exchanging a "Good morning" with the young policeman as they passed. Even though the officer had taken me to be fingerprinted the day before, I still had to show him ID and sign a receipt before he handed me a small brown envelope containing my keys.

The library was stuffy and smelled faintly of sweaty bodies. I opened a couple of windows, dropped my things in my office and went into the staff room.

Detective Gordon—or someone—had washed the coffee machine. The mugs and plate had been left to dry in the wire dish rack, and the counter and table had been wiped clean of crumbs and coffee rings.

I started the coffee machine, rationalizing that Susan would want a cup when she arrived for work. Every so often she would decide she was going to give up coffee. She'd given it up for peppermint tea with honey. That lasted about ten days. She'd given it up for water from an underground spring in a cave in Michigan—for a week. Currently she was drinking "green" juice she made with a Richard Simmons Superjuicer she'd bought at a yard sale. It smelled like lawn clippings that had been sitting in the sun for a week. She'd been on the juice kick for five days. It was only a matter of time before her twins tried to flush a ficus or each other, and Susan would stalk into the library, pour coffee into the largest mug she could find, add half the sugar packets and drink the entire thing before she said a word.

I was checking in the last few books from the book drop when Susan tapped on the main door.

"Well, remind me not to piss you off," she said when I let her in.

"Excuse me?"

"The maestro. One minute he's in here being a jerk and the next he's dead." She looked at me over her tiny glasses with mock seriousness. "You didn't sic your cat on him again, did you?"

I relocked the door and closed the security gate. "No, I didn't sic my cat on him. And Owen jumping on Mr. Easton's head the other day was an accident."

"Whatever you say," Susan said with a smile.

I followed her upstairs. "Would you like a cup of coffee?" I asked as she put her things in her locker and pulled out the vibrant pink sweater she wore when she was working.

"Oh, screw it. Why not? I had two devil's-food cupcakes for breakfast."

I poured a cup for her and one for myself and set Susan's on the table. "Why?" I asked.

She poured three packets of sugar into the cup and stirred. So much for green juice.

"Eric's on a chocolate kick," she said. "Brownies, cupcakes, chocolate mousse, chocolate cheesecake. He's making some changes to the menu at the café and he's trying everything at home first."

She drank a mouthful of coffee and pushed her black-framed glasses up onto the bridge of her nose. "So, is the rumor true? Did you really find Easton's body at the Stratton?"

I nodded. "I was trying to catch up with Oren. He wasn't there. But I did see him this morning."

Susan stirred another packet of sugar into her coffee. "So if Easton died at the theater, what were the police doing here? Why did they close the building yesterday?"

I took a sip of my own coffee. "I'm not sure. A detective came to ask me a few more questions. I told him he could look around. He found something over where the meeting room is going to be."

Susan leaned back in her chair and cupped her mug with both hands. "What were they looking for in here in the first place?" she asked. "The maestro had a heart attack, didn't he?"

I shrugged. "He had a cut on his head. That's all I know."

"So they think what? You whacked him with a big old *Encyclopædia Britannica*, or something? That's crazy." She drained her cup and got up for more coffee. "What did they find, anyway?"

I ran a hand back through my hair. "I'm not sure. There were some . . . stains . . . on the floor."

Susan froze, hand on the coffeepot. Today she had a chopstick in her updo. "Blood?"

"I'm not sure," I said again.

"Can't be. Easton wasn't bleeding when he left and he wasn't even over there. Do they think he came back?" She refilled her cup, then came around the table and topped up mine.

"Thanks," I said.

"I don't see how he could have come in again without me seeing him." Susan sat across from me again. "I didn't leave the desk, Kathleen."

"I know that." I poured a packet of sugar in my cup before it all ended up in Susan's.

"And I don't see how he could have snuck in. Or even why he would." She shook her head. "Easton wasn't subtle. He struck me as the kind of person who always made an entrance, who sucked all the air out of the room."

I tried to get a mental picture of Gregor Easton slinking back into the library, creeping past the circulation desk while Susan was busy. And to do what? Go bleed on the floor of a half-finished meeting room? What would that accomplish? From my one encounter with Easton while he was alive, I felt sure a showy, melodramatic scene was more his style. "You're right," I said to Susan. "Gregor Easton didn't seem like the kind of person to do anything unobtrusively. We don't know what the police found on the floor downstairs. We certainly don't know it was blood. And if, *if* it was, it's probably from one of the workmen."

"Yeah, that makes a lot more sense. One of those guys was carrying a piece of wood and almost took my head off last week. Then he turned around so fast he took out an entire shelf of paperbacks with the other end of the board."

"Not everyone is Oren," I said.

Susan grinned. "You've got that right."

I looked at my watch. It was five minutes to nine.

"That reminds me," I said, as I stood up and took my cup to the sink to rinse it. "The rest of the reference books are coming from Everett's warehouse this morning. Could you get them shelved, please?"

"Sure." Susan chugged the last of her coffee and set her mug in the sink.

"Mary will be here at ten," I said. "She can cover the desk and the phones. I'm going to see if I can figure out what we have for the computer room and what we still need. Oren will be here late this afternoon to at least get the furniture together."

The truck from Everett's warehouse pulled up to the back door of the library at exactly nine thirty. The driver used a small, wheeled dolly to move the crates of books into the building. He took off the tops with just a hammer and his hands, as if they were pull tops on cans of tuna, had me check each crate, sign for everything, *ma'am*ed me half a dozen times and was gone in less than fifteen minutes.

Susan started unpacking the books as soon as Mary arrived to handle the desk.

I got my trusty five-in-one, multipurpose Ginsu tool from my office. (It's a knife! It's a screwdriver! It's a corkscrew! It's scissors! It's a blade for opening anything encased in plastic! Wow!) And, yes, I'd bought it from a late-night infomercial—in between ads for spray hair in a can and the amazing panini press—but it really worked. It was great for cutting open boxes, hermetically sealed plastic packages and the occasional coffee cake from Susan's husband, Eric. And I liked knowing that if I ever needed to saw through a soda can, I could do that, too.

The soon-to-be computer room was piled with boxes and unassembled furniture. I set the three printer cartons under the window. The monitors were already stacked in the corner. I left them there. The chairs were shrouded in yards of plastic film, one upside down on another, as though someone had gone a little crazy with a giant-sized roll of sandwich wrap. I pushed those against the end wall. Leaning up against the last pair of chairs was a long, flat box—the other table for the children's department. I'd been looking for that for almost a week. I knew if I left it Oren would put that together, too, but all it needed was to have the legs attached to the top. How hard could that be for a woman with a multi-purpose, five-in-one Ginsu tool?

Harder than I thought. It took the better part of an hour to attach legs A1 through A4 to top B with screws DD, nuts FF and washers EEE. There were bits of plastic and bubble wrap all over the floor and clinging to my shirt when I was finished. I went upstairs and got the small vacuum we kept in the staff room, and prowled the walls looking for an outlet to plug it into. The re-wiring of that section of the library obviously hadn't been done. Another thing to talk to Will about when he showed up. Assuming he showed at all today.

Finally, under the end window, behind a printer box, I found an outlet. I leaned over the box and stretched to push in the plug. There was a loud snapping sound and sparks flew up. So did I, backward onto the floor. I lost a few seconds, maybe half a minute. I opened my eyes and looked up into Detective Gordon's blue ones. I struggled to sit up.

"Take it easy, Ms. Paulson," he said.

"I'm all right," I said. And I was, except for the tingling in my fingers, the buzzing ache in my arm and the high-pitched sound of crickets in my ear.

"I don't think you are."

At that moment Roma came around the end of the bookshelves. "Kathleen, what happened?" she asked. "I came in the door and Mary said you were hurt."

"I got a little shock when I plugged in the vacuum cleaner," I said.

"A little shock?" exclaimed Susan. I hadn't seen her standing behind Detective Gordon. "There were sparks and a big bang, and she went flying."

"Would you take a look at her, please?" Detective Gordon asked, getting to his feet.

"She's a vet," Susan said. She gave Roma an apologetic look. "No offense."

Roma smiled. "None taken. You're right. But I do have first-aid training." She knelt beside me.

"Roma, I'm all right, really," I said.

She laid a hand on my shoulder. "Kathleen," she said, "stop talking just for a moment, please." She began feeling my scalp, probing gently under my hair for bumps. "Did you hit your head?"

"No," I said. I shifted position and winced. "I did bang my hip."

She fished in her pocket, pulled out a set of keys and held them up to Susan. "My car is in the lot—it's the dark blue four-by-four. There's a black bag behind the driver's seat. Would you get it for me, please?"

"Sure," Susan said, taking the keys.

Roma turned back to me, reached for my arm and pressed two fingers to my wrist while she checked her watch. After that she sat back on her heels. "What happened?" she asked.

"I was plugging in the vacuum cleaner. There was a loud snap, sparks and I went over backward."

She glanced up at Detective Gordon, who nodded his agreement. "Which hand?" Roma asked.

"Excuse me?" I said.

"Which hand was holding the plug?"

"Oh. This one." I held up my right hand.

Susan came back then with Roma's bag and set it beside us. "Thank you," Roma said. She opened the bag and pulled out a stethoscope. As she put the round metal end on my chest I hoped the last place it had been wasn't a horse's rear.

"Take a deep breath and bark," Roma said. *Vet humor,* I figured.

She listened in several places, then pulled the ends of the stethoscope out of her ears. "Let's try standing up," she said.

Detective Gordon offered his hand. I took it and got to my feet. My arm still felt numb, but the high-pitched whine in my ear was almost gone. "See?" I said, holding out both hands. "I'm all right." I turned to Roma. "Thank you."

She bent to stuff the stethoscope in her bag. "You're welcome. But you should see a doctor—one who specializes in people, not pets and farm animals."

I thought about spending the rest of the morning sitting at the clinic, waiting to be seen by a doctor who wouldn't do anything more than Roma had done. "I promise if I feel sick or off in any way, I'll go," I said. Susan, standing with her arms crossed, shook her head.

"Kathleen, do you know why I became a vet?" Roma asked.

"No."

"Because my patients never second-guess me." She smiled to soften the criticism. Then the smile faded. "If you feel funny at all, go to the hospital. Don't wait around."

"I will," I said.

Roma swung the strap of her bag over her shoulder. She nodded at Susan and Detective Gordon. "I'll see you tonight," she said to me, and headed back to the checkout desk.

"You sure you're okay?" Susan asked. "You hit the floor pretty hard."

"I am, really," I said, rubbing my hip. "Just a bit sore."

"Okay. I'm going back to shelving. If you need anything, yell." She grinned. "Maybe not as loudly as last time, though." She disappeared around the corner.

I turned to Detective Gordon. "I won't ask you if you're really okay," he said.

"Thank you." I rubbed my arm. It still had a faint pins-and-needles feeling.

He walked over to the window to take a closer look at the outlet. There was soot on the wall plate and an ashy black scorch mark arced a good six inches above it on the wall.

"I don't think that's going to work anymore," he said, pointing to the electrical cord on the vacuum. The plastic plug had melted into a misshapen blob.

"I think we have a broom somewhere," I said. Then I remembered that the somewhere was the half-completed meeting room.

Detective Gordon was crouched down, studying the scorched outlet. He looked up at the ceiling. "I'm surprised you didn't blow a fuse," he said. "Still, I don't think it's a good idea to plug anything in here until it's checked out by an electrician."

I nodded. "You're right."

"Do you have any masking tape? We should mark this off so no one else uses it, either."

"I think there's a roll at the circulation desk. Let me check."

I walked around to the desk. Mary was just hanging up the phone. "Kathleen, are you all right?" she asked.

"I'm fine, Mary," I said, forcing a smile. "It was just a little shock." I didn't handle it well when people fussed over me. I was used to looking after other people, not the other way around. "Do we have any masking tape?" I asked.

"Uh-huh. Right here." She pulled open the drawer below her computer monitor and handed the tape to me with a smile. She smelled like cinnamon and Ivory soap and looked just like someone's sweet grandma—which she was. She was also state champion for her age and weight class in kickboxing.

"Mary, did Mr. Easton come back to the library Tuesday night after I walked him out?"

"No. Not while I was here."

"Okay, thanks."

I took the tape back to Detective Gordon. He crossed two pieces over the outlet in a large X. Then pulled a pen out of his jacket pocket and wrote DANGEROUS! DO NOT USE! on a third piece and stuck that above the X. "That should do it," he said, standing up and brushing off his hands.

"Thank you." He must have come to the library for a reason, I realized then. What was it?

"Was there something you wanted, Detective?" I asked. "You didn't just stop by to pick me up off the floor and safety-proof the building."

"No, I didn't." His smile disappeared. "Ms. Paulson, you said Mr. Easton was looking for an Internet connection when he came in Tuesday evening."

"That's right." Suddenly I felt cold. I folded my arms over my chest.

"So you would have been standing . . . here?" He held out his hands, palms up.

"Yes."

"Did Mr. Easton go anywhere else in the library?"

I shook my head. "Other than out the door, no."

He looked me straight in the eye and I met his gaze head-on. I didn't know where the conversation was going, but I didn't have anything to hide.

"Did Mr. Easton come back to the library?"

"No. He didn't come back while I was here. Susan and Mary covered the desk after that and they didn't see him."

He stared at me, hands jammed in his pockets, his face unreadable. If the guy who'd helped me off the floor was Nice Cop, then this had to be Mean Cop.

"Ms. Paulson," he said, finally. "Didn't your mother ever tell you what happens to people who lie?"

"Actually, my mother said, 'Always tell the truth, because it's much easier to remember,'" I said.

Detective Gordon said nothing.

"You think he came back?"

A tiny muscle twitched in his cheek.

"No," I said slowly. "You're certain he came back. That's why you won't let it go." I looked across the library. One of the heavy sheets of plastic had been taken down. "You picked something up off the floor after we saw those spots of blood. What was it?"

He cleared his throat. "Part of a cuff link."

"That doesn't make any sense." I played with my watch. "Easton didn't come back while I was here. Both Mary and Susan said they didn't see him, either. And they don't have any reason to lie."

"Do you?" the detective asked.

I closed my eyes for a moment and took a couple of deep breaths. "No," I said.

I held up one finger. "I met Gregor Easton for the

first and only time Tuesday night." I added a second finger. "I did not know Mr. Easton." Now three fingers. "Mr. Easton and I were not having an affair, a relationship or an encounter of any kind." Finally, I stuck my arm out and held up four fingers. "And if Mr. Easton came back to the library Tuesday night, I don't know when or how he did."

Detective Gordon's face was still unreadable, except for that tiny, pulsing muscle. He pulled out a piece of paper. "Then why did he have a note from you in his pocket?"

6

Single Whip

"What do you mean, a note from me?" I asked, my heart suddenly thumping in my ears.

He handed me the paper. It was a photocopy of an original, which had been written on library stationery. *Meet me at the library at eleven thirty. Kathleen*, was all that was on the page. I looked up at him. "I didn't write this," I said.

"It's your name and it's library stationery."

I made myself take a couple of deep breaths before I answered. "Yes, but it's not my handwriting. Mine's a lot messier. And I didn't write any note to Gregor Easton." I pointed. "Look, it's not addressed to him. It's not addressed to anyone. And as for the paper, that's not the library stationery. We found it in the workroom and we're using it for scratch pads. Look a little closer at the library name." I handed the sheet of paper back.

The detective squinted at the photocopied page; then he looked up at me. "Mabel Heights Free Public Library?" he said.

I nodded. "Uh-huh. I have one of these pads on my desk. There are a couple in the staff room and there's a stack of them under the counter at the circulation desk.

We all use them. I probably write half a dozen notes a day using that paper, to the staff, to the workmen, to myself, but not to anyone outside the library." I pointed at the photocopy again. "That's not even a full sheet of paper. It looks like it's been torn in half." I pointed over my head to the second floor. "You can have all the samples of my handwriting you want. I didn't write that note to Easton. I didn't lure him back here for a meeting."

"So you say." He tucked the paper back in his pocket.

"Why are you so certain he came back?" I said. "It can't be just that bit of cuff link." His face didn't give anything away. "Wait a second. Was it Easton's blood on the floor?"

"Why do you think it was blood on the floor?"

"Because when I asked you what you'd picked up when we saw the blood, you didn't correct me."

"No, I didn't."

Mary appeared behind him then. "Sorry to interrupt, Kathleen," she said. "Will Redfern is on line two for you."

"Excuse me, Detective," I said. "I need to take this." I followed Mary back to the main desk. It was faster than going to my office.

"Good morning, Mr. Redfern," I said.

"Morning, Miss Paulson. I was calling to make sure the library was open before I send my boys over to work."

I wondered where he was calling from. There was a hollowness to his voice that made it sound like he was talking to me from a bathroom stall—or the inside of a giant Spam can.

"I heard the police shut the building down yesterday."

"They did," I said. "But most of the library is open now, except for the meeting-room area where you were storing your tools."

"Not a problem. Tools we got."

"I need an electrician in here today, too," I said, pulling the phone closer so I could move to the side of the counter, out of Mary's way.

"An electrician? What for?"

"Because I plugged the vacuum cleaner into one of the old outlets in the computer room and was almost electrocuted."

"You're kidding," he said.

"No, I'm not. All the wiring in that part of the library needs to be checked, and I still need the new outlets for the computers."

"I can try to get someone there today." Was he chewing something?

"Thank you."

"Are you sure the problem wasn't with the vacuum?" he asked.

I glanced at Mary and shook my head. She smiled in sympathy. I took a deep breath and let it out. It didn't help. "I'm sure," I said.

"You know, Miss Paulson, the library's an old building, and just like an old gal, she's going to be a bit temperamental. You haven't been here long enough to know all her little quirks."

There it was, that slightly condescending tone Will Redfern tended to use with me.

I shut my eyes and imagined all my frustration filling up a big, red balloon coming out of the top of my head. It was a relaxation exercise my mother taught in her acting classes. "So, I can leave the electrician to you?" I said, picturing the balloon getting bigger and bigger and bigger. "Because if it's a problem, I can call Everett and ask him to recommend someone. I don't mind."

"You don't have to do that," he said quickly. "I'll find someone."

"Thank you." I reached above my head and flicked away the imaginary balloon with my thumb and middle finger.

"The boys will be there in about an hour," Will continued. "And I'll get an electrician there before the end of the day. Call me if you have any other problems."

"Thank you," I said again, but I was talking to nothing. I hung up the phone and pushed it across the countertop to Mary.

"Is Will planning on getting some work done here today?" she asked.

"Let's hope so." I turned to see Detective Gordon standing by the entrance. I walked over to him. "Are we finished?"

"For now," he said, pulling his keys out of his pocket.

"Thank you for your help back there."

"You're welcome." I almost got a smile then. "I'll be in touch." He pointed toward the taped-off section of the library. "We should be finished in another day."

I nodded. "Aren't you going to tell me not to leave town?" I said.

His lips twitched. He wanted to smile. "Are you going somewhere?" he asked.

"No."

"Then I don't see a problem." He turned and walked away.

I went back to the computer room. Susan was coiling the vacuum cleaner cord around the handle. "I'll stick this upstairs in the closet," she said.

I nodded. "Thanks. When Harry comes to mow again I'll ask him if he can fix it." I looked at the blackened section of wall above the outlet, hearing the bang, seeing the sparks, feeling the muscles in my hand and arm clench into twisted, painful knots.

"Does your arm hurt?" Susan asked.

I looked down and saw that I was rubbing my wrist without even realizing it. "No, it's just a bit sore—like I used it too much." *Like I used it to pitch nine innings of baseball*, I thought, but didn't say. "Will Redfern is sending over an electrician," I said, partly to change the subject.

"That doesn't fill me with confidence." Susan pointed at the wall. "You could have been electrocuted. And remember when they were taking out the radiators? You were burned by that shutoff valve."

I sucked in a breath, remembering the blast of steam that had just missed the side of my face.

"This is probably going to sound crazy," Susan began, "but have you noticed that every time something goes wrong here, you're the one who gets hurt?"

"Not every time," I said.

She made a face at me.

"Oh, Susan, c'mon," I said. "You think what? That Will Redfern is trying to sabotage the library renovation? Why? Does he have something against books? Or reading?"

"Well, when you say it like that it just sounds silly," Susan admitted.

I nodded. "Uh-huh. Will's just . . . disorganized. He's trying to do twelve things at once." *And he's sexist and way too cocky,* I added silently. "If he doesn't get an electrician in here today I'll get one myself," I said.

"Good." Susan picked up the vacuum with one hand and the hose with the other. She looked around the almost-deserted library. "What did the detective want?"

I didn't see any reason not to tell her. "He still thinks Easton came back to the library Tuesday night."

"No way," Susan exclaimed, so vehemently her

glasses slid down her nose. "He didn't come back, Kathleen. I would have seen him."

"That's what I told Detective Gordon." Just then a pretty redhead with two curly-haired toddlers, each clutching one of her hands, approached us. "Excuse me," she said. "Could you tell me where the board books are?"

I smiled. "They're in our new children's section," I said. "Let me show you." I pointed them to the far end of the library, looked back at Susan and mouthed, *Don't worry.* She rolled her eyes at me.

Will Redfern's "boys" showed up about half an hour later and started working right away on the new circulation desk. About twenty minutes after that, the electrician walked into the building, just as I was coming down from my office. He looked like a slightly younger, much blonder version of Harry Taylor, who took care of the library grounds. He offered his hand. "Ms. Paulson? I'm Larry Taylor. Taylor Electric."

"Please call me Kathleen," I said. He had Harry's green eyes. "Are you related to Harry?" I asked.

"Yep. Old Harry is my dad. Young Harry is my older brother. Harry, Harry and Larry—that's us." He grinned and I relaxed.

I explained briefly about the vacuum, the sparks and me flying backward through the air. Then I took him over to see the blackened outlet. He crouched down for a closer look. "I'll have to have a look at the panel," he said.

"It's in the basement," I said. "I'll show you."

He held up a hand. "It's okay. I know where to find it."

"Go ahead, then."

I walked over to Susan, who was shelving reference books again. "Tell me that was Larry Taylor," she said.

She was sitting cross-legged on the floor, dress tucked around her knees, slotting books onto a bottom shelf.

"It was."

"Good. He's like all the Taylors. He doesn't know how to do a half-ass job at anything."

"That's a catchy slogan," I said, handing her an over-sized atlas. "I wonder if he has it on his business card."

She made a face at me. I grinned back at her. "Could you help me carry a table over to the children's department?"

"Sure thing." She stood up and brushed her hands on her skirt.

We managed to get the table I'd put together across the library without banging into anything. Susan went back to shelving while I dragged the new table into place and set four chairs around it. Larry Taylor appeared just as I was putting a basket of foam puzzles in the middle of the table.

The problem was an old panel and even older wiring. "And that wall outlet?" Larry said. "I don't know why you haven't had a fire before now."

"Can you—*will* you—do the job?" I asked.

He thought about it for a moment, then nodded. "For Everett, for the library, yes."

My shoulders sagged as the tension drained out of them. "Could you put together an estimate for me?" I asked. "So I have some kind of idea of what it's going to cost."

"Sure." He pulled a pencil from behind his ear and wrote something on a small pad he had in his shirt pocket. "It'll be tomorrow afternoon before I can get started."

"That's fine. Drop off the estimate whenever you can. And send your bill directly here."

He nodded and stuck the pencil behind his ear again. "I've disconnected all the plugs and one set of lights in that area, so no one gets hurt."

"Thank you so much," I said.

"I'll drop an estimate back before the end of the day, and I'll see you tomorrow afternoon."

We shook hands and he left.

When you start the day almost being electrocuted, there's nowhere to go but up. Larry dropped off his estimate at about four thirty, just as Oren was arriving to start putting together the computer carrels and chairs. Will Redfern's crew had almost finished the circulation desk.

When I explained what had happened that morning, Oren's jaw tightened, but aside from asking if I was all right, he didn't say anything. I told him Larry was going to be fixing the wiring and he nodded his approval. That was all the recommendation I needed.

Hercules was sitting on the porch bench, looking out the window, when I got home. I unlocked the door, set down my bag and picked him up. "You little sneak," I said. "I didn't see you come out here behind me this morning. How did you do that?"

He didn't answer. He was too busy purring as I scratched his chin. I kept fresh water—a bowl for each cat, because they wouldn't share—and some dry cat food in the porch, along with a litter box, because they often snuck into the porch before I left. Hercules had even figured out how to push open the screen door so he could get out into the yard.

I unlocked the back door, set the cat down on the kitchen floor and went back into the porch to get my bag. When I stepped into the kitchen again Owen was sitting next to his brother.

"Hello," I said to him. "How was your day?" I bent to scratch the top of his head. His eyes narrowed in pleasure.

The cats followed me upstairs, waiting by the bed while I changed, then came back down to watch me get supper. I gave them both a little of the crabmeat from my pasta salad before starting to eat.

There were two brownies left from last night. I put one on my plate and left the other covered so I could pretend for a few minutes more that I wasn't going to eat both of them. I cut the brownie in front of me into four pieces and ate the first one. Owen looked expectantly at me as I picked up the second bite. "Forget it," I said. "Brownies are not good for cats." He glared at me, and for a second it looked like he'd crossed his eyes at me. I popped the bite of chocolate in my mouth, then stretched my arms behind the chair back. My right arm still ached a little and my mind was going around in circles, trying to make sense out of Gregor Easton's last hours.

"Why would Easton have come back to the library?" I asked the cats. Hercules was washing his face. He paused, paw behind an ear, to look blankly at me. "I know; it doesn't make sense," I said.

I looked over at Owen. "He didn't come back while we were there." Owen meowed his agreement and continued washing his tail. "Susan said she didn't see him, and neither did Mary. Why would they lie?"

Neither cat felt that thought was worth commenting on.

I reached for the last brownie and took a big bite. "So either he didn't come back, or he snuck into the building. If he didn't come back, how did the broken cuff link get there? And if he did sneak in, what the heck was he doing?"

Owen burped. It was as good an answer as any.

The phone rang then. I went into the living room to answer it.

"Hello, Katydid," the voice on the other end said.

My mother.

"Hi, Mom," I said, dropping into the leather chair beside the table that held the phone. I snagged the footstool with one foot and pulled it closer.

"How are you?" she asked.

For all that my mother could be incredibly self-absorbed, she also seemed to have some kind of mother radar that told her when something wasn't right with one of us.

"I'm fine." Because really, I was, except for a sore arm and a detective who had the idea I may have killed someone.

"I know you found that composer's body," she said flatly.

I slid down in the chair and propped my feet on the footstool. "How did you know?"

"I'm not a dinosaur, Katydid. I have a computer and I read the Mayville Heights Chronicle online every morning."

So it wasn't mother radar that had caught me; it was the Internet. "You read the Mayville paper every day?"

"Of course." Her tone was matter-of-fact. "I like to know what's going on where you are."

"Well . . . that's . . . nice," I said.

"Are you all right? Really?"

My throat tightened and I felt that lump of homesickness in my chest again. "I am. Really." I cleared my throat and tried to swallow down the lump.

"He was a randy old goat, you know," Mom said.

"You knew Gregor Easton?" I probably shouldn't have been surprised. My mother knew a lot of people in the arts. She'd been working in the theater since she started doing summer stock when she was sixteen.

"Just by reputation," she said. "Not that it was a good one."

"What do you mean?"

She sighed. "Mostly it was whispers and stories—you understand. I heard he couldn't keep his hands—and other body parts—to himself."

"Anything else?"

"It seems he liked younger women."

I thought of what Ruby had said about Ami Lester.

"He was there as the guest artist for your summer music festival, wasn't he?"

"Uh-huh. The Wild Rose Summer Music Festival. He was actually a last-minute replacement for someone else." Owen came around the side of the footstool and sat next to my chair. I shifted a bit so I could pet him.

"I'm surprised," my mother said. "Why was a musician of Easton's caliber at a small regional festival?"

"I don't know." I hadn't thought about it before, but she was right. Helping out from the goodness of his heart didn't seem like something the man I'd met would do. Then again, we'd only met once—while the man was alive—and Owen had jumped on his head, so maybe he hadn't been at his best.

"How's Dad?" I asked.

"Annoying," Mom said.

"What happened?"

"We're having artistic differences."

"Over what?"

"Over his interpretation of Nick Bottom. Your father is over-the-top."

I bit the inside of my cheek so I wouldn't laugh. "The character is kind of flamboyant," I said.

She snorted. "There's a difference between flamboy-ant and flaming."

I couldn't help it then. I laughed. "You'll work it out, Mom," I said.

There was silence for a moment. Then she said, "I saw Andrew yesterday."

Andrew. Tall, sandy blond hair, blue eyes, muscles in all the right places and a smile that could melt the elastic in your undies.

"That's nice," I said, working to keep my voice from giving away my feelings.

"He said to say hello."

Andrew, who went to Maine on a two-week fishing trip after we'd had a major fight and came back married. And not to me.

I swallowed. "How is he?"

"He looks thin."

"This is his busy time of year," I said. I checked my watch. "I've gotta go, Mom," I said. "I have tai chi class."

"And you don't want to talk about your ex-boyfriend," she said. So maybe she did have mother radar after all.

"You're right. I don't. But I really do have tai chi."

"I'll let you go, then," she said. "Call me soon, Katydid."

"I will," I said. "Bye."

I hung up the phone, then bent down and picked up Owen. He sat on my lap and studied my face.

"Andrew said hello," I said.

Owen tipped his head to one side and put a paw on my chest.

"I'm all right," I said. I scooped him into my arms and stood up.

"You know, Andrew said I didn't know how to be spontaneous," I told the cat as we headed for the stairs.

"So I quit my job in Boston and came halfway across the country to supervise a renovation that's never going to be finished, and to top it off, I'm a suspect in a murder investigation."

Owen lifted his head to look at me.

"Yeah, I guess I showed him," I said.

7

High Pat on Horse

I set Owen down on the bedroom floor. He stretched. Then something seemed to catch his eye. He moved across the room and stuck his head under the bed. "The only thing you're going to find under there is more dust bunnies," I said.

I looked in the mirror. My hair hadn't changed since morning. I combed my droopy bangs off to the side and fastened them back with a clip. It made me look about twelve. Assuming twelve-year-olds have permanent laugh lines.

Owen's backside was still poking out from under the end of the bed. "I'm leaving," I said. "Are you staying in or going out?" His back end gave an Elvis shimmy and he disappeared completely behind the hanging edge of the quilt.

I went back downstairs, stuffed my towel, sweatshirt, shoes and water bottle into my bag; grabbed my keys off the kitchen counter; and pulled on my sneakers. Hercules was nowhere to be seen. I locked both doors and started down the driveway, pulling the strap of my messenger bag over my head.

I'd tried Rebecca a couple of times in the afternoon

but gotten no answer. Would she be at class? I glanced back at the house and discovered Hercules was following me down the sidewalk. I waited for him to catch up.

"Where do you think you're going?" I asked. "And how did you get out of the house?" He stared unblinkingly at me. "Go home," I said, pointing back at the house. His eyes followed my fingers; then he walked several steps past me, stopped and looked back. "No. You're not coming," I said. "Just because Owen snuck down to the library doesn't mean you get to come, too."

I picked him up, walked back to the yard and set him on the grass. Then I crossed the lawn and started down the street. After half a dozen steps I stopped. "You're here, aren't you?" I said, not turning around. Herc rubbed against my leg. I looked down. He looked up. I swear he was grinning.

"I don't have time to do this," I said, checking my watch. I was going to have to hustle to make the start of tai chi class. I bent and picked up Hercules again. I half ran, half speed-walked back home. I unlocked the porch door, set Hercules inside, relocked the door and ran for the street, bag smacking against my hip.

I slowed to a fast walk to catch my breath and shifted the strap of my bag. Hercules was walking beside me along the edge of the grass where it met the sidewalk. I stopped and crouched down. Herc sat.

"How did you do that?" I asked him. "I put you in the porch. I locked the door." I remembered Owen chasing birds in the backyard and how I'd thought for a moment that he could disappear. Was that how Hercules had gotten out of the porch? Could he . . .

No. Crazy moment. Owen couldn't make himself invisible. Hercules couldn't walk through walls. And I was way more stressed than I'd realized. They were cats.

Real cats—fast and stealthy. They had no paranormal abilities. They were sneaky, not supernatural.

I lifted Herc into my arms and stood up. "What am I going to do with you?" I didn't want him to wander down the street and maybe get hit by a car.

"Okay. Fine. You win," I said. "You can come." I stuck my face close to his furry black-and-white one. "No getting out of the bag and no jumping on anyone's head. Are we clear?"

He nuzzled my cheek. I undid the side zipper of the bag, pulled out my sweatshirt and shoes and set Hercules inside. He twisted around and settled next to the rolled towel, tucking his tail around his back legs.

"Are you all right?" I asked, tying my hoodie around my waist. Hercules made a sound that was halfway between a meow and a burp. I closed the zipper. He peeked out at me through the side mesh panel. I settled the padded back of the bag on my hip and started down the street.

When I'd found the cats on the overgrown grounds of Wisteria Hill, I'd brought them home in this bag. Maybe that was why they liked being inside it. The bag couldn't collapse down on them and there were half a dozen mesh panels so the air could circulate. And they were getting carried instead of having to walk.

I looked through the top mesh window. Hercules was stretched out, with his head on one paw and the other over his nose. He opened one eye and looked up at me. "It does not smell in there," I whispered. The paw stayed on his nose and the open eye winked shut.

A truck passed, heading up the hill. *Maybe I should stop talking to the cat,* I thought. At least while there were vehicles driving by. I didn't want to be known as the crazy lady who talked to her gym bag.

Rebecca and I arrived for class at the same time. I waited by the door as she came up the sidewalk from the other direction.

"Hello, Kathleen," she said with a smile. "I like your bangs off your forehead."

"They're driving me crazy." I held the door open for Rebecca with one hand and took her canvas tote bag with the other.

"Thank you," she said. "You know, I think they just need a little more layering."

I sighed as we started up the steps. "I wish I'd never cut my hair," I said.

Rebecca's smile widened. "As soon as I can hold a pair of scissors I'll even up the ends for you and see what I can do with those bangs. I promise. You'll feel better."

At the top of the stairs I put Hercules down between my feet, untied the shirt from around my waist and hung it on one of the hooks by the studio door. At the end of the row a collapsible red umbrella dangled from the last hook. A green scarf with beaded ends was knotted around the middle of the umbrella.

Rebecca was sitting on the wooden bench opposite, changing her shoes. I hung her bag next to my sweatshirt. She glanced up and noticed the umbrella. "There's my scarf," she said. I reached over, unknotted the fabric and handed it to her. The long edges had been beautifully stitched by hand

She smoothed the material on her lap. "Thank you," she said. "I know it's just a scarf, but it was a gift and I couldn't remember what I'd done with it. I didn't realize I'd left it here."

She looked troubled. Was she afraid she was getting forgetful? I hadn't seen any signs that Rebecca was having problems with her memory. I smiled at her. "I forgot my rubber boots here once," I told her. "I didn't notice that I wasn't wearing them until I was starting up Mountain Road in the rain and the water was streaming down the sidewalk over my feet like a waterslide."

Rebecca stood up and reached past me to tuck the scarf into her tote. "What you're trying to say is that I'm not getting old and feeble." She smiled back at me.

I gave her shoulder a light squeeze. "I wouldn't let you cut my bangs if I thought you were," I said.

I grabbed the strap of my messenger bag, and we went into the studio. Violet raised her hand in greeting. Rebecca walked over to her.

I headed for Maggie, who was standing next to the tea table. "Hi," I said. "Can I leave my bag under the table?"

Her hand was on the top of her head, gently pulling it down to her shoulder. "Sure," she said. "Do you have something breakable inside?"

"I have a cat inside," I said.

"What?" Maggie's eyes widened, which looked a little strange because her head was tipped sideways. I lifted up the bag so she could look in the top. "Is that Hercules?" she asked.

"Shhh, yes," I hissed.

She let go of her head and peeked in the bag again. "Hey, Fuzz Face," she whispered. A soft meow came from inside. "Why did you bring a cat to class?" Maggie asked, grabbing the top of her head again and pulling it down to the opposite shoulder.

"He wouldn't stay home," I said. "He kept following me. I put him in the porch, but somehow he managed to get back out when I wasn't looking."

"Very sneaky," Maggie whispered to the bag. She gave me a sideways grin. "Stick him under the table," she said. "Can he breathe okay in there?"

"Thanks," I said, carefully sliding Hercules out of the way. "And yes, he can breathe."

Maggie started rolling her head slowly from one shoulder to the other. "Any more news on Easton?" she asked.

My hands were clammy. I wiped them on my shorts. "The police found part of his cuff link in the meeting room are at the library," I said.

"How'd it get there?"

"That's what Detective Gordon wants to know."

Maggie dropped her head to her chest. "So he thinks what? That you and the maestro made out in the meeting room? Then he ended up dead and you put him on a book cart and rolled him down the street to the Stratton, and no one saw you?"

"When you say it like that it sounds . . . silly," I said.

"Because it is." Maggie moved to the middle of the room, loosely shaking her arms.

Someone clattered up the stairs. Ruby. She came through the door, pulling off a yellow tie-dye T-shirt to reveal an orange tie-dye tank. I loved Ruby's clothes. I'd dressed a lot more conservatively when I'd been in my twenties.

Roma walked over, slowly rolling her shoulders. Violet and Rebecca trailed behind her. Roma touched my arm, turning me partly away from the others. "Kathleen, how do you feel?" she asked, keeping her voice low.

Slowly I flexed and extended my fingers. "I'm okay," I said. "These muscles are a bit sore, but the tingling is gone and everything works the way it's supposed to."

"Good," she said.

I glanced over at the table. Was it my imagination or could I see Hercules' green eyes watching through one of the front mesh panels? I turned back to Roma. I'd been meaning to ask her about Owen. "Roma, do you know anything about catnip?" I said.

"I know some cats love it and others don't," she said. "Why do you ask?"

I rubbed a hand across my neck. Sometimes I missed the weight of my hair on my neck. "Have you seen those little yellow chickens stuffed with catnip that they sell at the Grainery?" I asked.

"You mean Fred the Funky Chicken?"

I nodded. "Uh-huh. Rebecca's been buying them for my cats. Hercules isn't interested, but Owen—"

"—is acting like a catnip freak," Roma finished.

"Yes."

"Makes sense. About fifty percent of cats like catnip. The rest don't. It's probably genetic, the way tongue rolling is in people." She smiled. "It won't hurt him."

"Thanks. That's good to know," I said.

Roma twisted a wide silver ring around the index finger of her right hand. "You know, there's catnip growing wild on the grounds of Wisteria Hill. Maybe that's how Owen got a taste for it."

"Do you know much about the cats out there?" I asked, tugging at the bottom of my T-shirt, which had bunched up when I'd tied the hoodie at my waist.

"I do," Roma said. "Some of us have been taking care of them, making sure they have food and shelter. Over time we've managed to catch them all so they could be neutered and have their shots." She shrugged. "It wasn't easy."

I remembered the last time Roma had given shots to Owen and Hercules. Both cats had been yowling, scratching dervishes. Roma had worn a long, heavy Kevlar glove. Hercules had left teeth marks on the thumb and two fingers, and Owen, scratch tracks down the entire arm.

"Would you be interested in coming with me next time I go out to the estate?" Roma asked, pulling her ring all the way off and sliding it back on. Her nails were short, without any polish. "You seem to have a rapport with those cats."

I glanced over at the table again. "I would," I said.

Roma's smile grew wider. "I'll call you," she said.

We turned toward the others. Violet was asking a question about one of the movements, her hands in front of her body at about shoulder height. Maggie adjusted one arm and pointed down at Violet's knees.

"Cloud hands," Roma said with a sigh.

I wasn't the only one who had trouble with that part of the form. I couldn't coordinate my hands with each other, let alone the lower half of my body. I looked like I belonged in platform shoes and spandex in a bad disco revival show.

We all watched as Maggie demonstrated, moving slowly and fluidly through the movement. Rebecca tucked her arm across the front of her body. Her sleeve slid backward, uncovering her wrapped wrist.

Maggie stopped what she was doing. "Rebecca, are you hurt?" she asked.

Rebecca's face went pale and she put a protective hand over her arm. "It's just my arthritis acting up," she said, rolling her wrist slowly from side to side under her hand. "I'm using a poultice. The bandage is just to keep it clean and in place."

Maggie stepped in front of Rebecca, took her hand and ran her slender fingers gently over the bandage. "Can you bend it?" she asked.

"Yes." She pulled her arm away from Maggie and held it out from her body, slowly bending her wrist back and forth. "It's just a little stiff."

Maggie examined the bandage again. "Do you make your own cotton strips?" she asked.

Rebecca nodded stiffly. "Yes."

"You have a very fine hand. What do you use in your poultice? Red cedar? Marshmallow?"

"I use my mother's herbal remedies," Rebecca said, holding her wrapped arm against her chest with her good arm. "They're not like anyone else's."

"Oh," Maggie said, discomfort showing on her face. She dropped her hand to her side. "Just take it easy. Stop if anything hurts."

She took a step backward and a couple of slow, calming breaths. "Okay, everyone. Circle," she called.

Roma moved to my right side, next to Rebecca. A look passed between the two of them. Would that be me someday, exchanging looks with Maggie when someone younger urged me to take it easy?

We made the circle a little bigger and started our warm-up exercises. Maggie looked across at me and grinned. I knew what was coming. "Bend your knees, Kathleen," she called. I crossed my eyes at her from across the circle. Next to me I heard Roma laugh.

I was sweating by the end of class, even with the windows open and the fan running. I started for my bag and then remembered what else—who else—was in there. Instead I used the end of my T-shirt to wipe my face.

Ruby came up to me, her orange tank sweat stained. "I heard you found Easton's body at the theater yesterday," she said. "That true?"

I finger-combed my sweat-damp hair and refastened the clip. "Yes, it's true," I said.

Ruby held out her hand. "This is for you."

A coil of black cord lay in her hand. I picked it up. A

small purple crystal dangled from the cord. "What's this for?" I asked.

Ruby touched the crystal and started it swinging. "Keep it with you. Or wear it. Whatever. It'll keep negative energy out of your life."

For a moment I didn't know what to say. Between the problems with the library renovations and finding Gregor Easton's body, I was pretty sure there was a lot of negative energy in my life. "It's beautiful," I finally managed. "Thank you."

Ruby took the necklace from my hand and showed me how to slide the knotted ends along the cord to make it longer or shorter. I slipped the pendant over my head and tucked the crystal inside my shirt. I wasn't sure it could keep negative energy out of my life, but it couldn't hurt. I hugged Ruby. "This is so nice," I said.

Maggie came up to us, holding a steaming cup that smelled like lemons. "What's so nice?" she asked.

I pulled the necklace out from under my shirt so she could see Ruby's gift.

"Ruby, that's beautiful," Maggie said. "It's one of yours?"

Ruby nodded. "The crystal will help ward off negative energy."

"Do you think there was a lot of negative energy around Gregor Easton?" I asked, pulling my sticky shirt away from my body.

"Oh, yeah," Ruby said. "I know you're not supposed to speak ill of the dead, but from what I saw, the man was a lech. You put that kind of energy out into the world and who knows what will come back with it?"

I nodded, wondering what they'd all think if they

knew Detective Gordon thought I'd been sleeping with the dead conductor.

Rebecca and Violet had come over to where we were standing. Rebecca was blotting the back of her neck with a towel. Violet didn't sweat. She didn't wrinkle or get windblown, either. She looked at Ruby. "What do you mean, 'Who knows what will come back with it'?" she asked.

Ruby bent one arm behind her head and pushed down on the elbow with her other hand. "Whatever energy we put out into the universe—good or bad—stays connected to us, like there's a tiny, invisible thread attached to it," she said. "Eventually it comes back and there's no way to know what else it will pick up along the way. No way to know what will get entangled in the string." Ruby switched arms.

"My mother believed something like that," Violet said.

"Your mother believed in karma?" Ruby asked.

"My mother believed what goes around comes around," Violet said.

Ruby laughed. "That's karma all right. It's a bitch."

Everyone laughed at that, but I couldn't help shivering, for some reason. I felt a chill, as if someone had just drawn a finger up my spine.

Roma touched my shoulder. I jumped and sucked in a breath. "Oh, I'm sorry," she said. "It's just, well"—she pointed across the room at the tea table—"your bag seems to be moving."

8

Step Back, Seven Stars

*C*rap on toast! She was right. The bag was moving, rocking from side to side the way a kid might rock a rowboat to try and tip everyone into the water. Or the way a restless cat might rock a nylon bag because he was bored.

"Kathleen, dear, is there something in your bag?" Rebecca asked.

"It's my phone," Maggie blurted.

I stared at her. What the heck was she doing?

"Your phone?" Ruby said.

Maggie nodded her head vigorously. "Uh-huh." She caught my eye. "Sorry, Kathleen. I didn't want it to get broken so I tucked it in your bag." She held up both hands. "Who knew vibrate could be that vigorous?"

"That's okay," I said. I cleared my throat. "I'll, umm ... I'll get it for you."

I scurried over to the table. Keeping my body between the tote and everyone else, I squatted down and looked through the top mesh panel. Two green eyes met mine.

"Cut. It. Out," I whispered through clenched teeth.

Hercules made a noise that sounded an awful lot like a snort.

"Stay still and stay quiet. We're leaving in a minute." I straightened, bumping into Maggie. "'Who knew vibrate could be so vigorous'?" I said.

"You'd rather be known as the librarian who carries her cat in her gym bag?" she retorted.

"Good point," I said. I slid the bag onto my shoulder and kept it against my body with an elbow. "I'm going to get you-know-who out of here."

"Okay," Maggie said. "I'll see you in an hour or so."

Violet and Roma were standing just outside the door. Roma pulled a water bottle out of her backpack as I slipped past them and grabbed my hoodie off the hook.

"Violet, what's going to happen to the music festival now?" I asked as I tied the sweatshirt around my waist again.

Not a strand of Violet's silver hair in its sleek French twist was out of place. "I don't know," she said. "The committee is meeting tomorrow to try to figure that out."

"I'd hate to see the festival canceled," Roma said. Her face was flushed.

"So would I," Violet said. "But Gregor Easton was a last-minute replacement himself. I have no idea how we could get anyone of his caliber to take over at this point."

"How did you get him to step in for the original music director?" I asked.

"Actually, he contacted us."

Roma looked at her with surprise. "Really? I didn't know that."

"Oh, yes," Violet said, brushing invisible lint off of her T-shirt. "He'd heard about Zinia needing emergency surgery—apparently they're close friends—and he'd had an unexpected cancellation in his own schedule. So he told Zinia he'd step up. He got in touch with us, and that was that."

"That was convenient," I said.

"Yes, it was," Violet said. "Somehow I don't think we're going to be that lucky twice."

I heard the street door below open and someone started up the stairs. After a moment Ami appeared, in denim shorts and a tank top, eating what had to be a container of Tubby's frozen yogurt. She licked the stubby wooden spoon—at Tubby's they didn't use plastic spoons—and smiled at us. "Hi," she said. "I'm here to get Rebecca." Her voice went up at the end of the sentence, making it sound like a question, like she wasn't quite sure if she was at the right place at the right time.

"I'm ready," Rebecca said from the doorway. I lifted her tote bag down and handed it to her. *Thank you,* she mouthed. She pulled her scarf out of the top of the bag and held it up. "I found my scarf," she said to Ami. "I guess I left it here last time."

"I told you it was probably here," Violet said.

"Mmmm, good," Ami said around a mouthful of yogurt and strawberries. "But I would've made you another one."

"I like this one," Rebecca said, tucking the length of fabric back in her tote. "It's the first scarf you made."

Ami smiled at her over the cardboard cup in her hand. "You're such a mushball, Rebbie. You have everything I ever gave you—every present, every piece of paper."

"She has every piece of paper everyone ever gave her," Violet said tartly.

"Violet Cole, are you implying that I'm a pack rat?" Rebecca asked, hands on her hips in mock outrage, eyes twinkling.

"No," Violet said. "I'm coming right out and saying it. Rebecca, you are a pack rat."

Rebecca drew herself up to her full five-foot-three-inches. "I prefer to think of myself as an environmental-ist and conservator of history."

Violet shook her head slightly. "And I prefer to think of myself as twenty-five and hot as a two-dollar pistol. Doesn't make it true."

Everyone laughed. Hearing the elegant, composed Violet say "hot as a two-dollar pistol" was kind of like hearing a two-year-old repeat an off-color word. Maybe you shouldn't laugh, but you couldn't quite help it.

Ami came up the last couple of steps then and took Rebecca's bag.

Rebecca turned to me, reached over and pushed back a few stray strands of hair that had fallen on my cheek. "I'll get my scissors out this weekend and just give you a little more shape," she said with a smile.

I smiled back at her. "Thank you."

"Are you ready?" Ami asked. She held up her card-board cup. "I have one of these for you, packed in some ice down in the car."

Rebecca's smile got even bigger. "You are a darling girl," she said, hooking her arm through the younger woman's. She gave me a little wave with her free hand and they disappeared down the stairs.

I could feel Hercules wriggling inside the bag again. "I have to get going, too," I said to Violet and Roma. "See you next time." I started down the steps, holding my bag close to my hip. "Okay," I whispered. "We're going."

I walked quickly to the library. There were a lot of people out in the downtown, but it was deserted at the library. Jason was at the checkout desk.

"Quiet night?" I asked.

"Yeah," he said, brushing a lock of blond hair out of his eyes. "Nobody's been in since suppertime." He pointed to the book carts behind him. "All those new kids' books are ready to go on the shelves."

"Thank you," I said. "That's a big help." Jason was my summer intern, and a real find. He looked like a teen-magazine heartthrob, with blond hair and an easy smile, but he lived and breathed books. He wanted to be a writer and he was working his way through the classics—Faulkner, Dostoyevsky, Hemingway.

"Where's Abigail?" I asked.

Jason pointed over his head. "She's in the workroom, getting all those magazines ready for the yard sale."

I headed for my office first and let Hercules loose. He poked his head out of the bag, blinked and sniffed my desktop, then came all the way out and walked over a stack of files to the edge of the desk, where he jumped into my chair. Which set the chair spinning.

I darted around the side of the desk and stopped the chair. Hercules looked woozily up at me.

I reached down to pat his head. "Stay here," I said. "I'll be back."

I started for the second floor but couldn't resist detouring over to the computer room. True to his word, Oren had assembled all six carrels and chairs. I ran my finger over the closest table. There was no dust, no dirt on the light wood. That was Oren. A computer box sat next to each workstation. As soon as Larry had the wiring fixed and the new outlets working, I could set up the computers, and after a hundred years the Mayville Heights Free Public Library would be part of the electronic age.

Abigail was in the workroom next door to the staff lounge. She was sitting on the floor, two rows of stacked and tied magazines behind her. "Hi," I said.

She looked up and smiled. Her gray hair was pulled

back in a tight braid and her rimless reading glasses had slipped down to the end of her nose. She'd told me she'd started going gray in her twenties. Now, a couple of decades later, her hair was a beautiful mix of red and silver. Somehow it didn't make her look old—just smarter. Self-consciously I touched my own mussed hair.

"Did you do all this tonight?" I asked.

She pulled a knot tight in the string around a stack of magazines and set them behind her. "Yes, I did," she said. "It's been very quiet." She gestured to the back of the room. "I found some foam board in the cupboard. Do you mind if we use it for posters?"

"No. That's a great idea."

Abigail stood up and surveyed her work. "If it's like this tomorrow night I should be able to finish these and start on the hardcovers," she said.

"That would be great," I said.

I headed back downstairs. It was almost eight o'clock, closing time. Jason was going through each section on the main floor, turning off lights and shelving the occasional book as he went. I walked over to the magazines and gathered up a couple of issues that had been left out of their slots. Then I lined up the book carts at the desk and shut down the computer.

Abigail came down the steps carrying her bike helmet as Jason turned off the last bank of lights. Only the overhead above the circulation desk stayed lit. I walked Abigail to the entrance, let her out, and waited for Jason, who was gathering his knapsack, jamming even more books inside. He swung it up onto his shoulder and hurried over to me.

"See you tomorrow," he said.

"Have a good night," I said. I locked the doors and shut the ironwork gate, but left it unlocked.

Hercules was on the floor in front of the desk when I opened my office door.

"Do you want to look around before we leave?" I asked. He came right over to the open door and looked out, checking right and left. I crouched beside him. "No hiding, and you come when I call," I said, wagging my finger at him. He batted it out of the way, so I stood up and headed for the stairs. Herc padded behind me.

Except for a bit of trim the new reception and checkout desk was finished. There was some painting to do and lots more books to be shelved, and of course we didn't have a meeting room, but for the first time I had a sense of how the building was going to look when it was finally finished.

Herc prowled the computer area, twining in and out around the carrels, sniffing each cardboard box.

"Okay. Are you ready to go?" I said.

He looked back at me, then started purposefully across the library. "Hercules, where are you going?" I said. He ignored me.

I hurried after the cat, but when I bent to scoop him up he darted away. Only one of the large sheets of plastic that Will Redfern's men had hung was still in place. It was a blurry wall on one side of the door to the storage area/someday-to-be meeting room. The heavy paneled door was closed and locked and the space was marked off with yellow police tape.

"Don't you even think about it," I called.

Nonchalantly, Hercules walked past the police cordon toward the door.

"Hercules, come back here right now," I said sharply.

All I got for an answer was a low, rumbly "Meow."

"C'mon, puss," I coaxed. "Time to go."

His attention was focused completely on the heavy wooden door.

"You are never going to eat another spoonful of Tubby's yogurt in your life if you don't get over here right now," I said.

He tossed a quick glance back over his shoulder but didn't move. Okay, so the no-yogurt part was a bluff. Why was I standing on one side of a strip of plastic yellow tape when I could just duck underneath it and grab the cat? No alarm bells were going to go off. Detective Gordon wasn't going to rappel down from the ceiling and arrest me.

Still, I couldn't help checking around—for what, I didn't know—before I ducked under the tape.

"C'mere, you," I said, bending down for the little black-and-white cat, who walked out of my reach, through the closed door in front of us, and disappeared.

9

Slant Brush Knee

My knees started to shake. I sat down. Hard. Hercules had vanished. He hadn't darted past me. He hadn't run around the corner. He'd walked through a solid wooden door just as if it wasn't there. I could see it again in my head without closing my eyes. He'd vanished through that door and it was almost as though there was a faint pop as the end of his tail disappeared.

I closed my eyes and took a couple of deep breaths. "Be there," I whispered. I opened my eyes again. No cat.

Leaning forward, I laid my hand against the door. It was solid. I felt all over the panel, pushing at the curved wood. Maybe there was some kind of secret opening. Maybe Hercules had activated a hidden panel. Maybe the Hardy Boys and Nancy Drew would show up. The door was thick and unyielding.

"Hercules," I called. "C'mon, puss. Where are you?"

There was silence and then a faint "Meow" from the other side of the closed door.

He was in there. Somehow he was in there. I grabbed the doorknob. Locked. I twisted the knob in frustration. Of course it was locked. The room was part of a murder investigation. And I'd just been trying to get inside.

I yanked my hand away from the door like it was suddenly on fire.

Crap on toast! Now my fingerprints were all over the door. I used the hem of my T-shirt to rub the doorknob. Then I dropped to my knees and polished the bottom section of the door where I'd looked for some kind of hidden access panel.

I caught a bit of my reflection in the brass kick panel and realized what I was doing. "You're nuts," I said aloud, sitting back on my heels.

I shouldn't have touched the door at all. I took a couple of deep breaths. I should call the police, I realized. How else was I going to get Hercules out? Then I thought, *Oh, sure, call Detective Gordon and tell him my cat just walked through the door into the room. No, that won't make me look like a nutcase.*

Was that what was wrong? Was I crazy? I remembered a psych prof in first year telling the class that if you could ask the question, then you weren't. Of course, three-quarters of the time he came to class in his pajama bottoms.

Then I remembered how Owen had seemed to just materialize on Gregor Easton's head, just the way he'd suddenly seemed to appear in midleap, chasing that bird in the backyard.

I couldn't breathe. Was it possible? Did the cats have some kind magical abilities? I pressed my head to my knees and made myself take several shaky breaths. *Okay, no climbing on the crazy bus,* I told myself. I was tired. I needed glasses. There was a rational explanation for all of this.

I leaned close to the door and called Hercules again. Nothing.

I could picture him on the other side of the door, one

ear twitching at the sound of his name. I also knew he wasn't coming out until he felt like it.

I pulled the crystal Ruby had given me out of my shirt. If there was any negative energy around, maybe the crystal would keep it away. Then I shifted into a sitting position on the floor, wrapped my arms around my knees and waited. And waited.

Maybe five minutes went by, although it seemed a lot longer. Then I felt . . . something I couldn't define. It was as if the air around the door suddenly thickened and pushed against me, the way water pushes against your hand if you try to press it over the end of a garden hose.

And then Hercules walked through the door as if there wasn't any door there at all. He blinked and gave me an *Oh, you're still here* look. I grabbed him in case he got the idea to take another look inside the room.

"You are in so much trouble," I said sternly, heading for the steps.

He ducked his head. Translation: *No, I'm not.*

"That isn't going to work," I said, shifting him to my other arm so I could open the office door. Herc tilted his head to one side and looked, wide-eyed, at me. "Don't bother with any of that I'm-so-cute stuff," I said. I bent my face very close to his. "It's. Not. Working."

He licked my nose.

I pushed the door closed with my hip and set the cat on the floor. Closing my eyes for a moment, I rubbed the space between my eyes. It felt like something in my head had twisted into a pretzel, trying to make sense out of what I'd seen. I blew out a breath and opened my eyes. Herc was watching me as though I was the one who'd done something bizarre. I dropped into my desk chair and he immediately jumped onto my lap.

"How did you do that?" I asked. "Is there a kitty ver-

sion of 'abracadabra'? Do you click your back paws together or wiggle your whiskers?" I was asking a cat how
he walked through a solid door. Maybe I was losing my
mind.

I stroked the top of Herc's head. What if the police
weren't finished in the room? Could the cat have left
any DNA or hair behind? I felt a knot clench in my
stomach to match the one pressing behind my eyes. He
was a cat. How could he not leave hair behind?

And Will Redfern had been using that space for storage for weeks. It was a messy, dusty space. Would the
police find paw prints?

Or worse?

I scratched the side of Herc's face so he'd turn toward me. "Please tell me you didn't hack up anything in
there?" I said.

He looked at me, almost . . . smugly, nudged my hand
away with a push of his head, then bent over my hand
and spat out a small green glass bead.

My mouth went dry. I stared at the tiny glass sphere.
There were a few threads caught on it. Hercules had
found that in the storage room. How had it ended up
there? Before the damaged floor in the room had been
repaired, the baseboards had been pulled off and the
tile had been steam cleaned. It had been clean enough
to eat off of. Literally. And I couldn't picture any of
the burly workmen wearing anything with tiny, green
glass beads. Had Hercules found something the police
missed?

"How did you get this?" I said. He jumped off my
lap and stood in front of the window. He seemed to be
studying the wall. After a moment he started scratching
at the edge of the trim—where the old wood met the
floor—with one paw.

"Hey! Stop that!" I said.

As usual, Hercules ignored me. He caught the end of something with his paw and bent his head over it.

"No!" I snapped, so loudly my voice echoed around the room and startled both of us. I leaned forward. "Give that to me," I said. He moved his paw and a purple plastic paperclip skittered across the floor toward me.

I picked it up. Hercules looked from the twist of plastic to me to the baseboard trim. Then he sat, wrapped his tail around his feet, and looked at me again.

It was crazy, but it was like . . . he wanted me to *do* something. What?

I got up and knelt down in front of the window. Feeling along the edge of the baseboard I found a small gap, not much thicker than the blade of a butter knife, between the trim and the floor. No surprise in a hundred-year-old building. And because the building had shifted over the past century the floors had also moved a little. They slanted toward the window. Anything I dropped tended to slide or roll up against that wall.

I looked over my shoulder at the cat, who was patiently watching me. I was still holding the purple paperclip as well as the glass bead Hercules had found. I rolled the tiny bead under my thumb, along my fingers.

And then I got it.

I got to my feet, walking around the desk to stand with my back to the door. I shut my eyes, trying to see the meeting-room space before the renovations had started, before it had become the storage place for tools and supplies. The space below was almost identical to my office. Maybe that floor had the same slant toward the window. Maybe there was a gap between the baseboard and the floor in there, too.

I held the bead up to the light. I felt light-headed.

"Could this bead have something to do with Gregor Easton's murder?" I asked Hercules.

Okay, so now I had to deal with the idea that not only did my cats have magical abilities, but they were also trying to nudge me to solve a murder. I looked at Herc with narrowed eyes.

He continued to stare unblinkingly at me.

The mosaic tile floor on the main level of the library had been repaired and resealed early in the renovations, then covered for weeks with heavy brown paper—that had made me think of butcher's paper—and a layer of cardboard. The paper was still down in the storage area to protect the floor.

Vincent Gallo's crew had done meticulous work. They wouldn't have left a bead, a bit of paper or even a dust bunny behind. The old man, who could have been anywhere from seventy to ninety, had crawled all over the floor on his hands and knees, glasses perched on the end of his nose, to check the work.

I shook my head. "Maybe it does," I said. I crossed to the window again and looked down on the reading garden. "I should take this bead to the police or call Detective Gordon," I said to Hercules. I dropped onto my swivel chair again. "Of course, I can't do that, because how can I explain *why* it might be important without explaining *how* I have it."

I slumped against the back of the chair. Hercules came to sit front of me. I patted my leg. "C'mon up," I said.

He leaped into my lap. I stroked the top of his head and he began to purr. Slowly I rolled my head from one shoulder to the other, to try to loosen the knots in my neck. The cat continued to purr in my lap, warm and comforting.

Warm.

Solid.

He wasn't some superhero from the X-Men comics who could teleport or manipulate DNA. He couldn't shoot lightning bolts from his fingers. Hercules was a cat. A small, furry, black-and-white cat. That I'd seen walk through an inch-and-a-half-thick wooden door. That defied the laws of physics. It couldn't have happened.

Except it had.

What could I do? I couldn't go to the police. I couldn't tell the truth—not that I was even sure what the truth was. But how could I lie? Was there some option in between the two? I was tired. If there was a third option, I couldn't think of it right now.

"Let's go home," I said to Hercules.

I stood up and set him on the desk. He made disgruntled *murp* sounds but he climbed willingly into the bag.

I glanced out the window again. It was getting dark. I swung the cat bag over my shoulder, grabbed the rest of my things and left the office.

"We'll figure this out when we get home," I said as I locked the gate and the main doors. "Some chocolate for me, some tuna for you and we'll work it out."

"Work what out?" a voice said behind me.

Maggie was standing at the top of the steps. How could I have forgotten that she was meeting me so we could watch the *Gotta Dance* reunion special?

I turned, brushing my hair back behind one ear. "Umm ... ah ... I just meant everything that's happened since I found Gregor Easton's body."

We walked down the stairs together and out along the path to the sidewalk.

"Are you all right?" Maggie asked.

I blew a wayward strand of hair off my cheek, remembering that I hadn't had a chance to tell Maggie about the piece of paper the police had found on Easton's body. For a while I'd almost forgotten about it. "I can't believe I didn't tell you before, but the police found a note in Easton's pocket, supposedly from me, asking him to meet me here at the library."

Maggie stopped so abruptly I almost banged into her. "How could he have a note from you? That doesn't make any sense."

"I know." The shoulder strap of the bag was digging into the side of my neck. I shifted it a little. "I didn't write it. It's not my handwriting. But whoever wrote it signed my name."

She shook her head dismissively. "Of course you didn't write it," she said. "But somebody obviously wanted him to think you did."

We started walking again. "Why?" I said.

"Because that somebody knew Easton wouldn't show up for him . . . or her."

"But they thought he'd show up for me?"

Maggie shot me a wry sideways glance. "Kath, you're not exactly ugly, you know."

"I'm not exactly Easton's type, either. From what I've heard he liked women young enough to be his granddaughters."

We crossed the street and started up Mountain Road, and I switched Hercules to my other shoulder.

"After what happened with Owen in the library Easton probably thought you were looking to make amends."

I squirmed at the image. Then comprehension set in. I stopped walking and turned to face Maggie. "But that would mean whoever sent the note knew what had happened."

She nodded. "So who knew?"

"You. Susan. Mary." I held up my hand and ticked the names off on my fingers. "That's it. Oh, and Eric—Susan's husband—because I'd asked her to call him and have breakfast delivered to Easton as an apology."

Maggie stretched one arm behind her head as we started up the hill again. "Anyone else?" she asked.

"Just the cats," I said. "And I don't think they told anyone, but I have no idea who Susan or Mary or Eric—"

"—or even Easton himself might have told," Maggie finished. "Did you see the paper? Do you know what it said?"

"I saw it," I said. I pulled the image of Detective Gordon holding up the plastic bag with the note inside into my head. "It was written on a piece of paper from one of the library notepads. Remember? The ones that say 'Mabel' instead of 'Mayville.' There were two boxes in the workroom. There's a silhouette of an open book in the left corner and it says 'Mabel Heights Free Public Library' across the bottom." I rubbed the back of my neck again. "The note itself said, 'Meet me at the library at eleven thirty. Kathleen.'"

Maggie made a skeptical noise and touched my arm. "He sure had an overinflated idea of his appeal if he thought you were interested in a rendezvous among the stacks at eleven thirty at night."

"The man didn't lack confidence, Mags," I said.

She smiled and her hand, still on my arm, was warm. "Tomorrow I'll ask around and see what I can find out about Easton and what he'd been doing since he got here. No one's going to believe you killed the man."

Hercules meowed his agreement from my hip. Maggie held up both hands. "See? Even Furry Face knows that." She checked her watch, then patted the canvas bag she was carrying. "It's five minutes to showtime, and I have a bag of organic cheese puffs and another bottle of Ruby's homemade wine."

I opened the porch door and followed Maggie inside, tucking my keys in my pocket. My fingers touched the little sea-green glass bead. Okay, so I couldn't take it to the police. I could do some digging of my own. Because I was definitely going to figure out what was going on.

Someone had used my name to get Gregor Easton to meet him or her. And maybe kill him.

Not someone passing through town. Not some stranger.

Someone here in Mayville Heights. Someone I knew.

10

Play Guitar

I woke up early, and when I couldn't get back to sleep I cooked. By eight o'clock a batch of blueberry–poppy seed muffins was cooling on the counter next to a double recipe of Hercules and Owen's favorite kitty treats. There was a cat glued to each of my legs as I made coffee and scrambled an egg.

I poured a cup of coffee and put it, my breakfast and a big handful of cat nibbles on a tray. Then I snagged the newspaper from the front door and carried everything out to the backyard, followed, of course, by the cats.

I settled on my favorite Adirondack chair and spread my napkin on the grass. Half the cat crackers went on one side; half on the other.

Hercules sniffed the food carefully even though he'd been dogging me since the cookie sheets had come out of the oven. He must have liked what his nose told him because he began to eat, eyes half closed in enjoyment. Owen, as usual, was moving his stash, two or three pieces at a time, onto the grass.

"That's going to get soggy," I told him.

He shot me an annoyed glare and continued to deposit his food in little piles on the lawn.

I read the paper as I ate. There were very few details about the investigation into Gregor Easton's death, beyond a statement from Detective Gordon saying that the police were still investigating. The major story was what was going to happen to the music festival. The paper, via its editorial, took the position that without a well-known musician to act as music director, the festival should be canceled. The opinions in the letters to the editor section ran the gamut from continuing without a guest musician to bringing in the latest *American Idol* winner, to hiring Luciano Pavarotti, who was, unfortunately, dead.

Both cats finished eating. Owen set off across the lawn, probably heading for Rebecca's gazebo and a nap. Herc walked around the yard, doing his daily survey of things. I watched him for a moment, wondering if last night could somehow have been just a stress-fueled hallucination. Logically, I knew cats couldn't walk through solid doors or walls. Neither could dogs, monkeys, snakes, or people—although I'd seen some cockroaches come pretty close.

It wasn't like I hadn't heard rumors about the cats from Wisteria Hill, but there were no tales about paranormal abilities. Stories about the Wisteria cats ranged from innocuous (they all had six toes; mine didn't) to bizarre (the cats were more than a hundred years old). I'd never heard anyone suggest the cats had the ability to disappear at will. Not that I'd been able to find out much about them or the crumbling house. Most people changed the subject when I brought it up. Maybe I'd be able to find out more when I went out there with Roma.

Herc had finished his check of the yard and worked his way back to me. He gave the napkin, still spread on the grass, a cursory sniff and then jumped up onto my lap. I scratched the top of his head and he started to purr. The reality was, I couldn't ever say anything to anyone about what I'd seen him do. Because if I did and someone actually believed me, it was only going to end with my cats in a lab somewhere with wire mesh on the windows and electrodes stuck to their little shaved heads.

"I'd rather be the crazy cat lady," I told Hercules.

He purred even louder. I took that to mean living with a crazy cat lady was okay by him. Suddenly he lifted his head. His ears moved and he looked toward the side of the house.

I leaned sideways in the chair, but I couldn't see anyone. That didn't mean no one was there. I set the cat on the grass and stood up just as Everett Henderson came around the side of the house. "How do you do that?" I whispered to Hercules.

Everett Henderson looked a lot like Sean Connery— balding, close-cropped white beard, intense dark eyes, and a lived-in face—enough that when he spoke I always expected to hear Connery's Scottish accent. Everett was tall and lean, and when he walked into a room focus shifted automatically to him. If he said he was going to do something, it got done. I had no idea how he'd made his money, but, based on how much he was spending on the library, he seemed to have a lot of it.

"Hello, Kathleen," he said. "I'm sorry to bother you on your morning off."

"You're no bother," I assured him. "I was just having coffee and reading the paper. Would you like a cup?"

"It's not decaf, is it?"

I made a cross with one index finger over the other. "Bite your tongue," I said.

His smile widened. "In that case, yes, I would," he said.

I gestured toward the back door. "Come into the kitchen," I said.

Everett followed me into the house. Both cats had disappeared for the moment. I poured Everett a cup of coffee and got a new cup for myself. We sat at the kitchen table.

"Would you like a muffin?" I asked. "They're blueberry–poppy seed."

He shook his head. "I'm allergic to poppy seeds."

"I've heard of peanut and shellfish allergies, but never poppy seeds," I said.

"It's in the family." Everett picked up his mug and took a drink. "Mmmm, you make good coffee."

"Thank you," I said.

"So, I heard you found Gregor Easton's body," he said. Everett was not the kind of person to dance around things, I'd learned in the few months I'd known him.

"I did."

"Did you kill him?"

"No."

"I didn't think you had," he said. "I hope I haven't offended you by asking."

"You haven't." I smiled to show I meant it. "And since we're being frank, I didn't have an affair with Mr. Easton, either."

Everett laughed as he put his cup on the table. "Kathleen, you hardly seem the type to be sneaking around, engaging in hanky-panky with a man old enough to be, well, me."

"You're not an old man, Everett," I said.

"Yes, I am," he said, brown eyes twinkling. "But I do appreciate your flattery." Then his face turned serious. "Detective Gordon came to see me."

I should have realized the detective would do that.

"I gave him your references," he said. "And I told him I checked you out thoroughly and interviewed you myself before you were hired. And I told him I have complete faith in you."

"I"—my voice stuck in my throat—"I . . . thank you."

Everett drained his cup and set it on the table again. "Now, tell me how things are at the library."

I stood up to get us both refills as Hercules came into the kitchen from the porch. For a second I wondered if I'd left the screen door open. Then I remembered doors weren't exactly a barrier for Hercules. The cat stopped about halfway across the kitchen floor, his attention focused on our visitor.

Everett stared back at the cat. He looked stunned. "Where did that cat come from?" he managed to choke out. He didn't even look at me—he couldn't seem to take his eyes off the little tuxedo cat who seemed equally interested in the man.

"He's mine," I said slowly. "That's Hercules. Owen is out in the yard somewhere." I swallowed a mouthful of coffee, almost burning my tongue. "I was out walking, not long after I first arrived here. I stumbled upon Wisteria Hill and I realize I was trespassing, but the garden at the back was so beautiful. That's where I found Owen and Hercules. They . . . followed me home." I was babbling.

Hercules got up and walked over to stand in front of Everett, still looking intently at the older man.

"From Wisteria Hill," Everett said.

"Yes," I said. I cleared my throat. "Have I done something wrong by keeping them?"

That made Everett finally look at me. He shook his head. "No. No, you haven't." He glanced quickly back at Herc. "My mother had a cat. It disappeared when she died. I . . . We searched the house and the grounds for days, but . . ." He let the end of the sentence trail off and shook his head again. "I know it's not possible—cats don't live that long—but for a moment . . ." He pulled his hand down over his bearded chin and his gaze went back to Hercules. "Finn," Everett said, more to himself than to me.

Herc's ears twitched and he took a step forward. A shiver slid up the back of my neck.

"Here, Finn," Everett called again, holding out his hand.

Hercules started toward him. I held my breath and it seemed I could hear my own heartbeat thudding double time in my ears.

The cat took another step toward Everett. And then another.

And then he reached under Everett's chair and snagged something with his paw, completely ignoring the hand extended to him.

I started to breathe again. Leaning forward in my seat, I tried to see what Hercules was hiding. "What is that?" I asked the cat.

He jerked upright at the sound of my voice, almost bumping his head on the underside of the wooden chair. One white-tipped paw still covered whatever he had spotted.

"Let me see," I said. We had a little stare-down contest. I won.

Slowly Hercules raised his paw. It was a kitty cracker. It had probably fallen onto the floor when I was taking them off the baking sheet.

"Okay, you can have it," I said, straightening. "Cat treat," I said as an aside to Everett.

Hercules was already chewing the little cracker. He

took a couple of passes at his face, more to get any stray crumbs than to really get clean, I suspected, and then crossed under the table and came to lean against my leg.

I smiled at Everett, who smiled back at me and picked up his cup. Whatever memories Hercules had stirred up had been put away again. "You have another cat?" he asked.

I nodded, reaching down to scratch the top of Hercules' head. "Owen. He's a tabby."

"Owen?" Everett asked over the top of his mug.

"I was reading *A Prayer for Owen Meany*—John Irving—when the cats followed me home. Every time I put the book down Owen sat on it. It was either going to be Owen or Irving." I shrugged. "And he didn't look like an Irving." I reached for my coffee.

"And Hercules? From Roman mythology?"

"Uh, yes." That was sort of true. Herc was named after Hercules, son of Zeus, as portrayed by the delectable Kevin Sorbo. Or as Maggie sometimes called him, Mr. Six-Pack in a Loincloth. Mags didn't have a proper appreciation for trashy television.

"You were going to tell me how the renovations are going," Everett said.

Okay. We weren't talking about the cats anymore.

I brought Everett up-to-date on what had been happening—the wiring problems, the computer room, plans for the yard sale—downplaying my almost being electrocuted and leaving out Owen and Gregor Easton's encounter altogether.

"Were you hurt?" Everett asked, reaching across the table to pat my arm.

"I'm fine," I said. "Luckily Roma Davidson was at the library."

Everett raised an eyebrow and a hint of a smile played around his mouth.

I couldn't quite help smiling myself. "Yes, I know she's a vet, and I promise you I'm fine."

Everett relaxed all the way into a smile and sat back in his chair again. "I have every confidence that Lawrence will fix the problem with the wiring. And I'm confident that Roma took good care of you, even though you're not her typical patient." His expression turned serious again. "When Lawrence sends you a bill, send it directly to the office. That shouldn't have to come out of the renovation budget."

"Thank you," I said, feeling relieved I wasn't going to have to squeeze the already stretched budget after all. "I will."

Everett stood up. "Thank you for the coffee, Kathleen. I have to get back to the office. Is there anything else you need from me?"

For a moment I thought about telling him how Will Redfern kept giving me the runaround, how it seemed sometimes that he didn't want the library job to get finished. But it seemed like such a childish thing to complain about.

"No," I said. "I'll call Lita if I need anything."

I walked Everett out. He looked around, then crossed the grass to look at the roses, still blooming in the back corner of the yard. "You have a real green thumb, Kathleen," he said. "These roses have never looked so beautiful." He bent to smell one of the flowers, white petals edged in pink. "These bushes came from Wisteria Hill, you know. Harry Senior brought them down here. He said it was a sin to let them go wild out at the house."

There was my opening. I opened my mouth to ask him why the estate had been abandoned, but before I could get the words out Everett straightened and looked over at Rebecca's house.

"Have you met Rebecca?" he asked.

"The day I moved in," I told him, smiling at the memory. Rebecca had shown up with a plate of cinnamon rolls—still warm—and a stainless-steel carafe of coffee. I hadn't realized that Rebecca and Everett knew each other, which seemed silly, considering Mayville Heights was a small place and they were both in their midsixties, give or take. Sometimes I still thought like a city dweller.

"How is she?" Everett asked. For a moment I thought he was going to walk over to the hedge. Did he and Rebecca have a past, or had I been reading too many books by the Brontë sisters?

"She's fine," I said. "She's taking tai chi. She talked me into joining the class."

"I can see her doing that," he said, finally pulling his eyes back to me. He brushed his hand over his scalp. "Call the office if you need anything," he said. "And don't worry about this business with Easton. It'll straighten itself out." He patted my shoulder.

I watched Everett cross the yard to the street. I was just about to go back inside when Owen poked his head through the gap in the hedge. He meowed loudly when he saw me. Translation: *Come and get me*.

"C'mon," I called to him.

He sat down and yowled again.

"You can walk," I said. "I'm not coming to get you." I stood there, arms folded, doing my best Gary-Cooper-in-the-showdown-of-*High-Noon* impersonation, waiting to see what he'd do. After a minute Owen got up and started toward me, something hanging from his mouth. It was enough to get me to walk over and intercept him.

He looked up at me, all golden-eyed innocence, one end of what looked like a bit of fringe between his teeth.

"What is that?" I asked. I reached down and he obligingly let go. It was a twisted piece of fringe. "Owen, where did you get this?" I asked. It looked like the same fringe that was on the scarf Rebecca had left behind at tai chi Tuesday night.

"Owen," I said sharply. "Did you take this from Rebecca's scarf?"

The cat was suddenly intently interested in something crawling on the ground in front of him.

Great. I had one cat that could walk through walls and another that seemed to be turning into a kleptomaniac. I leaned down. "That was very bad." I shook the twist of fringe in his face. "Why did you do that?"

Owen lifted his head, looked around my legs, then sat down and started carefully washing his face.

"Ms. Paulson," a voice said behind me. *Detective Gordon.*

I closed my eyes for a second, pulled in a deep breath and slowly blew it out. Then I turned around, pasting a pleasant, innocent expression on my face.

The detective headed toward us.

"We are not finished," I hissed to Owen, bending to tug at my shoe as a cover so the police officer couldn't catch me talking to a cat.

Without really thinking about it, I tucked the piece of fringe into the back pocket of my pants.

"Good morning, Detective," I said.

He looked at Owen, who continued washing his face. I didn't think I'd ever seen the cat be quite so meticulous about his face washing in, well, ever.

"Is that your cat?" the detective asked.

"Yes, that's Owen," I said.

"Hello, puss." He held out his hand for Owen to sniff. Owen ignored it and continued his elaborate face-washing routine.

The detective gave a slight shrug and straightened. "Ms. Paulson, I have a couple more questions, if you don't mind."

I wondered what he'd do if I said I did mind. Instead I said only, "Go ahead."

"Tuesday morning, how did you get into the theater?"

"Through the side door."

"Did you touch the alarm panel?"

"I didn't know there was an alarm panel." Why wasn't he writing this down? Was his memory that good, or was he more interested in my reaction to the questions than my answers? Owen finally finished washing his face.

"Did you turn on any lights?" Detective Gordon asked, pushing his rolled shirtsleeves back a bit more. His forearms were deeply tanned.

I shook my head. "No."

"Do you remember which lights were on?"

I closed my eyes for a second and let the image of the Stratton fill my head. "There was one light by the side door and several of the stage lights were on. That's how I noticed that little silver musical note."

"Is that it?"

In my mind I looked out over the audience seating. "No," I said slowly. "There was a light—not very bright—at the back of the theater."

I held up both hands to put the image in perspective. "This side," I said, wiggling my left fingers. I opened my eyes. "The light was on the left as you look toward the back of the audience."

He nodded. Did that mean I'd given the right answer? Owen was still leaning against my leg. I bent down and picked him up. Detective Gordon held out his hand again. Owen shifted in my arms, and his attention focused on something just over my right shoulder. "I'm sorry," I said. "Owen doesn't like to be touched by anyone other than me. He was feral. Both cats were, actually."

"From the old Henderson estate?"

I nodded.

"How did you get them to come with you?"

I scratched under Owen's chin. He rubbed his head against my neck, but I could still feel his body, under his fur, tensed in case he had to defend my honor by—I don't know—jumping on Detective Gordon's head, maybe?

"Actually, they followed me," I said. "They were so small, and I couldn't find their mother." Owen licked my chin then. It tickled and I laughed.

"They followed you?" The detective seemed . . . surprised. "I've never seen any of the cats out there come anywhere close to a person—not even Dr. Davidson."

It was my turn to look surprised. "You've been out to Wisteria Hill?"

He stared at his feet, his face suddenly tinged with pink. "A few of us have been helping Dr. Davidson."

He'd been helping Roma. *Damn!* That made it harder to dislike the man.

Owen started squirming, so I set him on the grass. He headed for the house.

"Detective Gordon, would you like a cup of coffee?" I asked. He was helping Roma. It seemed wrong to hold a grudge. "I made muffins. Blueberry."

He smiled. "I would love a cup of coffee," he said. "And I wouldn't say no to a blueberry muffin."

We crossed the yard to the back door, where Owen

was waiting. He followed us into the kitchen. The detective leaned against the counter while I poured coffee. The cat sat by the refrigerator, eyeing the remaining cat treats still on the wire cooling rack. I handed Detective Gordon a plate and dipped my head in the direction of the muffins. "Help yourself," I said.

I set the mugs on the table and turned to find him about to pop a sardine-flavored kitty treat into his mouth. I burst out laughing.

He looked at me in surprise, cat cracker halfway to his mouth.

"I meant help yourself to a muffin," I managed to choke out between laughing fits. "But if you prefer sardine-and-cheese cat snacks, that's okay, too."

He dropped the cracker as though it had suddenly ignited.

Owen was across the floor in a flash. He snatched the cat snack and retreated back to the fridge, where he set it on the floor.

"Sorry," the detective mumbled. "They smelled so good."

"Yeah, there's nothing like the smell of sardines in the morning." I snickered. I reached behind him, set two muffins on the empty plate and put it on the table by his cup.

Owen had already eaten the cracker and licked all the crumbs from the floor. He watched Detective Gordon pull the paper off one of the muffins and break it in half.

Since the detective had taken a break from asking questions, I decided I might as well ask a few of my own. "Detective, did Mr. Easton somehow get into the storage area at my library?"

To his credit, he didn't even look surprised by the

question. "It looks that way," he said, before taking a mouthful of coffee.

"Was that his blood on the floor?"

"I'm not sure yet. There may be more than one sample."

I drank from my own cup. "But you found something else that tells you he was there, more than the cuff link." His mouth was full of muffin now so he just nodded.

I flashed back to the night before as I'd tried to rub my fingerprints off the door like some crazed criminal. "You found his fingerprints," I said.

"Very good," he said, brushing crumbs from his mouth.

I needed more coffee. I got up, refilled my mug and leaned across the table to top up the detective's. "Thanks," he said.

I sat back down, glancing over at Owen, who had moved a few steps closer to us.

"Do you know yet how he died? Did he have a heart attack?"

He shook his head. "It wasn't a heart attack."

I gripped my cup tightly with both hands. "That gash on his head. Someone hit him."

"I didn't say that."

"You didn't say it was natural causes, either. And you wouldn't still be asking questions if you thought it was."

He nodded. "True." He started carefully peeling the paper cup off the second muffin. "Okay, I can tell you Mr. Easton's death is suspicious."

I'd kind of already figured that out. "Are you going to arrest me?" I asked.

That question didn't seem to surprise the detective, either. "No," he said.

"Why not?"

"Excuse me?" He'd been watching Owen out of the corner of his eye.

"Why aren't you going to arrest me?" I really did want to know. I wasn't asking just to needle him—well, not for the most part.

"Harry Taylor saw you walking up here at about eight thirty. Mrs. Nixon said your lights went on just as *Entertainment Tonight* was ending. And Dr. Davidson saw them go off about eleven thirty, as she was leaving Mrs. Nixon's house." He ticked off each person on the fingers of his left hand.

I remembered waving to Young Harry, who had passed me as I walked up the road, but I wouldn't have been able to say if Rebecca's lights had been on or if Roma's car had been in her driveway. It was a good thing that they were more observant than I was.

"So if I'd been meeting Mr. Easton at eleven thirty—the time on the note—then I would have been late," I said.

"You would." He smiled at me. He was unflappable, which, childishly, made me want to try to get a rise out of him.

"I could have had the lights on a timer," I said, raising one eyebrow at him. (I love doing that. It's very Mr. Spock.)

He drained the last of his coffee and stood up. "Yes, you could have."

His attitude had changed. Was it because of all the people who had vouched for me, or did he have another—a better—suspect? I got to my feet, as well. "Would you like to look around the house to see if I have a timer?" I asked.

"It's not necessary," he said. "Thank you for the coffee and the muffin."

"You're welcome," I said.

He paused in the doorway to the porch, bent down

and set a tiny pile of cat treats on the floor about a foot and a half in front of Owen.

Owen had whipped his head around before all the little crackers had made it onto the floor.

"Hey, puss," Detective Gordon said softly before he straightened up.

Owen eyed the detective. He eyed the small heap of treats. (And how had Detective Gordon managed to palm them without me noticing?) His nose twitched. His whiskers quivered. He lifted a paw.

Detective Gordon caught my eye and gave me a small, smug smile.

Owen started washing his face.

I smiled back—magnanimously, not at all smugly. "Really, it's not you," I said with a slight shrug. "The cats won't get close to anyone except me."

The detective acted as if I hadn't spoken. He kept his eyes on Owen. "C'mon," he said again softly.

The cat paused, one paw behind his ear. And then he set it down. And took a step forward. And another.

When he got close enough he reached out with one paw and pulled the crackers toward him, taking a couple of steps backward, his kitty gaze never leaving the detective's face. Finally he bent and ate one treat from the top of the pile, actually sighing with pleasure.

Detective Gordon looked at me then, giving me a small smirk—a small, restrained smirk, but a smirk nonetheless. "Have a nice day, Ms. Paulson," he said. And he was gone.

The sound of crunching filled the kitchen. "Nice to know you're on my side, Owen," I said. He burped without bothering to look up.

Note: Sarcasm is wasted on a cat.

11

Wild Horse Separate Mane

"**Y**ou are a little cat fink!" I said to Owen.

He glanced up at me. There were crumbs stuck to his nose and whiskers. As far as Owen was concerned, there was kitty integrity and then there were kitty treats.

I heard a "meow" from the porch. I left Owen spreading the rest of his snack over the floor and his face, and went to see what Hercules was up to.

He was sitting on the bench by the window. "Your brother is consorting with the enemy," I said. Herc nuzzled my hand.

Okay, so Detective Gordon wasn't exactly the enemy. He wasn't exactly my friend, either.

I looked out through the screen door and caught sight of Rebecca in her gazebo, trying awkwardly to sweep. "C'mon," I said to the cat. "I don't see Ami, and Rebecca could use a hand." He jumped down and went to stand by the door. I stopped to step into my gardening clogs, which I'd kicked off when I brought Detective Gordon in for coffee. Herc meowed impatiently.

"A closed door didn't stop you last night," I said, pushing the door open for him.

He flicked his tail at me, went down the steps and started for Rebecca's.

I felt the brush of fur against my leg. Owen leaned out around me to look across the yard. "We're going over to see Rebecca," I said. At the sound of her name Owen trotted down the steps and headed purposefully for the back hedge. I followed the cats, even though I couldn't see either one of them anymore.

"Hello, Kathleen," Rebecca said when she spotted me. "Isn't it a beautiful morning?"

"Yes, it is," I said, climbing up the three steps to the main floor of the gazebo and taking the broom from her hands. "I'll finish up."

"You don't have to do that," she protested. Just then Hercules meowed from behind us. Rebecca turned. I started sweeping.

Herc's front paws were on the top step.

"Hello, Hercules," Rebecca said, leaning down toward the cat.

I swept my way toward them.

"Your fur is looking especially glossy," she said.

The cat ducked his head—embarrassed by the compliment?

"Sardines," I said.

Rebecca looked at me, puzzled.

"His fur. Susan told me to add sardines to the cats' diet. She claims they're what keep her dog's coat looking so good."

Rebecca patted her cheeks with both hands. "Do you think they'd work on my wrinkles?"

"Maybe," I said with a grin. "But they'd be hell on your social life."

I swept the last of the gazebo floor and the three shallow steps leading up to it. "There," I said, "what else can I do?"

"Not a thing," Rebecca said. "Thank you. Ami should be back from the theater in a couple of hours, and I thought we could have lunch out here."

"The theater? Does that mean they're going ahead with the festival?"

Rebecca shrugged and picked up a flowered tablecloth she'd set on the bench seat by the steps. "Your guess is as good as mine."

I grabbed an end of the fabric and helped unfold the cloth. Hercules climbed onto the railing to supervise.

"The board called a meeting with all the performers," Rebecca said. "I don't think anything's been decided yet."

We spread the cloth over the table and Rebecca smoothed out the wrinkles. The breeze caught a corner of the material and blew it up over the tabletop.

I looked around. "Rebecca, where are your corner weights?" I asked.

"Oh. They're in the shed," she said, pointing to the small outbuilding in the far corner of the yard.

"I'll get them," I said, starting down the steps.

"They're on the shelf under the window," she called after me.

I snagged the broom as I passed it so I could put it away.

Rebecca's garden shed, painted the same gray-blue as the house, looked like a tiny cottage, somewhere the three bears or Hansel and Gretel might live. The door was open. I stepped inside, blinking to adjust to the change in light. I set the broom behind the door and turned to the window. The weights were on the shelf, just as Rebecca had said.

Tablecloth weights were Maggie's creation—whimsical pottery elves, fairies or gargoyles, hanging from a cord with a clip at the other end. The idea was to attach one to each corner of a tablecloth. The weight was enough to keep the breeze from blowing the edge of a picnic cloth into the potato salad on all but the windiest days.

I scooped up Rebecca's weights—four grinning, zaftig and slightly lecherous-looking winged fairies—and turned around.

My eyes had completely adjusted to the dim light in the shed, so it was impossible to miss Owen, standing with his paws on the top edge of the recycling bin just to the right of the door. He had a piece of paper in his mouth.

"Owen!" I snapped. He turned at the sound of my voice. "What are you doing? Put that back!" I kept my voice low so Rebecca wouldn't hear.

Owen dropped to all four paws, the sheet of paper still in his mouth.

I jerked my head toward the bin and took a couple of steps toward him. "Put it back!" I said, my voice sharp with warning. "Now."

Owen looked at the recycling box, craning his neck to see the cardboard and paper stacked to the top.

And then he bolted.

I lunged, but I didn't have a hope of grabbing him. I couldn't catch what I couldn't see. At the same moment Owen had run he'd also . . . vanished, faded out in less than a second.

I slumped against the doorframe of the shed. I had one cat that could walk through walls and another that could disappear—and also seemed to be developing into a kleptomaniac. My cat was turning into a cat burglar.

I rubbed the back of my neck. This would be funny if it were happening to someone else.

I was still holding on to Rebecca's weights. I didn't have time to obsess, figure out why my cats had superpowers and, in the case of Owen, flagrant disregard for the law. I didn't even have time to figure out where Owen was. And any more deep breaths and I was going to hyperventilate and pass out on the floor of Rebecca's shed. So I tucked my hair behind my ears and went back to the gazebo.

"You found them," she said.

"I'll fasten them for you," I said. I dropped to one knee by the table. While I attached the fairies to the cloth I did a quick scan of what I could see of the yard beyond the steps to the gazebo. I didn't catch so much as a glimpse of gray fur or even a piece of disembodied paper bouncing around the yard. I switched to the other side of the table and hung those weights, as well, before standing up to see if the cloth was hanging properly.

"That's perfect. Thank you," Rebecca said, smoothing out a small wrinkle in the cloth. "Why don't you come over later and join us?" she asked. "I made lemon meringue pie."

I sighed loudly, making my bangs flutter against my forehead. "I love your lemon meringue pie. But I have to be at the library early today."

"Then at least take a piece home."

How could I say no? "I'll get a couple of chairs for you from the shed," I said.

Rebecca made a dismissive gesture with her good hand. "You don't have to do that," she said.

"I don't mind. And for a piece of your lemon pie, I'd walk down to the library to get you chairs."

She laughed. "All right, then. I'll go get you a piece of that pie."

Owen wasn't in the shed. At least I couldn't see him. I did a quick check of the backyard. I didn't see the cat anywhere, which, I realized, didn't mean he wasn't around.

Tucking a chair under each arm, I headed back to the gazebo, still watching for the cat. Maybe he'd gone home. I looked over into my own yard. I didn't see Owen, but I did see Maggie. "Mags," I called. She turned, grinning when she saw me and holding up a brown paper bag.

I was guessing she'd brought the blueberries she'd promised me. She ducked through the gap in the hedge and walked over to where I was standing.

"Blueberries?" I asked.

"Picked this morning."

"Thanks," I said. "I have muffins in the house. Just let me open up these chairs for Rebecca."

"I'll give you a hand," Maggie said, setting the sack of berries above her on the wide gazebo railing and taking one of the folding wooden chairs from me.

We set the chairs on opposite sides of the table. Maggie stood, mesmerized, looking up at the cedar timbers above her head. "This is beautiful," she said, continuing to stare at the gazebo roof. "Look at the joints, the symmetry." Maggie tended to look at everything from the perspective of an artist.

She ran her hand down one of the long posts that supported the roof of the structure. "I bet Harry built this."

"Actually, it was his father." Rebecca spoke from behind us.

I hadn't heard her come out of the house. She was holding a plastic food container. Based on the size, there had to be more than one piece of pie inside.

"Hello, Maggie," Rebecca said. "It's a beautiful day, isn't it?"

"It is beautiful. And so is your gazebo," Maggie said.

Rebecca reached out to pat the railing with one hand. "Thank you. But Harrison—Old Harry—deserves the credit. I told him what I wanted and he built it."

"No plan?" I asked.

Rebecca shook her head. "He said he could see the gazebo in his mind's eye and all he had to do was put the pieces together."

Maggie was looking up again. "Incredible," she murmured. Then she looked down at Rebecca. Her face grew serious and she pressed her lips together. "Rebecca, I owe you an apology," she began. "I was rude to you at the last class, asking personal questions about your herbal remedies." Her cheeks were tinged with pink and she clasped her hands in front of her like a child.

"And I acted like a sour, suspicious old woman," Rebecca said. "I'd be happy to tell you more about my mother and her medicines . . . if you're still interested."

Maggie's face lit up. "Yes, I'm interested."

"Mother's notebooks are in the attic." Rebecca looked back at the house. "If you don't mind some dust and cobwebs, you can look around up there for them."

"Dust, cobwebs, giant spiders—I don't mind," Maggie said eagerly.

They put their heads together and quickly agreed on Sunday afternoon. I heard Maggie mention blueberries and Rebecca say something about pie. Neither of them noticed a floating piece of paper go bobbing by the gazebo steps.

Owen.

I leaned over and grabbed the paper bag of berries as a cover, so I could make shooing gestures in the direction of the fold of paper, now hanging immobile about six inches off the ground.

"Go!" I whispered.

The paper started around the side of the gazebo, and, I hoped, toward the gap in the hedge. It occurred to me that maybe I should have said, "Appear" instead.

I leaned over the railing. The paper wasn't moving very fast. "Go!" I whispered again.

"Did you say something, Kathleen?" Rebecca said behind me. Both she and Maggie were looking at me.

I crossed my fingers that Owen was out of sight and then realized that was the problem. "I, uh, just that I have to go," I stammered. "Is there anything else I can do for you?"

"You've done more than enough, Kathleen. Thank you." She held out the plastic container. "Don't forget your pie."

"Never," I said, taking the box with my free hand and hugging it against my chest. "If you need anything, if Ami isn't around"—I pointed at my house—"you know where I am."

She nodded.

"I'll see you Sunday," Maggie said over her shoulder, as she followed me down the steps. Rebecca gave a little wave of acknowledgment.

"What kind of pie?" Maggie asked, eyeing the container as we cut through the hedge.

I was busy scanning the yard for a small gray tabby or a small piece of paper that seemed to be self-propelled.

Nothing.

"What?" I said, then remembered what she'd asked. "Oh. Lemon meringue."

"I like lemon meringue," she said.

"Yeah, everyone does," I said distractedly. Where was Owen? Maybe by the back door, and, I hoped, three-dimensional.

Maggie had been talking and I hadn't been paying attention, I realized.

"So, you'll help me?" she said, looking expectantly at me.

"Umm, yeah, of course I will." I wondered what I'd just agreed to.

Maggie burst out laughing.

"What? What's so funny?" I asked.

"I just told you that I'm giving up art to become an exotic dancer in Vegas, and you agreed to help me make a costume out of pigeon feathers."

I felt my face redden.

"What's with you this morning?"

What could I say? One of my cats is adding new meaning to the term "cat burglar," Everett mistook my cat for his dead mother's cat, and, oh, yeah, the police were still asking questions and trying to seduce Owen over to the dark side. Plus, I'd had way, way more caffeine than I should have. I decided just to share the last two things on that list.

Maggie stared at me, decidedly dumbfounded. "The police were here and you gave them breakfast? Again?"

I tried not to cringe. "It was just one police— Detective Gordon—and I didn't give him breakfast, I gave him coffee."

She folded her arms across her chest and continued to stare at me.

"And a muffin . . . okay, two muffins, but they were right there on the rack on the counter, and not offering any to him would have been rude." I stopped to take a breath.

"The man thought you and Gregor Easton were playing musical mattress and you don't want him to think you're rude?" Mags shook her head.

I couldn't help laughing. "Can I help it if I have nice manners?"

Grinning herself, Maggie shook her head at me. "You're hopeless," she said. Then her expression got more serious. "What did he want? Aside from a free breakfast."

I pushed my bangs back off my face. "Well, it looks like I'm moving down on the suspect list."

"I told you." Maggie pointed a finger at me. "No one is seriously going to believe you killed someone."

I saw movement over her shoulder. It was Owen, sitting on my blue Adirondack chair, watching us, still as a statue and just as solid, the piece of paper under one of his paws.

I felt my shoulders loosen a little and I nudged open the screen door. "It helped that both Roma and Rebecca could confirm where I was, at least part of the time. Harry, too."

I remembered how Detective Gordon had turned down my offer to look through the house to see if I had a timer for my lights. "I have the feeling the police are focusing somewhere else now," I added.

Maggie nodded with satisfaction. "About time."

I paused in the doorway. "You want a cup of coffee?" I asked. "And a blueberry muffin?" I gave her the eyebrow. "I have cheese-and-sardine crackers," I wheedled.

Maggie grimaced, then pasted on a decidedly fake smile. "As tempting as a good cheese-and-sardine cracker can be, I'm afraid I'll have to pass. I'm working an extra shift in the store today. Rats!" She gave a huge, exaggerated sigh before smiling for real. "You going to the market in the morning?"

"Uh-huh."

"Want to have breakfast at Eric's?"

Breakfast at Eric's. Homemade cinnamon bread. An omelet with cheese and mushrooms. Granola with gobs of raisins. And I knew a lot of the people involved with the music festival had been hanging out at Eric's—the menu was eclectic, but very good. I didn't know if any of them would be around early on a Saturday, but it was worth a shot, and I hadn't had breakfast at Eric's in ages. "Okay," I said.

We settled on a time and Maggie left. I waited until she'd had enough time to make it to the street; then I backtracked to where Owen still sat on my chair like some furry lawn ornament. One paw was still holding down the piece of paper he'd taken from the recycling bin in Rebecca's shed.

"What is with you?" I said. "First you chew a piece of fringe off Rebecca's scarf and now you swipe something from her recycling bin." I reached for the paper, but he kept his paw firmly on it. "If this is some kind of protest because I told Rebecca not to buy you any more catnip, it's not going to work." I pulled at the paper again. "Give it here."

He looked at me, narrowing his golden eyes like he was actually thinking over my request. "If you ever want me to make you another batch of those crackers you'll move your paw now."

Owen didn't even hesitate for effect. He lifted his paw and I picked up the page. It was a photocopy of a piece of sheet music. Written by Gregor Easton. For a moment I half expected to hear the music from *The Twilight Zone*. First Hercules found something that may have been connected to Easton's murder, and now Owen. Could they actually be trying to . . . help me? I shook my head. That was crazy. On the other hand, a cat that could disappear kind of defied logic, too.

Owen was watching me. Feeling a little foolish, I looked around to make sure no one else was. "Okay, I'm going to . . . take a big leap and believe that you brought me this for a reason. Why?" I waved the piece of sheet music in front of his face. "Ami is over there all the time and she's singing in the festival. Nice try, but this doesn't mean anything."

Owen made disgruntled muttering sounds low in his throat. I scooped him up with one arm and dropped onto the lawn chair, settling the cat on my lap. "C'mon," I said, scratching under his chin. "You don't actually think Ami had something to do with Easton's death, do you?" I tried to picture Ami, who just last night I'd seen carry a spider out to Rebecca's gazebo in her china gravy boat instead of squishing it, killing Gregor Easton. Killing anyone.

I looked at the piece of sheet music again. "You know what I don't understand?" I said to the cat. "Why did someone want Easton dead? He was a stranger. He hadn't been here long enough to make anyone angry enough to kill him."

Owen's response was to knead my stomach with his front paws—"Claws!" I reminded him as one foot snagged skin through my shirt.

"Do you think maybe Gregor Easton wasn't a total stranger here?"

Owen gave a loud meow.

"You could be right," I said. "Violet was a music teacher. Could she have known him?" It was hard to imagine elegant, confident Violet luring Easton to a clandestine rendezvous at the public library.

I shifted in the chair so I could stretch out my legs. "And then there's Ruby. She's in the festival choir." I couldn't picture her enticing Easton to a private meeting, either. Ruby was more likely to call someone out in public. At great volume

The paper had said Easton had done a graduate degree at University of Cincinnati College-Conservatory of Music. Hadn't Everett told me that the University of Cincinnati was where he'd studied business? I couldn't imagine Everett tied up in Easton's death, either. I couldn't imagine anyone I knew involved. But the truth was, someone I knew had used my name to get Gregor Easton to meet him or her. And wasn't admitting it. Someone I knew was willing to let me be tied up in a murder. In the few months I'd been in town I thought I'd made friends. Now? Maybe I was still more of an outsider than I'd realized.

Owen was stretched out on my lap, eyes closed. I stroked his fur. I couldn't take feeling this kind of suspicion about everyone I knew. I had to do something. The most logical place to start was with the dead man himself. Maybe if I knew more about Easton I'd be able to figure out whether he did have a connection to someone in Mayville Heights and whether that someone wanted him dead.

Owen suddenly opened his eyes, shook himself and jumped off my lap. He headed for the front yard.

I got up, as well, stuffing the note Owen had swiped into my pocket along with the bit of fringe he'd taken from Rebecca's scarf.

I started for the house just as Harry came from the front yard, pushing a lawn mower. I detoured over to him. "Good morning," I said.

Harry mowed the lawn at the library and at my house. I had no idea how old he was, but if I had to guess, I'd say late fifties. His face was lined from years of working in the sun, and the one time he'd taken off his Twins cap to mop his sweating forehead, I'd noticed he was mostly bald with just a little salt-and-pepper hair.

"Morning," Harry said. "Do you mind if I get at the lawn early? It's going to rain later."

I shook my head. "No."

The sky overhead was clear, bright blue with only a few puffy clouds like little bits of cotton batting that had been blown up into the sky by the wind. Still, if Harry said it was going to rain, it was going to rain. It didn't matter what this morning's forecast said. He judged the weather by the birds, the leaves, the smell of the wind and how his left leg—which had been broken twice—felt.

He was also very well-read. He'd borrowed Solzhenitsyn's *The Gulag Archipelago* and renewed the book twice, which made me think he'd actually read it all.

Harry had the kind of face that somehow smiled even when he wasn't actually grinning. I smiled at him now. "Thank you for telling the police you saw me Tuesday night."

"I did see you," he said.

I felt a little awkward. "I know," I said, sliding my hands into my back pockets, "but you didn't have to get involved."

Harry pulled off his cap and ran a hand over his scalp before pulling the hat back on again. "Kathleen, I don't know what happened to Mr. Easton, but I know whatever it was, you had nothing to do with it. You love books and you've spent months working on restoring the library building. There's no way on God's green earth you're going to whack someone over the head and let him bleed all over your library." He shook his head from side to side for emphasis. "And I told that to Detective Gordon," he added.

Was that why the detective had seemed less suspicious? Did Harry's words carry that much weight?

"Well . . . thank you." I cleared my throat. "I met your brother yesterday."

Harry nodded. "Said he's doing some work for you."

"Oren says he's a good electrician."

"He is. And if he gives you any trouble, let me know." Harry bent over the mower. "He's not so big that I can't hang him off the roof by his ankles." He grinned, which I hoped meant he was kidding, and pulled the starter cord on the mower.

I went inside, cleaned up the kitchen and made a turkey salad sandwich to take to work with me. The necklace Ruby had given me was lying on the table. I slipped it on over my head. I didn't know if the crystal could keep negative energy away or not, but it couldn't hurt.

Harry and the mower moved from the back to the far side of the house. I went out into the porch to look for Owen and Hercules.

There was no sign of the cats, but Santa Claus was in the backyard, sitting in my blue Adirondack chair.

12

Fair Lady Works at Shuttle

Okay, it wasn't really Santa in my Adirondack chair, but the elderly gentleman in my backyard definitely looked like Saint Nick, minus the belly that shook like a bowlful of jelly. He had thick white hair and a white beard that looked as soft as dandelion fluff.

I opened the door and walked across the grass to find out why Santa Claus's doppelganger was sitting in my favorite chair. He struggled to get to his feet when he saw me approaching—Adirondack chairs are not always easy to get out of.

"Hello, my dear," he said, offering his hand. His grip was strong and his blue eyes actually seemed to twinkle.

I didn't think I'd ever seen the man before; still, there was something very familiar about him.

"You're trying to decide if we've ever met," he said.

Okay, not only did he look like Santa Claus, he seemed to be able to read minds like the Amazing Kreskin. The old man was still holding my right hand and now he covered it with his left. I could feel the warmth of both of his hands, sinking into mine.

"I'm Harrison Taylor," the Kriss Kringle look-alike said. "But everyone calls me Old Harry." He gestured at the chair behind him. "I hope you don't mind me making myself at home."

"Not at all." I gave his hand a gentle squeeze. "I'm so glad to finally meet you."

"I'm happy to meet you, as well," he said. "I was feeling a little like someone's big, old, smelly dog, left in the truck with the window cracked just a little. Plus, I'm a nosy old man and I wanted to see what you've done back here." He patted my hand before letting go of it.

"So what do you think?" I asked.

He looked around and slowly nodded his approval. I felt a small, warm bubble of pride spread inside me. Young Harry kept the yard mowed and trimmed, but I'd cleaned out all the overgrown flower beds.

"Those roses are from the homestead," Old Harry said, gesturing with a heavily veined hand.

"Yes, they are. So are the blackberry canes."

"How was the rhubarb this year?"

"Delicious," I said. It had been, once I'd figured out rhubarb needed a lot of sweetening.

The mower stopped in the front yard, replaced in a moment by the sound of the trimmer.

"Please sit down," I said, dipping my head at the chair. Old Harry eased back into the seat and I sat on the grass.

He patted the wide arm with one hand. "I didn't like this color, you know, when Harry started painting the chairs. I thought all the colors he chose looked like something from a box of those fancy little mints you get at the end of a la-di-da dinner party." He smiled, which made him looked more like Santa than ever. "Turns out he was right." His gaze shifted to something behind me. "Well, bless my soul," he said. "Hello there, puss."

I shifted to see which cat was coming. It was Hercules, probably returning from Rebecca's gazebo, stalking across the lawn like one of his jungle cousins. He paused beside me for a moment—long enough for a quick stroke of his fur—then went to stand in front of the old man. Old Harry patted his leg. I opened my mouth to explain about the cats, and Hercules jumped up onto his lap.

My lips moved—I could feel them—but no sound came out. If someone had poked me with a feather I probably would have fallen over onto the grass. In fact, I almost did fall over when Owen came out of nowhere and brushed against my back. I turned, but like his brother he moved around me, stopping in front of the big wooden chair.

"Hello. I didn't realize there were two of you," Old Harry said. He didn't even have to pat his lap. Owen jumped up without an invitation. As usual, it took him a moment to get settled. He shifted, kneading Old Harry's leg, apparently without claws, nudging Herc a tiny bit sideways.

I just sat there, staring at the three of them, wondering when I'd fallen down Alice's Wonderland rabbit hole. I didn't say a word. I wasn't sure I could trust my voice to work, anyway.

"I see the rosebushes and the blackberry canes aren't the only thing you have from Wisteria Hill," Old Harry said. He was scratching Owen behind his ears and Herc just at the top of his white face patch. How he knew what each cat liked was beyond me. The whole thing was so . . . weird. The White Rabbit in his waistcoat, glasses and watch could have come around the rosebushes muttering, "I'm late, I'm late for a very important date," and I wouldn't have been surprised.

Old Harry smiled kindly at me. "It's all right, my dear," he said. "They know."

From somewhere I found my voice. "Know what?"

"That I'm dying," he said, in the same matter-of-fact tone you might use to say it's Tuesday.

"But . . . but you look fine," I said stupidly, shifting on the grass so I could pull up my knees and wrap my arms around them.

"You've probably heard the expression 'Looks can be deceiving.'" Both cats were purring now. Loudly. "What are their names?" the old man asked.

I pointed. "That's Hercules and that's Owen."

"This one looks like Anna's cat, Finn."

I rubbed my damp hands on my shorts. "Everett's mother? You knew her?" I asked.

"My first job was out at Wisteria Hill," he said. "Everett's father—Carson— built the place for Anna when she said she'd marry him. He was older than she was and hard as nails, except when it came to her." He smiled. "She had that effect on people."

I leaned forward. "What happened? Why was everything just abandoned?"

For a moment I wasn't sure he'd heard me. He gave Hercules a last scratch under his chin and said, "Time to go." The cat jumped down, shook himself and came to lean against my leg. "You too, puss," Old Harry said to Owen. Owen yawned, stretched and hopped down, as well. He came across the grass and leaned against my other leg, pushing his head under my hand in a not-so-subtle attempt to get me to pet him.

The old man finally looked at me. "I don't know why Everett gave up on the place. I was in St. Cloud—had been for six months." He shook his head and I could see the sadness in his eyes. "By the time I got home again Anna was . . . gone. Everett didn't completely abandon the house, mind you—there was a caretaker—but I don't think he ever went near the place again."

He stroked his beard with his gnarled fingers. "There was a lot of loose talk, but nothing you could hang your hat on. And by the time Everett came back to stay"—he shrugged—"he wasn't saying anything, and nobody liked to push."

Old Harry gestured to the cats, both still leaning against me, and his face softened. "Now, they're most definitely descendants of Anna's Finn." He pointed at Hercules. "That one looks just like the old cat. And that one"—he gestured at Owen—"has the same eyes." He pulled himself forward in the chair. "The old mother cat, she picked Anna, you know. Showed up one day at the back door of the house. Didn't care much for anyone but her. Just the way these two chose you. They know how things are meant to be."

Before I could ask him what he was talking about he started getting to his feet. I jumped up to help him and saw Young Harry was headed toward us.

"Time to put me back in the truck," the old man said, giving one of my hands a squeeze. "It was a pleasure to finally meet you."

I squeezed back gently. "For me, too."

"Are we headed down the hill?" he asked Young Harry, who had joined us.

"Yes, we are. I have to mow at the Stratton and the library."

"Good," Old Harry said, his blue eyes twinkling. "Maybe I'll crank down my window, stick my head through with my tongue hanging out, and see if it's as much fun as it looks when Boris does it."

His son was unfazed. "Yeah, well, try not to shed all over my front seat, Dad," he said as they headed for the street.

I crouched down so I could talk to the cats at their level. Owen put a paw on my knee. Hercules, on the other hand, decided it would be a good time to catch up on his grooming. "What was that all about?" I asked. Owen suddenly decided that he should wash his face, too.

Was Old Harry really dying? Was it possible the cats could tell? Neither cat so much as twitched an ear in my direction. I sat back on my heels. I was turning into one of those people who talked to their cats and actually expected an answer.

I got up and went back to the house. It didn't take long to get my things together, change and fix my hair. I put fresh water out for the cats. When I went to the back door, they were waiting to come in. They moved past me, avoiding eye contact. I locked up and headed down the hill.

The library was deserted—again—but two of Will Redfern's men were there, pulling the temporary desk into sections so they could take it out. Mary waved at me from the new circulation desk, where she was getting organized.

"Isn't this great?" she beamed, pointing to the new book drop with separate slots for fiction, nonfiction and other media like CDs and DVDs.

"It looks good," I agreed.

"What are you doing here so early?" she asked.

"I have some paperwork I need to get at," I said. "Is Jason here?"

She nodded. "He's shelving, and Abigail is upstairs, sorting books for the sale." She looked at the boxes piled on either side of the counter. "I could stay an extra couple of hours, if it would help," she offered.

I looked at the boxes. "It would help, yes," I said. "Thank you."

Mary nodded with satisfaction. Organizing things, making labels, setting up files were her idea of fun—aside from kickboxing. She'd be able to get the circulation desk organized faster and better than anyone else.

I let myself into my office, closing the door behind me. I had an open-door policy, generally, but I had only an hour to see what I could dig up on Gregor Easton.

I turned on my laptop, spreading lunch on the far right side of my desk, and started Googling.

The basics were easy to find—concerts Easton had given to great acclaim, a catalogue of his CDs, a bibliography of the music he'd written. There were photos of the man at Carnegie Hall, at the Grammys, joining an eclectic group of other musicians to record a song for charity—always with some beautiful, younger woman on his arm. But I could find very little about his early life. It was almost as though Gregor Easton hadn't existed before graduate school. What little information I could find was sketchy and one source seemed to contradict the next. There was lots of information about the public Gregor Easton. But I wanted to know about the private man. How could I get the personal details, the rumors, all the things that didn't seem to make it into the public record?

Then it hit me. Who knew more about music—classical and contemporary—than Dr. Lise Tremayne, curator and librarian for the music collection at Boston University? I didn't even have to look up the number.

It was early afternoon in Boston. "Dr. Tremayne," she answered on the third ring. The sound of Lise's voice, with its perfect enunciation and touch of French accent left from the years she worked and studied in Paris, immediately made me homesick.

"Hi, Lise. It's Kathleen," I said.

"Kath! How's life in the land of a thousand lakes? You haven't been carried off to become the consort of Bigfoot, have you?"

I laughed. Lise might seem like a big-city intellectual, but I knew she'd grown up in rural Maine, so far north that the next stop was Canada. She'd dug potatoes and stacked firewood and could dress a deer. Her highbrow friends would have been shocked to find out that the braised partridge they'd savored at one of Lise's elaborate dinner parties had been running around the Maine woods right before her annual "fall retreat."

"No, I haven't been abducted by Bigfoot." I swiveled in my chair so I could look out over the lake. Even though there were more clouds—which meant Harry was probably going to be right about the rain—the sun still sparkled on the water. The grass, which Harry must have come and cut right after he left my house, was a deep, rich green and the flower bed was an artist's palette of color. My homesickness eased a little.

"It's beautiful here, Lise," I said. "I'm sitting here at my desk, looking out over the lake. The sun is shining. The air is clean—"

"—and all the little forest animals come into the library to help you shelve books while you whistle a happy tune," she said drily.

"No, but you'd be surprised how useful squirrels can be for getting books up on the top shelves." She must have known what was coming next. "And," I added, "they work for peanuts!"

"I miss you, Kath," Lise said, laughing.

"I miss you, too." I had to swallow a couple of times to get rid of the sudden lump in my throat.

"So, tell me about your library." I pictured her leaning back in her chair, propping her feet, in some ridiculously expensive pair of sandals, on the edge of her desk. "Is it really one of the original Carnegie buildings?"

"It is," I said. I told her about the stone building and the renovations. I left out the fact that it was a possible crime scene and I was a possible suspect.

I took a deep breath. "Lise, the reason I called is I'm looking for some information. Do you know anything about Gregor Easton, the conductor?"

"I know he died just a couple of days ago."

"He died here, Lise."

"There? What was Easton doing in Smallville, Minnesota?"

"Mayville," I said. I held the phone with one hand and stretched my other arm over my head. "He was here for the Wild Rose Summer Music Festival. He's—he was—guest conductor and clinician."

"I've heard of the festival." Lise's voice turned pensive. "I didn't realize that was where it was." I could hear her tapping a fingernail against the side of the phone. "But what was Easton doing there? It's not his usual type of venue."

I shifted in the chair and pulled my legs up under me. "He was a last-minute replacement for Zinia Young."

"Now, your festival would be Zinia's type of event."

"She had to bow out at the last minute, so Easton volunteered to fill in."

"Volunteered? I don't think so."

"That came straight from someone on the festival board," I said. "I guess he offered because he and Zinia are close friends."

An inelegant snort of laughter came through the receiver. "Gregor Easton doesn't have friends," Lise said. "He has—had—sycophants and people he was using. Easton and Zinia were not friends. Trust me, if he volunteered, there was something in it for him."

The man Lise was describing did sound like the man Ruby and Maggie had talked about in class, like the man I'd encountered at the library.

"What else do you know about Easton?" I asked. I kept waiting for Lise to ask me why I was asking for information about the man.

"He wasn't well liked in the classical music world," Lise said. "He was arrogant—even for a conductor."

"So I've heard."

"Now, to be fair, he was considered to be a first-rate composer, deservedly so, from what I've heard. But technically he wasn't anywhere near as gifted."

"What do you mean, technically?" I asked. I heard Lise's feet drop to the floor and I knew she was probably reaching across her desk for her coffee.

"His playing—and conducting, too—weren't close to the caliber of his composing. Do you remember Dr. Mitton?"

I thought for a moment. "Wasn't he musician in residence a couple of years ago? He was English."

"That's him." I imagined Lise nodding on the other end of the phone. "He once compared Easton's piano playing to that of a three-year-old on a toy keyboard."

"That's harsh," I said.

"That's the kind of response Easton generated in people," she said. "I heard him play once, years ago, and while he was good, he wasn't great. The music was beautiful, but he didn't seem to connect with it. It was almost as though he hadn't written his own score. It was so much better than his playing. The best versions of his compositions have been played by other people."

That was interesting, though I had no idea how it might help me. I glanced at my watch. There was a lot more I wanted to know, but I was running out of time.

"Lise, do you know anything about Easton's background?" I asked. "Where he grew up, where he got his first degree?"

"I don't." I pictured her shaking her head, blond curls bouncing. I felt another sting of homesickness. "But I can ask around, discreetly, of course, if you'd like me to."

"Please," I said. I gave her my home phone and my cell number. If we missed each other, I didn't want a message about Gregor Easton left for me at the library.

"So, Kath," Lise said. "Why all the interest in a dead conductor?"

So I wasn't going to get away without answering some questions myself after all. "This stays between us?"

"Absolutely."

"I found his body."

"Oh, Kath, I'm sorry. Are you all right?"

"Yeah, I am. Thanks," I said. "The thing is, the police still have some questions and so do I."

"Do you mean there was some kind of accident, or are you saying someone killed him?" I heard the surprise in her question.

"Lise, I honestly don't know for sure," I said. "I can tell you that it looks like the library is one of the last places he was before he died. Somehow he got into the building after hours."

"And you want to know why a renowned composer was breaking into your library."

That, and why would someone want to kill him at all, not to mention who did. But I didn't say that out loud.

"I thought the biggest problems you'd see out there would be grizzly bears and killer mosquitoes."

"Maybe I'm just being nosy. It's probably going to turn out that Easton had a stroke."

"Well, let me see what I can find out and I'll get back to you."

I thanked her and we both said good-bye. I hung up the phone and stood up, giving my right foot—which had fallen asleep—a shake. I stood in the doorway of my office. And looked down to the main floor of the library. In the time I'd been on the phone, Will Redfern's men had taken the temporary circulation desk apart. One of the workers was spreading a heavy canvas tarp over the floor where the desk had sat. The front doors were propped open and another man came in, carrying what looked to me like pieces of steel staging.

Something was up. I headed down the stairs. "Excuse me," I called, walking quickly over to them. "Are you setting up staging?"

The man spreading out the tarp turned at the sound of my voice. I recognized him as Eddie, a cousin I wasn't sure how many times removed, of Abigail's. He was a big, barrel-chested man with a great, booming laugh, but as Abigail had observed wryly, he wasn't very "work brittle."

"Yes, ma'am, we are settin' up stagin'," Eddie said. "We brought this 'cause we didn't know if we could get into the storage room to get the other stagin'."

The other worker set the pieces he'd carried down on the tarpaulin. I knew from watching Eddie work, or, more correctly, not work, who'd be assembling that staging.

"What's the staging for?" I asked.

"Well, we need to reach something up to the ceilin' and the ladder don't go that high."

Talking to Eddie could be maddeningly slow. I wasn't sure if he doled out information so slowly just because he truly was literal-minded or whether he secretly enjoyed playing people.

I blew out a breath and rubbed the knot that was forming between my shoulders. "Why do you need to reach the ceiling?" I asked.

Eddie scratched his stubbled chin. His hands were huge. One of them could have covered my entire head. "Well, ma'am, the ceilin's where that big, old plaster medallion goes."

Plaster medallion?

I looked up. The front entry of the library ran up two floors. I could see where a ceiling medallion could fit, but I hadn't signed anything to order one and it wasn't part of the original renovation plans.

The knot at the base of my neck tightened.

"Where's your boss, Eddie?" I asked.

He scratched his ear and frowned. "Well, I can't exactly say," he said. I noticed he hadn't said he didn't know.

His cell was tucked in his T-shirt pocket. "Give me your phone," I said. I knew if I called from the library phone Will Redfern wouldn't answer.

Eddie hesitated. "This is a work phone," he said.

"Good." I grabbed the cell from his pocket and flipped it open. "Because this is a work conversation." I stepped away from Eddie and punched in Will's number. He answered on the third ring. "Hey, Eddie boy," he said, all macho good humor.

"Hello, Will," I said. "It's Kathleen Paulson. Eddie very kindly let me use his phone." I looked back over my shoulder and smiled at Eddie, who looked as if he were still trying to figure out how I'd managed to get his cell.

There was silence on the other end of the phone. "Will, are you still there?" I said.

"Umm, yes, Miss Paulson, I'm here. What can I do for you?"

"According to Eddie there's a ceiling medallion to be installed in the front entry of the library."

"That's right."

Like Eddie, Will could stonewall. "There were no ceiling medallions on the renovation plan." I was certain of that. I'd gone over the list of renovations, as well as the actual plan, before the work started. And I knew how to read a floor plan.

"Well, you see, the medallion is from before."

"Before what?" I asked, struggling to keep the growing aggravation out of my voice.

"Before you got here," Will said. "Roof leaked, right after Thanksgiving last year."

"I know," I said.

"Caused quite a bit of damage to the medallion that was up there—part of it came down. Made a helluva mess. So the boys took the whole thing down and we sent it away to be repaired. No one around here can do that fine work. Took a long time to get it back."

What didn't, if Will were involved? I cleared my throat. "Thanks for explaining," I said. "Sorry to have bothered you."

"No problem," Will said. He was full of that good-humored machismo again. "When you're from away, how could you know what happened last year?"

From away. It wasn't the first time Will had pointed that out. The words stung and I suspected sometimes they were meant to. Did the person who had used me to lure Easton to the library set me up because I was from away?

"Tell the boys I'll be over there shortly," Will said, and hung up.

I closed the phone and handed it back to Eddie.

"That wasn't a long-distance call, was it?" he asked suspiciously. "You weren't callin' Taiwan, were you?"

"Not unless your boss was in Taiwan," I said with a smile. "He said to tell you he'll be here soon."

I started for the stairs. "Call me when Will Redfern gets here, please, Mary," I said as I passed the desk.

"Will do," she said.

I closed the workroom door, slumped against it and threw back my head in a silent, head-shaking scream. I opened my eyes to find Abigail watching me with amusement.

"Feel better?" she asked. She was sitting cross-legged in the center of the floor.

I thought for a moment. "Actually, yes," I said. I also felt more than a little embarrassed.

"Let me guess." She made a show of closing her eyes and pressing her fingertips to her temples. "I'm getting an image," she said in a singsong voice. "I see workmen. I see wood and tools. But I don't see any work being done. I see . . . I see . . ." She opened her eyes and dropped her hands. "Let me guess: You were talking to Will Redfern."

"Very good."

Abigail grinned and set four paperback books into the open box in front of her. "It was an easy guess," she said. "Will hasn't exactly made the renovations run smoothly—especially lately." She closed the flaps of the carton, fastening them down with a strip of clear tape.

There were a dozen boxes behind her, all labeled in Abigail's slanted printing: MYSTERY, MYSTERY, ROMANCE, ROMANCE, ROMANCE, FANTASY, SCIENCE FICTION. There were more, but I couldn't see the writing on all of them.

"Maybe my expectations were too high," I said with a sigh. "I'm used to a big city where things go at double speed." I snapped my fingers rapidly several times.

Abigail shook her head. "Don't let Will pull that small-town slash country-boy routine on you. No, we're not Boston, but we do know how to do a job properly and on time."

"I'll keep that in mind," I said. "You're doing a great job, by the way." I gestured at the stacked boxes. "Is there anything you need?"

She sat back on her heels and looked around. "More boxes would be a help."

"That's easy," I said. "There's maybe a dozen flattened behind the door of the lunchroom."

"Then I'm good," Abigail said.

I left her sorting books and went back downstairs. Will's workmen had the first lift of staging assembled. Mary was checking someone out at the new desk. Jason was pushing a cart full of books over to the shelves.

For the moment, everything was running the way it was supposed to.

I went back to my office, turned on my computer and pulled up the budget spreadsheets. I spent the next hour going over the numbers, stopping only once to give Mary the key to the back loading dock for Larry, so he could bring in his supplies. I didn't realize how dark the sky had gotten until I finished the last column of numbers, leaned back in my chair and swung around to look outside. Heavy gray clouds seemed to be pressing on the lake. Spits of rain began hitting the window. Harry was a lot more accurate a forecaster than the weatherman on this morning's news.

The rain was beating steadily on the window now. I got up to turn on the overhead light and put paper in the printer.

The last copy of the budget was coming out of the printer when Larry knocked on my open door. "Sorry to bother you, Kathleen," he said. "But it looks like you've got a leak in the computer room."

I sighed and stood up. "Where?" I asked.

"Window on the far left." Larry looked back over his shoulder. "I wouldn't have bothered you, but it seems Will's guys are on a break."

"They take a lot of breaks," I said, coming around the desk. I followed Larry to the computer room. Just as he'd said, the end window—a brand-new-three-weeks-ago window—was leaking. A small stream of water ran along the inside edge of the unit, between the actual frame holding the glass and the build-out, across the wide ledge and onto the floor. Actually it was running into a large white bucket with SHORTENING written on the side. The floor around the base of the bucket was wet.

"Do you have any rags or paper towels to soak up that water?" Larry asked.

"There's a plastic crate full of clean rags under the sink in the lunchroom upstairs," I said.

Larry touched my arm. "Stay here. I'll get them." He headed for the stairs. I checked the other windows.

I was thankful there was only the one leak.

Larry came back with the box of cloths in one hand and a couple of heavy drop cloths in the other. He handed me the drop cloths. "I thought it might be a good idea to put these under the other windows—just in case," he said.

Together we spread the painting tarps under the two dry-for-now windows. Then I mopped up the small pool of water around the bucket. The leak hadn't slowed down, but it wasn't any faster, either.

"There's probably something wrong with the flashing outside around that window," Larry said.

I looked at the little river of water running down the side of the window. I took a couple of deep breaths, but they did nothing for the anger simmering in my stomach.

"Looks like I need to track down Will," I said to Larry, rubbing my wet hands together.

"Good luck with that," he said with a wry smile.

I went back to my office and called Will's cell phone. No surprise; all I got was voice mail. I left a tense, brief message.

Then I hung up and called Lita at Everett's office. I explained about the leak, and after a moment's hesitation gave her the highlights of what it had been like working with Will, especially lately.

"You have more patience than I do, Kathleen," Lita said. "Everett's out of the office right now, but I'll have him call you when he gets back."

I thanked her and hung up. I went back out to the desk to see if Mary had any idea where Eddie and the other worker had gone. "They might be in the parking lot," she said. "Will's here."

"He is?" I said. "Where?"

Mary gestured at the staging. "He was checking that when I was on the phone."

The staging filled all the free space inside the front doors. Neither Will nor his crew was in evidence anymore. How could they have gone off and left it like that?

I threaded my way between the wall and the metal framework. The floor was damp in spots. I hoped it was because the sections of staging had been outside in the rain, not because there was another leak.

I tipped my head back to check the ceiling overhead. My foot skidded on the wet tiles and my shoulder banged into the metal frame.

"Kathleen, look out!" Mary called.

Startled, I put a hand against the wall just as a large roll of plastic fell from the top of the staging above my head.

13

Wave Hands Like a Cloud

The roll of plastic glanced off my shoulder and thud-ded to the floor, where it unrolled for several feet before hitting the circulation desk. The impact knocked me into one side of the staging and onto the floor. It also knocked the breath out of me. Wheezing, I clutched my shoulder.

Mary scrambled over the unraveled plastic and around the staging to get to me. I looked up at her, wide-eyed, mouth gaping like some kind of fish that had jumped too high and ended up on the shore. Mary used a swear word that I didn't even think she knew. It was so out of character, I would have laughed if it hadn't been for that pesky breathing thing.

"Kathleen, are you all right?" Mary asked, kneeling beside me.

I nodded, making squeaky sounds as I tried to get a full breath.

Larry appeared behind Mary. "Do you want me to call nine-one-one?" he asked.

"Yes," Mary said.

I shook my head vigorously, which only made the wheezing squeaks sound worse. I was not going to the hospital, because if I did, I wouldn't be here when Will Redfern came in from the parking lot or wherever he was. I wouldn't be able to take a couple of swings at him with that three-foot roll of vapor barrier that had just whacked me on the shoulder. I closed my eyes for a second and had a Walter Mitty–esque moment, in which I imagined myself swinging the roll of plastic like I was Big Papi swinging for the stands, as I chased Will over the rock wall and down to the lake.

"Kathleen, you need to see a doctor," Mary said.

"I . . . I'm . . . fine," I managed to gasp.

"Mary's right," Larry said, pulling out his cell.

Without thinking I reached for the phone, grimacing as I moved my left shoulder.

"See?" Mary said.

I sighed, mentally, if not literally. Truth be told, I had a bit of a phobia about hospitals. When I was seven I'd gotten lost in an old hospital in Key West. My parents had been doing Alan Ayckbourn's *Table Manners*. My dad had skidded on the edge of a rug during his entrance in act two. By the end of the play one side of his face was a gigantic bruise and his eye was swollen shut. We ended up at the emergency room, along with the rest of the cast, the stage manager and the young woman who worked the last shift at Dunkin' Donuts and had a massive crush on the actor who played Tom.

In all the uproar, I went for a walk and got lost. Let's just say that when you're seven, it's close to midnight and you've spent most of the evening hiding backstage with a big bag of cheese puffs, the sight of an artificial leg can scare the life out of you—or at least a lot of half-digested cheese puffs.

Larry flipped his phone open just as Roma came

through the library doors. Mary caught sight of her at the same time I did and waved her over.

Roma knelt beside me on the tiled floor. "What happened?" she asked.

"That roll of plastic"—Mary pointed—"fell off the staging and hit her. She doesn't want us to call an ambulance."

"I've heard that before," Roma said. She held up a hand. "Hang on a second and let me take a look." She began to probe the back of my head with her fingers. "Kathleen, this is getting to be a habit and not a good one."

"Not my head," I wheezed, reaching for my right shoulder. "Hit my shoulder."

Roma's fingers moved down to my shoulder. "You had the wind knocked out of you, too," she said. She laid the palm of one hand flat against the front of my shoulder, holding it steady, while her fingers felt around my shoulder blade and up along my neck. Then she took my arm and moved it slowly forward and back. "Does that hurt?" she asked.

I shook my head. She sat back on her heels and studied me. "You don't need an ambulance," she said.

Larry and Mary exchanged looks before he slid his phone back into his pocket.

"Thank you," I whispered. I was just about breathing normally again.

"It doesn't look like anything is broken," Roma said, lightly touching the top of my shoulder. "But I'd feel more confident saying that if you had four legs instead of two." She extended a hand to help me up.

Larry took my other arm. He looked over at the unwound plastic and shook his head, his face tight with disgust. "That's vapor barrier," he muttered. "Why did they need that up there?"

"Could you please roll that up before someone trips on it and get hurt?" I asked.

"Sure thing," he said.

Gingerly, I rolled my shoulder slowly forward, trying not to grimace.

Roma folded her arms over her chest. "You're going to have a nasty bruise," she said. "Try an ice pack."

"I will," I said. The shoulder was making popping sounds. "Thank you for taking care of me again." Embarrassingly, I felt a sudden prick of tears and had to blink them away.

Roma smiled and shook her head. "Oh, you're not getting off that easy this time. This is the second time in just a couple of days that you've been hurt. You need to see a doctor—the kind that specializes in patients that don't lick themselves clean. That shoulder needs to be X-rayed, just in case."

I opened my mouth to argue and Roma held up a hand. "Save your breath, Kathleen," she said. "I've held down a nine-hundred-pound cow in labor. Don't make me toss you in my truck."

Mary gave me a triumphant smirk. I felt like sticking my tongue out at her, but that didn't seem very responsible and I was supposed to be the one in charge. "All right," I said. "But it's Friday afternoon. It'll be next week before I can get an appointment at the clinic."

"Who's your doctor?" Roma asked. I told her. She pulled out her phone and punched in a phone number, walking a few steps away from us.

I turned to Mary. "Thanks for being so concerned," I said. "I'm okay—really. You can go back to the desk."

She glanced over at Roma. "Okay."

Larry had rolled up the plastic vapor barrier and leaned the roll up against the side of the circulation desk.

"Eddie knows better than to leave something like that up above people's heads and then just take off," Mary said. "So does Will. You could have been badly hurt."

I could have. Or Mary. Or Abigail or Jason or anybody coming into the library. I'd let Will get away with too much because I'd wanted to be reasonable. "I'll take care of it," I said to Mary. She didn't look convinced, but she went back to the desk.

Roma walked back to me, slipping her phone into her pocket. "You're all set. Four thirty at the clinic. They'll X-ray your shoulder and then the doctor will take a look at it."

"Thank you," I said, feeling a little overwhelmed by her kindness. "How did you manage that?"

Roma stifled a yawn. "Sorry," she said. "Early start to the day. As for the appointment, I used to babysit your doctor." She laid a hand on my shoulder. "So go to the clinic and take care of that shoulder."

"Thank you, Roma," I said, "for looking at my shoulder and getting the doctor's appointment for me. I owe you."

She smiled and turned toward the music department. "Yes, you do," she said over her shoulder.

Mary was back behind the desk, on the phone. I went over to the entrance and looked outside. There was no sign of Will's truck in the lot. I walked back to the staging and circled it slowly, checking it carefully from every angle. There was nothing else that could fall on someone, but I wasn't taking any chances.

There were four yellow plastic sandwich boards that said DANGER, WET FLOOR in the janitor's closet. I dragged them out and roped off the scaffolding by linking the sandwich boards with a roll of fluorescent orange streamers from a box of Halloween stuff in my office.

The leak in the computer room had slowed to a trickle. "Larry, did you by any chance come past the Stratton on your way here?" I asked the electrician.

"Uh-huh," he said. "Why?"

"Was Oren's truck there?"

He thought for a moment. "Yeah, it was. Are you going to see if he'll take a look at this window?"

I nodded. With my right hand flat against my chest I bent my arm and moved it up and down and back and forth. It didn't hurt that much, or maybe it was just that I didn't want it to.

"I'll keep an eye on the bucket for you," Larry said.

I smiled. "Thanks." I went back to my office for my raincoat, and stopped at the desk to tell Mary where I was going. "If Will Redfern comes back while I'm gone, don't let him leave," I said.

Mary eyed the roll of plastic still leaning against the desk and a slow, mischievous smile stretched across her face. "Don't worry," she said. "I won't."

It had stopped raining completely. I started down Old Main Street. The breeze was blowing in off the water and the air smelled clean.

Oren's truck was in the parking lot at the theater. I felt like doing a happy dance right there on the sidewalk. The stage door was unlocked. I hesitated, feeling a sense of déjà vu. The image of Gregor Easton slumped over the piano flashed in my head. I remembered how unnaturally still he'd been. Even in sleep our bodies move. We breathe and shift, our eyelids flutter, our fingers twitch. The stark paleness of his skin made the bruised gash on the side of his head look almost as if it had been painted on by some makeup artist.

I shook my head to clear the picture from my mind, but it wouldn't go. The injury to Easton's head—I'd almost forgotten how severe it was. And Detective Gordon hadn't asked me about it, either. I closed my eyes for a moment and concentrated on picturing the side of Easton's head. Yes, it had reminded me of stage makeup, probably because I'd seen gallons of fake blood and so many "gruesome" wounds—decapitations, amputations, prop knives buried in gaping chest wounds—over the years that horror movies generally put me to sleep.

The surprising thing about Easton's wound was that it was clean. His head had been bruised and the cut was raw and red-edged, but there was no dried blood on his skin or in his silver hair, no bits of dirt or grit in the scraped skin. I was certain it would have been a difficult spot for Easton himself to see and care for easily.

I opened my eyes. I was betting he hadn't. So if Gregor Easton didn't clean up his head wound, who had? Was that person with him when he got hurt? Was that how the blood had ended up on the floor at the library? Had someone hit him? I ran a hand down over the back of my head, sucking in a sharp breath as my shoulder reminded me of my own injury and the fact that right now I needed to find Oren and do something about the leak at the library.

The backstage lights were on inside the theater. I threaded my way down the hallway, past light stands and other equipment.

Someone was playing the piano onstage. I paused at the edge of the curtains. I didn't know the music but it made me want to move, to start swirling and twirling in place the way the tune seemed to be dancing all around the stage. I forgot about Gregor Easton. I forgot about leaky windows and missing contractors. I forgot about my bruised shoulder.

I took a couple of steps forward, just past the edge of the curtains so I could see who was playing. Violet, maybe? Or Ruby. Or Ami. To my amazement Oren was at the piano, his strong fingers sweeping over the keys.

I couldn't have moved even if the building had suddenly been on fire. I was both stunned and transfixed. That beautiful music swept around me and then it stopped. And Oren looked up and saw me.

He looked away. One arm went behind his head, fingers digging into the back of his scalp. He pulled into himself. I walked slowly across the stage, stopping at the back of the piano. He tipped his head sideways and looked up at me.

"That was wonderful," I said. I was almost at a loss for words. "I didn't . . . I didn't know you played."

Oren dragged his hand down over his neck and let it drop into his lap. "I . . . uh . . . don't. Very much," he said. His eyes kept sliding off my face. "What are you doing here? Is there a problem at the library?"

I nodded. "One of the windows is leaking. The end one in the computer room."

"Did you call Will Redfern?" He shook his head. "If you could find Will, you wouldn't be here. Would you?"

"I'm sorry," I said. "I know you still have a lot to do here, but Will came and went before I could even lay eyes on him, and I can't leave the window leaking all weekend."

"No, you can't. I'll come take a look at it." He stood up. "I need to get a few things."

"I'll head back," I said. "I'll see you there."

I didn't even zip up my coat to walk back to the library. Will hadn't called or shown up. No surprise.

By the time I'd hung up my jacket Oren had arrived. He headed for the computer room, raising one hand in acknowledgment of Larry, on his way back down to the basement electrical panel.

The leak was even slower now, a steady *drip, drip, drip*. "Looks like the flashing," Oren said.

"Larry had the same thought," I said.

Oren nodded. "I'm going to get the ladder and take a look outside."

I studied the window frame, hoping the problem was nothing more than a bent piece of metal or a missing bit of caulking.

"Kathleen," Mary called.

I swung around.

"Everett Henderson for you."

I nodded and pointed toward my office to let her know I'd heard and would take the call there.

I closed the office door and reached across the desk for the phone. "Hello, Everett," I said.

"Hello, Kathleen. Lita said you needed to talk to me."

I explained what had been happening with Will and the renovations. I tried very hard to keep my frustration out of what I was saying. "Oren's outside on a ladder right now," I said, "trying to find the source of the leak. I've left two messages for Will, and I didn't want to let this go any longer."

There was silence on the other end of the phone. Finally Everett spoke. "Kathleen, I apologize. Lita advised me very strongly not to hire Will." He sighed softly. "I went to school with Will's father and I let sentiment and nostalgia influence my decision."

I chose my words carefully. "How Will is handling this job has nothing to do with you, Everett."

"That's very kind of you," he said. "I have to go out of town on business. I'll be back Monday. I'll stop by the house Monday evening and we'll figure out what to do about the rest of the renovations. Will that work for you?"

"Yes, it will," I said.

"Good. Now, are you sure you're not hurt? Have you seen a doctor?"

I rubbed the top of my shoulder, wincing as my fingers hit a tender spot. "I'm okay, Everett. Really," I said. "Roma is pretty good with two-legged patients."

"Good to know," Everett said drily.

"And I'm going to the clinic to get checked out later this afternoon. I'm fine."

"I think you'd say that even if you weren't. If you need anything—"

"—call Lita," I finished. "I will."

"Is Oren handy? I'd like to talk to him, if I could."

"Hang on," I said. I stepped out of my office just as Oren walked back into the building.

"It is the flashing," he called up to me. "I can fix it for you."

"Good," I said. "Everett's on the phone. He'd like to talk to you."

Oren didn't seem surprised. "Okay," he said, swiping his hands on the bottom of his shirt. The phone at the desk was closer.

While Oren talked to Everett, I walked around the staging again. I didn't like having it stay there all weekend, and it didn't look like Will or Eddie or anyone else was coming back today.

Oren hung up and joined me. "Everett asked me to fix the window," he said.

"Thank you," I said.

"He asked me to take the staging down, too—if Will's boys don't get back before the end of the day." He studied me for a moment. "He said something fell off it and hit you."

"That roll." I pointed to the plastic, still leaning against the desk.

"Are you all right?" Oren asked.

I nodded. "Just a sore shoulder."

"I don't know where Will's head is," he said.

I could guess, but it wasn't anatomically possible.

"I'll get started, then," he said.

I walked over to Mary, sorting a pile of picture books. "Break time," I said.

"You sure?" she said.

"You're working extra hours. You're entitled to a break." I looked at my watch. "Where's Jason?"

"Upstairs."

Mary stood up and I slid into her place. "Tell him to take his break now, too."

"Sure thing," she said, heading for the stairs and the staff room.

I kept busy until Mary returned; then I went back to my office to print off a copy of the library renovation budget and the running list I'd been keeping of what was finished and what still had to be completed. The painting had to be finished and the computer area wasn't ready, not to mention the meeting room. And there were about a dozen other little tasks still undone. If Will would stop messing around we could get back on schedule. Big "if."

While I waited for the printer I checked my e-mail. There was one message from Lise. Subject: *Easton*. I clicked on the message.

Gregor Easton was born Douglas Gregory Williams.
Curiouser and curiouser.
Lise

Douglas Gregory Williams. I copied the name on a blue library pad. So Easton had changed his name. Why? Maybe that was why I hadn't been able to find anything online about his early life. "Curiouser and curiouser" was right. All I had were questions, questions, questions. Who was Gregor Easton, really? Why had he been in the library after hours? Who was he meeting? What happened to him? Not to mention the biggie: How had he died?

Lise was very good at ferreting out information. I was hoping she'd be able to tell me more about Easton/Williams. And now that Detective Gordon seemed to be less suspicious of me maybe I could find out exactly how Easton—I couldn't think of the man by any other name—had died.

There was a tap on my open door. I looked up. Oren stood in the doorway.

"I have the leak patched for now," he said. "When things dry out a bit tomorrow I can do a permanent fix. I've checked the other windows and I don't see any problems, but I left the bucket and the drop cloths down just in case."

"Thank you for coming to the rescue," I said.

He shrugged and ducked his head. "I'll be back at the end of the day to take care of the staging." He hesitated, then took a couple of steps into the room. "You've done a good job here, Kathleen," he said. "When I was a boy I spent a lot of time in this building, my nose buried in a book—chasing pirates, solving mysteries, going on safari. No video games back then." He smiled. "It was one of my favorite places. Before you got here everything—the books, the building—was worn out. You're turning the library back into that kind of place—somewhere special."

It was the most Oren had ever said to me at one time. I swallowed a couple of times, uncertain how to respond. "Thank you. That, uh, means a lot," I finally managed.

Oren shifted from one foot to the other. "So, I'll be back," he said. He glanced down at my desk as he turned to go and saw the pad with Easton's real name scrawled across it. He touched the pad with his index finger. "Easton wasn't a good person."

He cleared his throat and shook his head. "I better get going," he said, and he was gone before I could ask him how he'd known that Douglas Gregory Williams and Gregor Easton were the same man.

14

Snake Creeps Down

Oren knew Gregor Easton's real name. How? Did he know Easton?

I sank onto the edge of the desk. Oren knew Gregor Easton. There was no other explanation. I could feel my stomach tying itself into a knot. Was it Oren that Easton had met here at the library? Did Oren have anything to do with Easton's death? *No. No. No.* I couldn't believe Oren had hurt Easton. I wouldn't believe it.

The stiffness in my shoulder had turned into a throbbing pain all the way down that side of my back. I fished in my top drawer for a couple of ibuprofen.

It was almost time to leave for the clinic. What was I going to do about Oren? Call Detective Gordon? No. Talk to Oren? I wasn't sure. I just couldn't fit the idea of Oren hurting anyone—even by accident—into my mind. There had to be some logical explanation for Oren knowing Gregor Easton's real name. I'd just have to figure out what that was.

I went to my clinic appointment. My shoulder was bruised, not broken. The doctor suggested ice; the same advice Roma had given me, which just proved to me that she was a pretty good people doctor, too.

I stopped at Eric's for Chinese chicken salad to go and a giant brownie, because it had been an I-deserve-a-giant-brownie kind of day. When I got back to the library Abigail had given up sorting books for the yard sale and was at the desk. The staging was gone.

I looked up at the foyer ceiling. No medallion, so I was pretty sure neither Will nor Eddie and the crew had been back. But what the heck, I asked Abigail, anyway.

She gave a snort of laughter. "Friday afternoon? Not likely."

"I didn't think so." I set my take-out bag on the desk.

"How's your shoulder?" she asked.

"Nothing broken, just a big bruise."

"Glad to hear it," she said, smiling. "Oh"—she snagged the notepad at her left elbow—"the electrician said to tell you he's finished, except for one plug by the window and that'll have to wait until Oren has fixed the leak. He'll be back Monday."

Upside down, Abigail's handwriting looked like a cross between cave-wall drawings and the Cyrillic alphabet. I leaned over the desk to look at it right side up. It looked the same. "How do you read that?" I asked.

"It's code," she said, flipping her braid over her shoulder.

"Seriously, is it some type of shorthand?"

"Seriously, it's code."

"I don't understand," I said.

"That's the point." She set the pad on the desk and spun it around so I could see it. "I have five older brothers, Kathleen." She held up five fingers. "Five. They gave Malibu Barbie a Mohawk and a Sharpie tattoo when I was eight." She shook her head. "A tattoo that says 'Bite Me' is not a good look for Barbie."

"Not really," I said sympathetically.

"I had zero privacy, so I came up with the code. I was reading *Pippi Longstocking* and a book about pirates at the time." She laughed at the memory. "It was so complicated in the beginning I couldn't remember all the rules, but over time I made up something that was a cross between shorthand and my own private language" She shot me a sideways look. "It does make me seem like a nutcase, doesn't it?"

"Not even close," I said. I pushed the notepad back to her. "Abigail, my parents are actors. When they get into a part they become entirely different people—twenty-four hours a day. Creating your own language seems pretty tame to me." I picked up my food. "I'll be in my office," I said.

The rest of the evening went by quietly. The walk home up Mountain Road seemed longer than usual. My shoulder ached, and while I'd managed to push Oren out of my mind for a while, what to do with what I knew was niggling in my brain again.

The cats were waiting just inside the kitchen door. "Hi, guys," I said. "My day was pretty crappy. How was yours?" Hercules meowed but was immediately drowned out by Owen, who yowled louder. "Okay, okay, it's not a competition," I said.

I made us toast and peanut butter, propped a bag of ice between my shoulder and the back of the chair, and told the cats all about the leak, my shoulder, Lise's e-mail and Oren. They listened intently—although that may have been because I was the one with the toast—but they didn't offer any insights.

I had a shower and went to bed.

In the morning my shoulder actually felt a little better. On the other hand, it looked worse. I felt a bit like a circus contortionist, trying to look at my back in the bathroom mirror. There was a black-and-purple bruise, about the size of a slice of bread, on my right shoulder blade. Seeing it made me angry with Will Redfern all over again, and at myself for being nice a lot longer than I should have been.

The cats followed me around while I dressed, dried my hair and then sighed at my reflection, regretting, the way I did every morning, my ill-advised haircut. I fed Owen and Hercules, and when I was ready to head out to meet Maggie they were both waiting by the back door.

"I'm not going to be that long," I told them. "Stay in the yard. No going over to Rebecca's to mooch treats." I glowered at Owen. "Or anything else."

Maggie was already at Eric's at a table by the window. Our waitress appeared with coffee before I'd even settled into my seat. Eric waved from behind the counter. I waved back.

"How's your shoulder and why didn't you call me?" Maggie demanded.

"Good morning to you, too," I said. "I'm fine. Thank you. And, yes, it's a lovely morning." I put cream and sugar in my coffee, stirred and took a long sip.

Maggie waved her hand as though shooing away a fly. "Okay. Good morning. Nice day. I'm fine. Is your shoulder all right?"

I set the cup on the table. "I'm fine. I have a bruise but nothing's broken. Roma checked me over and I went to the clinic and I had X-rays. I'm fine." I stage-whispered the last two words.

Mags twisted her teacup in its saucer. "Why didn't you call me?"

"Because all I wanted to do was go to bed." I took another sip of my coffee. "How did you know, anyway?"

"Mary told Susan. Susan told Eric. Eric told me."

"Ah yes, the information superhighway," I said wryly.

The waitress came back to take our orders. While Maggie changed her mind half a dozen times about what she wanted in her omelet, I looked around the café. It was mostly families stopping for breakfast before or after a trip to the farmers' market. So much for questioning people involved with the festival. Not that it was a really practical idea. What was I going to do? Go from table to table saying, "Good morning. Did you kill Mr. Easton?"

Maggie finally settled on tomatoes and asparagus. While we waited for the food I brought her up-to-date on what had been happening at the library.

"I'm glad you're going to talk to Everett," she said.

"I should have done it before now."

"Will's always been the type to start late and finish early. If I didn't know better I'd say he doesn't want the job to get finished."

"Susan said the same thing," I said. "But there's no reason for Will to want this job to go badly. In the end, the only person that's going to be hurt is him."

Maggie edged her chair sideways into a patch of sunlight. "Will's always been the kind of person who takes the easy way, but he wasn't always so careless. A little lazy, but not irresponsible."

"Maybe he's having a midlife crisis." I looked around for our waitress so I could get more coffee.

"You could be right about that," Maggie said. "He's dyeing his mustache."

"What?"

She nodded.

"How do you know?"

Eric came over with the coffeepot before she could answer. He was a much more serious person than his wife. Eric and Susan seemed to prove the old adage that opposites attract. "Hi, Kathleen. How are you?" he said, filling my cup.

"I'm good, Eric," I said. "I owe you for the breakfast you sent to the hotel for Mr. Easton."

Eric shook his head. He'd cut his salt-and-pepper hair very short and it suited him. "I never sent it. I called over there to get Easton's room number—we do their continental breakfast, so I thought I'd send everything at once—and they said he'd gone out the night before and hadn't come back. The next thing I heard, he was dead."

"Okay," I said.

"Your order will be out in a minute," Eric said, heading for another table with the coffee.

So, after Easton had been at the library he hadn't gone back to his hotel room. Did that mean he'd gone directly to the theater? And had he been alone? More questions to add to my list.

I turned my attention back to Maggie. "How do you know Will dyes his mustache?"

She took a sip of her tea. "Ruby saw him buying a box of L'Oréal Excellence number forty-six at Walgreens."

"It could have been for his wife," I said, adding cream to my coffee.

"Forty-six is Copper Red, and Will's wife is a blonde," Maggie said. "He dyes his mustache, Kath. It's not even the same color as his hair. And he traded his old truck for that huge thing he drives now—long bed and extended cab. How Freudian is that?" She held out both hands. "Midlife crisis," she said, lightly banging the table to make her point.

Our breakfast arrived then, which meant, thankfully, that we didn't have to talk about Will Redfern's midlife crisis—real or not.

After breakfast we walked down to the farmers' market, one street up from the hotel. The market was actually open all week. Like the artist's co-op that Maggie was part of, the farmers' market was a cooperative—vegetables, fruit, a small bakery, a butcher and a tiny cheese shop. But on Saturday morning the market expanded out into the parking lot, weather permitting. Farmers sold directly to customers from the backs of their trucks. Maggie was looking for Swiss chard and new potatoes. I wanted carrots for salad and maybe muffins.

"I think I see potatoes over there," Maggie said, pointing to the far end of the lot.

"Okay, I'll be there in a minute." I'd caught sight of what I hoped was rhubarb jam being sold from the tailgate of a dusty old Ford.

I was trying to decide between plain rhubarb jam and rhubarb-strawberry jam when someone said, "Good morning, Ms. Paulson," by my left ear.

I turned and looked up. Way up. "Good morning, Detective Gordon," I said.

He looked different in jeans and a gray T-shirt. He had a flat stomach and wider shoulders than I'd noticed before, and . . . *What the heck was I thinking*?

"Looking for something for your sweet tooth?" he asked.

I flashed back to Andrew teasing me about my habit of putting jam on everything. Andrew, who'd married someone he'd only known two weeks. I wondered what Detective Gordon would think if he knew how many nights I'd sat in the dark in the living room and eaten jam right out of the jar.

I pulled my hand away from the bottles. "Umm, no." I cleared my throat and caught sight of several dozen bunches of fat, red radishes, farther back in the truck bed. "I was looking for radishes." *Why had I said that?*

"Oh, well, let me reach a bunch for you," he said. He stretched over the side of the bed and handed me a clump of plump radishes, each about the size of a jawbreaker.

"Well, thank you," I said.

"My pleasure." I waited for him to walk away so I could put the radishes back, but he just stood there, smiling at me. "I think you can pay right there," he said, pointing to the other side of the truck.

"Ah, great." I handed over the money for the radishes, tucking them in my bag next to a bunch of carrots and some peas. Then I turned. "Have a nice day, Detective," I said, with a not exactly genuine smile.

"You too, Ms. Paulson."

I threaded my way across the parking lot. He didn't follow me. I found Maggie, who'd found her potatoes.

"Did you get your jam?" she asked.

"No," I said. "I . . . I changed my mind." I pulled the radishes out of my cloth bag. "Here," I said to Maggie, thrusting the bunch at her.

"You bought radishes instead of jam?" she said. "Why? You know how they make you burp."

"Just take them," I said.

Maggie shrugged. "Okay."

We walked around a while longer. We both bought a couple of loaves of crusty French bread from the bakery inside, and Mags had a long conversation with one of the vendors about the upcoming fall harvest of Honeycrisp apples, which, she assured me, I was going to love. We parted company on the sidewalk.

I headed up the hill with the delicious smell of bread coming from the bag over my shoulder. Mentally I kicked myself for not buying the jam. Andrew had a new life, and so did I.

There was no sign of the cats in the yard. I stood on the back stoop for a moment. No sign of them in Rebecca's yard, either. It was awfully quiet. I went inside and put everything away, after tearing the end off one of the baguettes. The crisp brown crust left crumbs down the front of my shirt. While brushing them off, I found a smear of marmalade from breakfast on my shirt. I went upstairs to change and gathered the laundry. I put in the first load and went back up to the kitchen.

Hercules was waiting at the top of the stairs. I bent down and picked him up. "Hey, fur ball," I said. "Where were you?" He leaned in and licked my chin. "What?" I laughed. I'd had marmalade on my shirt. Did I have omelet on my chin?

I carried the cat out to the porch, set him on the bench and sat down beside him, rubbing at my chin, just in case there were remnants of my breakfast stuck to it. I reached over to scratch the side of Herc's face.

"What am I going to do about Oren?" I asked him. He rubbed his head against my hand. "You're no help," I said. He shook his head, jumped down and went over to the porch door, where he turned and looked back at me. "Are you going somewhere?"

Hercules scratched the bottom of the screen. "Hey!" I said. His green eyes firmly on my face, he lifted one paw and raked his claws across the door's kick panel. I opened my mouth to snap at him again and it occurred to me that he was trying to tell me something. "What?" I said. "I don't understand."

He smacked the screen with his paw and it came unlatched. Herc almost tumbled out the open door. Shaking himself, he stalked out, flipping his tail at me.

It would have been a lot easier if his superpower was talking instead of walking through walls.

I rubbed the space between my eyes with the heel of my hand. I was afraid Oren could be tied up in Gregor Easton's death somehow, and I wasn't completely convinced I'd dropped off Detective Gordon's suspect list. Plus the cats were acting strangely. Well, more strangely than walking through walls and becoming invisible.

I stepped into the kitchen just as the phone rang. I headed into the living room, thinking for the hundredth time that I probably should get a cordless phone.

"Hello, Kathleen. It's Roma."

"Hi, Roma," I said.

"How's your shoulder?"

I hadn't thought much about my shoulder since breakfast. I rotated it slowly forward and backward. It was stiff and a bit sore, but otherwise okay. "A lot better," I said. "I have an ugly bruise, but nothing's broken."

"Glad to hear it," Roma said. "I realize it's short notice, but are you available to come out to Wisteria Hill with me this afternoon? My helper had to cancel."

Stay home, clean house and obsess, or help Roma and maybe learn a little more about the cats?

"Yes," I said.

"Wonderful. I can pick you up at two o'clock."

"I'll be ready."

"I know it's warm, Kathleen, but you'll need long pants and long sleeves," she warned.

"That's okay. I can find something."

"I'll see you at two, then," Roma said, and hung up.

I had laundry to finish. I needed to find some clothes to change into, and I had to have lunch.

I took the clean clothes out of the washer, threw in

another load and headed for the clothesline, using the basket heaped with sheets and towels to bump my way out of the porch door. Which is why I almost tripped over Owen coming up the steps, carrying a paper bag in his mouth.

15

Slant Flying

"**O**wen! Not again," I said, dropping the laundry basket on the stoop.

He held his ground and glared at me, the little brown bag clamped between his teeth.

Is there a twelve-step program for klepto cats? I wondered. Then I caught sight of the logo on the bag: GRAIN-ERY FEEDS & NEEDS.

"Owen, do you have a Fred the Funky Chicken in that bag?" I asked.

His furry gray face was unreadable.

I crouched down. "Let me see," I said.

He sat down but didn't let go of the bag.

"I'll give it back, I swear." I held out my hand.

After a long moment Owen dropped the bag in my outstretched palm. I unfolded the top. I'd guessed correctly. Inside the paper sack was a little yellow catnip chicken. Owen shoved his nose down into the top of the bag.

"Hey, hang on a second," I said. I pulled the bag away from him, which got me a sharp meow in return. "I'm not taking it. I'm trying to get it out of the bag for you."

I finally managed to fish out Fred the Funky Chicken

despite Owen crowding me. I held it out to the cat, who immediately snatched the chicken from my fingers. I stood up and held the porch door open for him. "Please don't leave fuzzy chicken parts all over the kitchen," I said. Owen already had that glazed/gleeful look in his eye as he brushed past me. I was pretty sure he wasn't listening.

I picked up the laundry basket again. As I pegged the last bath towel on the line Rebecca came through the hedge with Violet. I folded my arms across my chest. "Rebecca. You're spoiling my cat," I said, smiling to show I really wasn't mad.

"I'm sorry, Kathleen," she said, matching my smile with one of her own. "But it wasn't me. It was Ami. She loves animals and she's taken a great liking to Owen." She pushed her glasses back on her nose. "And I think he likes her. He follows her around the yard."

"That's because he's a moocher." I dropped the clothespins into the empty laundry basket.

"How many cats do you have, Kathleen?" Violet asked.

"Two," I said. "Owen and Hercules. Owen is the one with the catnip fetish."

"They came from the old Henderson estate," Rebecca said.

I nodded. "They were just kittens. They literally followed me home."

"Roma has spent hours and hours at Wisteria Hill, taking care of the cats that are still out there. She's managed to trap and neuter all of them so there won't be any more kittens," Rebecca said, rolling her sore wrist under her opposite hand.

I leaned against the stoop railing. "I'm going out with her this afternoon to see if I can help."

Rebecca smiled. "Make sure you wear long pants and

long sleeves. It's really grown up out there, especially around the outbuildings."

"I will," I said, returning her smile.

"Kathleen, Rebecca and Roma are coming for dinner tonight," Violet said. "Please join us." She was all smooth elegance in a pale green shirt and flowered skirt.

"Thank you, Violet. I'd like that."

"Do you know how to find my house?" she asked.

Violet lived in a historic two-story house downtown, Llŷn House. I nodded. "Yes, I do. I've passed your house several times. I'm eager to see the inside."

Violet smiled. "Don't let me forget to show you around, then. We'll see you tonight, about six."

"Give Roma a nudge so she doesn't keep you out at Wisteria Hill too late," Rebecca said.

"I will," I promised.

"We'll see you later," Rebecca said.

I grabbed the laundry basket and went back inside. Owen lay on his back in the middle of the kitchen floor, eyes closed, blissed out. The body of Fred the Funky Chicken was strewn in pieces around him. The chicken's head was on Owen's belly, the yellow fabric bright against his white fur. And he was purring.

I stepped over him without comment. At least if he was decapitating chickens, he wasn't raiding the neighborhood recycling bins.

By the time Roma pulled into the driveway all the laundry was on the clothesline, and I'd eaten lunch and changed into a long-sleeved cotton T-shirt, paint-spattered pants and a denim ball cap. Owen had wandered off with his chicken head, and Hercules was sleeping on the bench in the porch.

"I brought my gardening gloves," I said. "In case I need a pair of gloves for . . . well, anything."

"Good idea," she said.

"And I brought my big thermos. I made lemonade."

Roma glanced over at me. "When you say you made lemonade, you mean the powder in the can, not the fizzy stuff in the bottle?"

"No," I said. "I mean, I made lemonade. Lemons, sugar syrup, cold water, ice."

"You're kidding."

I shook my head. "Roma, my mother knows how to make only two things, if you don't count toast"—I held up a warning finger—"which you shouldn't count, because most of the time she either forgets to press the little lever so the bread doesn't toast, or she forgets about the bread altogether and it burns."

I couldn't help grinning, thinking about my mother's efforts at cooking. "However, she makes the best lemonade—from scratch—and the very best baking-powder biscuits."

"In other words, your mother is a picnic looking for a place to happen," Roma said. "I think I'd like her."

I smiled. It was a pretty good description of my mom.

Roma jerked her head toward the backseat. "I brought a thermos of ice water. Lemonade sounds a lot better."

"How long have you been going out to Wisteria Hill?" I asked.

"A bit more than a year." She raised her hand in greeting as we passed a woman walking a large black lab. I recognized the woman's face, but I couldn't think of her name. She was working her way through the various ethnic cookbooks we had at the library—Indian, the last time I'd checked her out.

"I worked with a cat-rescue group in Des Moines," Roma continued.

"You lived in Des Moines?"

"For years. I've only been back here about a year and a half."

"Why did you come back?" I asked. "If that's not too personal a question."

She didn't take her eyes off the road, but her smile grew wider. "I don't mind. I guess it was mostly because I was homesick."

I knew that feeling. On the other hand, there was a lot I'd miss about Mayville Heights if I left—when I left.

We waited while two cars and a pickup, most likely headed for town, went by; then Roma turned left onto the road that would take us out to the old estate. "Don't get me wrong," she said. "This is a small place. And everyone seems to know what's going on in your life. But everyone knows who you are, too. When someone asks, 'How are you?' they truly want to know. It's not just some meaningless pleasantry. I missed that."

She put her window down a couple of inches. "So when I heard Joe Ross was retiring it seemed like divine providence. I sold my practice, bought this one and here I am."

There were no houses on this stretch of the road, just trees, huge, old trees. Except for the asphalt, it probably didn't look much different from how it had when Everett's mother was alive.

"How long has Wisteria Hill been abandoned?" I asked.

"Years," Roma said, driving around the remains of a dead skunk and closing up her window at the same time. "Must be close to twenty-five."

I stared at her, incredulous. "Twenty-five years? But why? Why would Everett let his home deteriorate for twenty-five years?"

"That's the question, isn't it?" Roma slowed and put on her blinker for the turn into the lane out to the old house. "To be fair, the place wasn't really abandoned in the beginning."

I put a hand on the dash as we bounced over the rutted dirt drive. "Everett closed the house after his mother died, didn't he?" I asked.

"Yes, he did," Roma said. "He closed off all but one section at the back. He had a caretaker who lived in it and took care of things, and, I'm guessing, looked after the cats."

We pulled into a open area then, in front of the house, and I couldn't help staring, just the way I had the first time I'd stumbled on the estate in the spring. The old house looked neglected. It looked . . . lonely. The windows had been boarded over. The right end of the verandah sagged. The yard was even more of a tangle of overgrown grass and weeds, prickly rosebushes, and saplings about knee-high, new trees taking root as the forest slowly spread out. I thought about the remnants of the English country garden in the backyard. Someone had clearly cared about Wisteria Hill at one time. "What happened?" I said softly. "How could . . ." I let the end of the sentence trail off.

Roma sighed. "I truly don't know. No one does." She studied the house. "George and Clara Anderson took care of the place. They're related to Everett's secretary, Lita, somehow. Then they decided they wanted to move to Michigan to be closer to their daughter and grandkids. It was before I came back, but not by a lot."

She reached into the backseat for her ball cap and pulled it on. "Everett spent most of his time in Minneapolis and just came home for weekends. When George and Clara left everyone thought he'd hire someone new. But he didn't. He moved his business and himself back here, but he left the house empty. If he even comes out here, no one's seen him."

"How could Everett leave the cats out here to fend for themselves?" It was clear to me that Everett was an intense, hardheaded businessman, but I would never have said he was cruel.

"He didn't," Roma said. "No one knew there were any cats out here." She reached over the seat again, this time for a dark canvas backpack. Then she opened the car door and got out. So did I. She glanced over at the house, then looked at me over the roof of the car. "The Andersons took four cats with them when they moved. Clara was the kind of person who would carry a bug outside rather than squish it."

Like Ami, I thought.

"She wouldn't have left a cat behind. Second week I was back here someone brought in an injured cat—attacked by something, probably a coyote. It was Desmond." Roma popped the trunk.

"I didn't know Desmond was feral," I said, as I helped her take two large animal cages and a couple of blankets out of the trunk.

"What? Did you think he was just cranky?" Roma said, giving me a sideways grin.

"I didn't even think he was cranky."

Desmond was Roma's cat. Or, more accurately, he was the animal clinic's version of a guard dog. Sleek and black, Desmond had only one eye and was missing part of an ear. Even though he wasn't a particularly big cat, his appearance and his demeanor made him seem larger and decidedly imposing. I'd seen him glare a barking golden retriever under a clinic chair. But he'd also sat companionably beside me in the waiting room while Owen and Hercules were being neutered.

"It never occurred to me that Desmond was a Wisteria Hill cat."

Roma tucked the blankets under one arm and picked up one of the cages with her other hand. I grabbed the remaining cage. She started for the house and I followed.

"Des was almost full-grown when Marcus brought him in. He's learned to tolerate people, but he hasn't gotten close to anyone—not the way Hercules and Owen are close to you, although he does seem to like you better than pretty much anyone else."

I stopped. "Marcus?"

Roma looked back over her shoulder. "Uh-huh. Marcus Gordon. The detective who's working on the Easton case." She started around the house to the backyard and I hurried to catch up with her. "Even hurt, Desmond was wild," she continued. "He clawed the back of both of Marcus's hands and caught the side of his face, as well." She smiled. "You weren't my first two-legged patient, Kathleen."

Using her elbow to push a clump of blackberry canes out of her way, she gestured for me to go around her. "That encounter with Desmond would have put anyone else off of cats," Roma said. "But not Marcus. In fact, he's the helper who had to cancel today."

Roma set down the cage she'd been carrying just in front of a large outbuilding. It was bigger than a garage, but not quite as large as a barn.

"What was this building?" I asked. "It's too small to have been a barn."

"It was the carriage house. Now it's where the cats live." She took the backpack from me, set it on the grass and opened the top.

"What happens in the wintertime?"

Roma pulled out a couple of sections of newspaper

and set them on top of one of the cages. "We take care of the cats all winter, just the way we do the rest of the year." She stood up and looked around the unkempt yard. "It took six weeks before I'd figured out how many cats there were in the colony. There were nine—a tom, three females and five kittens. It took four attempts to collect them all for neutering."

"I don't understand why you brought them back here." I was already sweating a bit in my long pants and sleeves.

"Because they're feral," Roma said. "They're not used to people and they don't adapt well to living with them." She held up a hand. "I know, I know. Owen and Hercules are different and I can't completely explain that. In fact, I'm not even sure they were part of this colony. And as for Desmond, I don't think he was feral. I think he was someone's pet that was abandoned."

"Is there a difference?"

Roma nodded. "An abandoned cat—a stray—will eventually form a relationship with you if you start feeding it. A feral cat will learn to trust you and depend on you if you feed it, but it will always be skittish."

Roma crouched down and began to fold the newspaper so it would fit on the bottom of the two cages. "With caretakers the cats do quite well in the colony— the family—that they've formed."

I bent beside her and took the other section of newspaper, folding it the way she had. "What do you mean by 'caretakers'?"

"Pretty much what it sounds like," she said. "Like I said, we trapped and neutered all the cats and made sure they were healthy. Of the original nine, one was too ill to return here and one of the kittens died several months later."

"So there are seven cats now." I set the folded paper on the bottom of the cage the way Roma had done with hers.

"That's right. We have a feeding station set up. Volunteers come out once a day to feed the cats. In the wintertime Harry keeps the road plowed." She brushed off her hands and stood up. I did the same.

"How do the cats stay warm all winter?" I asked.

"We have shelters for them—cat houses, if you will. They're made from plastic storage bins, insulated and with straw inside for warmth. Rebecca built three of them for us."

That didn't surprise me at all.

Roma rooted around in her backpack again and pulled out a can of tuna and a fork.

"Are you making lunch?" I asked with a grin.

"Sure," Roma said, standing up and grabbing a cage with her free hand. "As long as you can climb in here."

I picked up the other cage and followed her across the grass to a shaded space close to the front of the carriage house.

"So if all the cats are neutered, why are we here?"

Roma set her cat trap down near the base of a maple tree. "Marcus was out here yesterday and noticed that Lucy—one of the older cats—is limping. Based on his description, I think her leg may be broken." She took the cage I was holding and set it several feet away from the other one.

I pulled at the neck of my T-shirt. "But how are you going to trap just one cat?"

Roma popped the top on the can of tuna. "That's why we're using more than one trap. And Lucy is the ... boldest of the cats. I'm hoping she'll come out first."

"Out?"

She pointed at the carriage house. "See that hole just to the side of the doorframe?"

The wood had rotted or broken away, leaving a small, jagged opening to the right of the carriage house doors.

"The cats go back and forth through that hole. We use the door. The feeding station is inside. That's also where the cats sleep."

I nodded. "So the tuna goes in the trap and when the cat steps inside to get it—"

"—she steps on the trigger mechanism and the door drops down," Roma finished for me. She pressed on the trigger plate and the door fell onto her arm. "And we cross our fingers we have the right cat."

"Pretty simple."

"Uh-huh. But I swear before we'd finished catching all the cats to be neutered, a couple of them had pretty much figured it all out." She adjusted the newspaper slightly. "The only way I could get one of the females was to bring out a chicken breast I'd roasted with rosemary and garlic, and believe it or not she tried to grab the chicken with a paw and pull it out."

"All it would take with Owen would be one of those glow-in-the-dark yellow catnip chickens."

Roma grinned. "Is Rebecca still buying those for him?"

"Ami bought him one today," I said, brushing away a bug that was trying to land on my neck. "But I suspect Rebecca had a hand in that. I came in from the backyard, and Owen was on his back, paws in the air, with a goofy look on his face and the chicken head balanced on his chest."

She laughed. "Hey, change the chicken head to a carton of mocha chocolate chip ice cream and you've just described my typical Friday night."

Now it was my turn to laugh.

Roma stirred the tuna with the fork, breaking it into small chunks in the can.

"What are the blankets for?" I asked. "I'm guessing they're not so we can go lie down in the shade."

"No, they're to cover the cages because it keeps the cats calmer. But having a couple of blankets to lie on in the shade isn't such a bad idea."

I watched as she put a forkful of tuna toward the back of the cage and then made a trail of small tuna bits back to the opening. She repeated the process with the other cage. "Now we wait," she said, standing up and wiping her hands on her pants.

We backed up all the way to the house and sat on the peeling stairs. I could still see the carriage house and the two traps. Roma leaned against the stair railing and stretched out her legs.

"What's back behind those trees?" I asked, pointing behind the carriage house.

"More trees," she said. "And eventually the most beautiful field of wildflowers I promise you'll ever see— black-eyed Susan, lavender hyssop, evening primrose, milkweed and a lot more I don't know the names of. Come back out with me again sometime and I'll take you up there."

"Is that a bribe?" I asked, leaning my elbows on my knees.

Roma grinned. "I prefer to think of it as offering an incentive."

"I'd like to come back and help, if I can," I said, smiling. "But I'm also open to an incentive."

"I'll keep that in mind," Roma said, shifting a little to the left so she could keep an eye on both the traps and the carriage house door.

"Roma, what would happen to the cats if Everett decided to do something with this property?"

She ran a hand down her throat. "There's a farm about an hour from here that's run by a couple who do a lot of work with feral cats. I guess I'd try to send the cats there."

"The cats would go live on a farm?" I made a face. "When I was six we lived for a while next door to the Bartletts, who had a little black dog named Farley. Farley got hit by a car and they took him to the vet. Mrs. Bartlett said that after Farley got better he was going to live on a farm in the country where he could run around and not have to worry about cars." I eyed her with suspicion. "This isn't the same kind of farm, is it?"

Laughing, Roma shook her head. "It's not. I promise you." She stretched both legs along the step.

"Did you always want to be a vet?' I asked.

"Actually, no," she said. "It was a really good teacher who pointed me in this direction. What about you?"

"I wanted to live in the library from the moment I discovered that's where they kept the books."

"Do you miss Boston, Kathleen?"

I pushed my hair back off my sweaty face. "Sometimes I do," I said. "Especially when I talk to my family, my friends. On the other hand, look at that sky." There was nothing but endless blue overhead. "Sometimes I'm in my office and the sun is shining through the windows and sparkling on the lake, and I can't think of a more beautiful place to be working."

"Wait till January." She leaned forward then and without shifting her gaze, stretched out an arm and tapped me on the leg. "Look," she said, "by the door."

I sat up, leaning left to get a better view. A small calico cat squeezed out through the hole next to the carriage house door.

"Yes!" Roma hissed.

"Is that Lucy?" I asked.

She nodded.

I watched the cat approach the closest cage, taking slow, careful steps and sniffing the air. She was definitely limping.

"C'mon," Roma whispered. "C'mon."

Lucy hobbled closer and closer to the cage. Finally she reached the opening. She sniffed the tiny bit of tuna Roma had set there. Then she ate it.

"Good girl," Roma said, softly.

And then she turned and walked away. Roma groaned. Lucy paused, ears twitching. I held my breath. The little cat looked around, sniffing the air again. She changed direction, toward the other cage.

Roma grabbed the back of her scalp with one hand, resting her forearm on the top of her head. Lucy approached the trap. Again she sniffed the scrap of tuna by the opening, then ate it. Neither Roma nor I moved. Lucy leaned into the cage and ate the next bite of tuna. She stepped inside with one paw and then the other. One more step, I guessed.

I was right. Lucy stepped on the trigger plate and the door snapped down. She howled with anger and threw herself at the door.

Roma headed for the cage, unfolding the blanket and talking softly to the cat. She draped the blanket over the top of the trap, but Lucy continued to yowl and throw her weight against the cage door.

"She's going to hurt herself," Roma said. "I'm going to get my bag. I'll have to give her something." She headed for the car.

I didn't know what to do. I crouched down near the cage, out of Lucy's line of sight, and spoke softly to her, the way I did when I had to take Owen or Hercules to Roma's clinic. I told her it was going to be okay. I wasn't sure the cat could even hear me. And then suddenly she stopped.

Stopped yowling. Stopped flinging herself against the cage. I took a chance that I wouldn't spook her and peeked around the edge of the blanket. She was crouched low, her eyes wide.

"You're all right," I said softly. I kept talking as Roma came up behind me. I turned to look at her.

She stared at me, shaking her head. "You're either Dr. Doolittle or the Cat Whisperer," she said. "So which is it?"

16

Needle at Sea Bottom

There was a bottle of wine on the counter and Barry Manilow was on the CD player, and my bangs were miraculously staying off my face. All was well, at least for the moment, in my small corner of the universe.

Not so much for Owen. He was hiding under the bed and had been from the moment the first notes of "I Write the Songs" floated up the stairs. Hercules walked to the end of the bed, dipping his head so he could look under the frame.

"Forget it," I said. "You know how he is. He won't come out until I take the CD off." I bent down and picked up Herc, dancing him in a circle while I sang along with the music. A slightly muffled howl came from under the bed.

I danced Hercules over to the closet and set him down. "So, what am I going to wear?" I asked him.

He sneezed at my first choice and yawned at my second. My third choice, a white top and blue skirt, got two paws up. Well, actually, he just looked the outfit up and down and walked away, which either meant "Great choice" or "You're hopelessly fashion challenged—I give up."

Violet's house was downtown, close to the market and the artists' co-op. It was a big two-story colonial with a beautiful yard and a converted carriage house in the back. White and pink impatiens bloomed on either side of the walkway to the front door. The lawn looked like a green carpet. It had to be Harry who took care of Violet's yard. No one else would be so meticulous, except maybe Violet herself. And I couldn't quite picture her trimming the edge of the grass by the walk with a Weedwacker slung over one shoulder.

Rebecca opened the door. "Kathleen, come in," she said. "Violet's in the kitchen."

I stepped into a foyer that was as well cared for as the outside of the house. I guessed the hardwood floors and wide trim were original, but someone had restored and refinished them at some point. Overhead a lavish brass and crystal chandelier shone down on us. "Wow!" I whispered to Rebecca.

She patted my arm and grinned like a little girl. "Isn't it spectacular?" she said.

"It's beautiful." Everything seemed so right, from the framed painting of sunflowers to the small antique table next to the curving staircase that led to the second floor.

"Wait until you see the piano," Rebecca said conspiratorially, dipping her head close to mine. She led me into a large room to the right of the foyer. A massive grand piano sat by the window.

"How did they get that in here?" I asked.

Rebecca frowned. "I don't know. It's been here since Violet was a girl."

A fireplace dominated the wall beyond the piano. There were two sofas covered in a deep sky blue fabric, and several comfortable-looking chairs.

"Hello, Kathleen," Violet said behind me.

I turned. "Hello, Violet," I said. "Your house is beautiful."

"Thank you," she said. "I haven't forgotten I promised you a tour."

"I'm looking forward to that."

Violet wore a green flowered apron over a yellow blouse and tan skirt. She didn't look like she'd been anywhere near a kitchen.

Was the woman ever rushed? Did she ever get rumpled or messy like the rest of us?

"How did things go at Wisteria Hill?" Rebecca asked.

"Very well," I said. "Roma thought one of the cats might have a broken leg. We managed to catch her."

"Good."

"Please sit down," Violet said, gesturing to one of the sofas.

We sat, Rebecca and me on the sofa and Violet in one of the chairs.

"So, was the cat's leg broken?" Violet asked.

"Roma wasn't sure," I said.

"I'm glad she came home," Rebecca said. "I don't like to think about what might have happened to those cats without her."

"They would have frozen to death or been trapped the first winter," Violet said.

I looked at her. "Trapped?"

She nodded. "More than one person was nosing around out at the old house and had the run put to them by the cats. Next thing you know, there's a lot of loose talk about trapping the cats and euthanizing them for their own good."

Rebecca shuddered. "How can killing another living creature be good for it?" she said softly.

The doorbell rang. "Excuse me," Violet said, getting up.

I turned to Rebecca. "Roma told me that you helped make the winter shelters for the cats."

She folded the edge of her sleeve back over the top of the bandage on her arm. "I couldn't stand the thought of those poor animals out there with no way to stay warm." She glanced around. Violet was at the door, letting Roma in. Rebecca leaned toward me across the sofa. "I'll tell you a secret. Vi bought the plastic bins we used. She didn't want anyone to know. She's really a big softy."

I put my finger to my lips. "Your secret's safe with me."

Roma and Violet came in from the foyer. "Hi," Roma said, lifting a hand in greeting. She took a deep breath. "Violet, something smells wonderful."

Violet smiled. "Which means I probably should go check on dinner. Have a seat, Roma. I'll be right back," she added over her shoulder as she disappeared toward the back of the house.

Roma dropped into the chair where Violet had been sitting. She looked troubled.

"How's Lucy?" I asked. "The cat," I added, as an aside to Rebecca.

"The leg's broken. She needs surgery."

I sighed.

"David Thornton—he's a small-animal vet—is coming from Lake Forrest tomorrow to help me set it. He has some experience with a new technique that uses a mesh made from pig bladder. Lucy should be all right."

"Let me know if you need any help when it's time to take her back," I said.

"I will." She turned to Rebecca. "Kathleen seems to have a rapport with animals. Lucy panicked in the cage, but Kathleen talked to her and she settled down."

"Kathleen has a rapport with everyone," Rebecca said with a smile.

Violet appeared in the doorway. "How about a glass of wine? Is anyone driving?"

"I walked," Roma said. "So I'll have a glass. Thank you."

"Ami's going to pick me up," Rebecca said. "I'll have a little, as well, please."

Violet looked at me.

"I walked, too," I said. I held up my thumb and index finger about an inch and a half apart. "Just half a glass for me, please."

"I'll be right back," Violet said.

I turned to Rebecca. "Any news about the festival? Did Ami say if they've made any decisions?"

"They're not going to cancel, are they?" Roma asked.

Rebecca shifted sideways so she could see both of us. "If the committee can't find a replacement conductor they'll have to cancel the festival." She sighed. "In fact, they may have to cancel even if someone is willing to step in."

"Why?" I asked.

"Because without a director slash conductor there's no one to continue rehearsals."

"Actually, there is." We all turned toward Violet.

She smiled as she crossed the gleaming oak floor. "The festival board has asked me to continue rehearsals for now." She was carrying a wooden tray with four wineglasses on it. She offered one to Rebecca, who picked up a glass and gave Violet a warm smile.

"Violet, that's wonderful news. Ami didn't tell me."

"She didn't know," Violet said, turning to me with the tray. "I only got the call about an hour ago."

"I'm glad you're going to take over," I said, taking a

glass. "I've heard so much about the festival. I'd hate to see it canceled."

Violet handed a wineglass to Roma and took the last one for herself. Roma sipped her wine. "Oh, that's nice," she said, leaning back in her chair. "Violet, why can't you just take over as the festival director?"

Violet took a sip from her glass and then set it on a round glass coaster on the coffee table. "Because no one knows who I am," she said.

"That's ridiculous," Rebecca said. "Everyone in Mayville Heights knows who you are. You've lectured at the University of Michigan and the Cleveland Institute of Music."

Roma glanced over at the piano behind us. "I've heard you play," she said. "You're very talented."

Violet held up a hand. "Thank you," she said. "I've had a wonderful career—lots of opportunities—but I have no name recognition."

"And that's what the festival needs to draw people in. That's what sells tickets, as much as the music," I said.

Violet nodded. "Exactly."

"But the festival should be about the music, not about personalities," Roma said. "Not about whether the conductor went skinny-dipping at the Playboy Mansion."

"Gregor Easton went skinny-dipping at the Playboy Mansion?" I said.

"No, Zinia Young did," Roma said drily.

"And how did you know?" Violet asked.

Roma turned the same shade of pink as Rebecca's blouse. "I might have seen something about it on *Access Hollywood*," she mumbled.

"*Access Hollywood?*" Rebecca tried and failed to keep a straight face.

"Now, don't tell me you've never picked up a supermarket tabloid, Rebecca," Roma said.

"Only for the articles," Rebecca replied, deadpan.

Roma laughed and took another drink.

I finally took a sip from my own glass. The wine was light and slightly sweet. Its warmth slid down into my stomach and spread out like a sunburst. I took another sip and turned to Violet. "This is Ruby's wine, isn't it?"

"Yes, it is," she said, picking up her glass again.

"It's very good." I tilted my glass so the clear liquid swirled around the inside. "But it does sneak up on you."

Violet held up her own glass and studied the contents. "So I've noticed," she said. She got to her feet. "Excuse me again, everyone," she said. "We should be ready to eat very soon."

"Kathleen, did you say Ruby made the wine?" Roma asked.

"Uh-huh." I set my glass on a coaster on the coffee table.

Roma nodded thoughtfully. "Makes sense. I went to school with Ruby's mother, Callie. Her father, Ruby's grandfather, was the bootlegger around here."

"You mean he made—"

"No, no," Roma interjected. "He didn't make it. He sold it. Resold it, actually."

"He did usually have three or four swish barrels on the go," Rebecca said. "So technically he was making it, too."

I held up a hand. "What's a swish barrel?"

Rebecca pushed her glasses up off the end of her nose. "It's an oak barrel used to age whiskey and other spirits. People would buy the used barrels, put water in them and eventually the alcohol would leach into the water and you'd have a barrel of, well, swish. You know, both Oren's father and grandfather made barrels for the Union Distillery."

"Oren used to work summers with the old man, didn't he?" Roma said.

Rebecca nodded. "Yes, he did. But Oren's not just a carpenter; he's an artist, too. He gets that from his father."

"What happened to those sculptures?" Roma asked, shifting in her chair.

"I hope they're still out at the homestead. Maybe Oren has them in the barn."

I looked from one to the other, trying to figure out what they were talking about.

Rebecca noticed my confusion. "Oh, I'm sorry, Kathleen," she said. "We're talking about people and things you don't know anything about." She adjusted the pillow at her back. "Let me see if I can explain."

I picked up my glass again and leaned back against the arm of the sofa.

"Oren's father, Karl, was a carpenter and a house painter. He worked for Harrison Taylor—Old Harry—as well as making barrels for Union. You know the stairs that go up to the top of Wild Rose Bluff? Karl worked on those. But in his spare time he made these incredible metal sculptures. They were massive things. Sadly, very few people got to see them."

She must have seen the surprise on my face. "In those days young men from Mayville Heights, Minnesota, did not become artists, no matter how talented they were. And he was."

I thought of the sun Oren had made for the library entrance. "Rebecca, you haven't been in the library lately," I said. "You haven't seen the sun Oren carved for just inside the doors."

"Oren made the sun?" Roma asked. She was picking at the nail of her left ring finger. I wondered if she was more worried about the injured cat than she'd let on.

I nodded.

"I had no idea. It's absolutely beautiful."

"He also made the new wrought-iron railing for the steps."

"All that skill, that talent, it's in his blood," Rebecca said. "Karl Senior and Anna's father was a blacksmith."

"Anna?" I said. "Everett's mother?"

"Yes." Rebecca nodded. "Everett's mother and Oren's grandfather were brother and sister."

At that point Violet appeared in the doorway. "Dinner's ready," she said. "Please bring your glasses."

The dining room overlooked the backyard. I'd been expecting a formal room, but it was actually very relaxed and welcoming. The table was set with a cream tablecloth and matching cream napkins with blue flowers, and flanked by six black leather Parsons chairs. Very comfortable chairs, I discovered when I sat down. Violet was at the head of the table, with Rebecca to her left and Roma and me to the right.

Dinner was sole with spiced vegetable stuffing, rice pilaf, tiny carrots and salad with mustard vinaigrette. Violet was an excellent cook. As she refilled our wineglasses I wondered how she'd ended up with a bottle of Ruby's wine. They both loved music, but I didn't know they were friends. Roma had apparently been thinking the same thing.

"Violet, why do you have a bottle of Ruby's homemade wine?" she asked.

Violet set down her fork. "That's right. I didn't tell you," she said. "Ruby's going to move into the apartment over the carriage house." She turned to me. "You probably noticed the carriage house at the end of the driveway."

"I did," I said.

"There's an apartment on the second level. I haven't had a tenant there for a long time, but I decided having a little more life around here would be a good idea."

"When is she moving in?" Roma asked.

"End of the month. Unless the festival is canceled, in which case she may move in a bit sooner."

Roma speared a carrot with her fork. "What do you think happened to Gregor Easton?" she asked. It seemed like a casual question; then I noticed how tightly she was clutching her fork.

"I think he was a debauched old goat who had most likely been engaged in something he shouldn't have been doing with someone far too young for him," Violet said.

"You think he had a heart attack or a stroke, then?"

"Don't you?" Violet asked.

"It makes the most sense," Roma said slowly. "From what I'd heard he was a man of large appetites. But if it was just a heart attack why are the police still investigating?"

I didn't say that Easton's death hadn't been a heart attack—or most likely not even an accident. I wanted to see where the conversation was going.

"Because Gregor Easton was a celebrity of sorts. He died here, in Mayville Heights. To a lot of people that's Nowhereville." Violet poured a little more wine into her glass. "Why wouldn't the police be extra thorough? As it is, there's probably going to be some comments made about our 'hick' police department." She looked at me. "Kathleen, you used to live in Boston. There is a big-city perception that a small town can be a little slow, isn't there?"

"With some people, yes," I admitted.

"What about you?" Rebecca said teasingly. "Did you think we were all a bunch of lumberjacks running around the woods in plaid flannel shirts?"

She popped a bite of fish and stuffing in her mouth.

"Not in the beginning, I didn't," I said. "Then my first week here Susan came to work one morning wearing a pair of fur-trimmed Sorels, a hat with earflaps and a red-and-black plaid jacket."

Violet and Rebecca both laughed. "I think Susan feels the cold," Rebecca said. "She's a tiny person."

"And plaid was in last winter," Violet added.

"So, Susan didn't leave you with the impression we were all a bunch of hicks?" Rebecca asked, setting her knife and fork side by side on her plate.

I took the last bite of fish and did the same. "No, she didn't," I said. "I've lived in a few small towns myself, so I'm aware of the stereotypes."

"I thought you grew up in Boston," Violet said. She stood to clear our plates.

"No," I said. "I've lived all up and down the East Coast. My parents are actors."

"Theater?" Violet asked.

"For the most part. My father has been in a number of commercials over the years. But most of the time they've been onstage." I realized Violet had very skillfully turned the subject away from Gregor Easton and his death. Why? Was it just that she didn't think that was suitable dinner conversation? Or did she have another reason? Beside me Roma sat silently playing with her fork.

"And you didn't want to act?" Rebecca asked, finishing the last of her wine.

"No," I said emphatically. "First of all, I didn't inherit

a drop of my parents' talent. I can memorize lines, but I'm a big block of wood onstage."

"You couldn't be that bad," she said.

"I could and I am. And sometimes I think acting held no interest for me because there was no lure to the exotic, the unknown."

"What do you mean?" Violet asked, turning from the sideboard with a blueberry tart in a clear glass pie plate.

"I know how hard being an actor can be. I've seen the work, the rejection, the uncertainty. There's nothing glamorous about it. Not to me."

Violet cut a slice of the tart and handed it to Rebecca.

"What about the rest of your family?" Rebecca said, taking the plate. "Do you have any brothers or sisters?"

"I have a younger brother and sister. Twins." Violet passed plates to both Roma and me.

"Do they act?"

I shook my head. "No. Sara is a screenwriter and filmmaker. She's made several short films. She's working as a makeup artist, as well. There have been enough movies made in and around Boston to keep her working pretty steadily." I took a forkful of pie—juicy blueberries, a light custard filling and flaky pastry. "Mmmm, Violet, this is delicious," I said.

"Thank you," Violet said. "It's Rebecca's recipe."

I raised my fork to Rebecca across the table. "Then thank you, too," I said.

"It's my mother's recipe, actually," she said. "Although I think you added a little nutmeg to the berries, didn't you?" She looked at Violet, who was pouring coffee.

"Yes, I did," Violet said. She handed me a cup. "You were telling us about your family. What does your brother do?"

"He's a musician," I said. "A drummer. He teaches

jazz drumming and he's in a band called The Flaming Gerbils."

That pulled Roma back into the conversation. She almost choked on her coffee. "The Flaming Gerbils?"

"Uh-huh. Ethan has been in one band or another since he was a little kid. He put his first band together when he was in kindergarten. He called it Up Your Nose."

They all laughed.

"What about you, Violet?" I asked. "Were you in a group when you were younger?"

"Not unless you count rhythm band in grade two. I played a mean triangle."

"She did," Rebecca said, solemnly. "Violet was a triangle virtuoso."

"I did play rehearsal piano for pretty much anybody and everybody when I was getting my first degree," Violet said.

"Where did you go to college?" I asked. Was it possible she'd known Gregor Easton at university?

"Oberlin College. It's in Ohio. What about you?"

Easton had gone to the University of Cincinnati. "I went to Husson in Maine." I smiled, remembering. "I may not have had any stereotypical ideas about Minnesota, but I definitely had them about Maine. I showed up with a suitcase full of sweaters, and they were in the middle of a late-summer heat wave."

Thank heavens Lise had been my roommate. I wondered when I'd hear from her again. If anyone could dig up information about Gregor Easton, it would be Lise.

After we finished dessert Violet took me on a tour of the house. Every room was as beautiful as the living room and foyer. "Llŷn," I said as we walked back into the living room. "That's Welsh, isn't it?"

Violet nodded. "It is. It means 'lake.' My mother's parents were from Wales."

Roma was looking at a large photograph that was hanging in the dining room. It was a street shot of the downtown by the lake, from, I guessed, at least fifty years ago. Violet joined her as Roma tried to pick out old landmarks. I sat beside Rebecca on the sofa.

"Violet's a wonderful cook," I said to Rebecca.

"She is. Even when we were girls she would take a recipe and change it just a little to give it her own unique touch."

"Have you been friends a long time?"

"Forever. From the time we started school. Violet's like my sister." She settled back against the arm of the sofa and folded her hands in her lap. "I had two older brothers who teased me constantly. Violet was an only child. But she was fearless."

Rebecca shook her head, smiling at something she'd remembered. "We weren't allowed down by the lake," she said, lowering her voice so we wouldn't be overheard. "But we used to sneak down all the time. My brother Stephen told on us. The next morning when he got up his shoes were filled with wet sand—the pair he wore for school and his good pair for church." She laughed at the memory. "It was Violet, but to this day I don't know how she did it."

I glanced toward the dining room. "It's hard to picture Violet as a rebellious girl."

Rebecca rubbed a hand over the sofa cushion between us. "I know she comes across as very reserved. Some people think she's cold, but she's not. Life has just made her seem that way." She looked around the room. "Violet grew up in this house. She was only twenty-five when her mother and father died within six months of each other. Ten years later she was a widow with two little boys. If she seems unfeeling, well, is it any wonder? But inside she's warm and loyal. I've always been able to count on her. I'd do anything for her and she'd do anything for me."

"That's what my mother calls sisters of the heart," I said.

Rebecca glanced over toward Violet again. "I like that," she said. She turned back to me. "You come from a very colorful family, Kathleen. How did you end up in Mayville Heights?"

Andrew's face suddenly filled my memory—his big smile, his deep blue eyes, his blond hair that curled down over his collar when he was overdue for a haircut. Maybe it was what seemed like Rebecca's genuine interest, or maybe it was two glasses of Ruby's wine. Whatever it was, I answered honestly. "I ran away."

Rebecca's eyes widened. "From what?"

"From my life at the time. From my family—I love them, but they can use up all the air in the room."

Rebecca nodded her understanding.

"And from the man I thought I was going to spend the rest of my life with."

I looked away for a moment. Violet and Roma had a photo album out now.

Rebecca leaned over and squeezed my hand. "I'm sorry," she said. "Do you mind my asking what happened?"

I twisted my watchband around my arm instead of looking at her. "He married someone else."

"Then perhaps you're better off without him."

"That's what my friend Lise said. She also called him a no-good, scum-sucking elephant turd."

Rebecca was silent for a moment. "I think I'd like

your friend Lise," she said finally, a bit of a smile playing on her lips.

"It's a bit more complicated than that," I said.

"I'm listening," Rebecca said.

"Andrew—that's his name—wanted me to take a leave of absence from my job and see the country. All of it. With him."

"I take it you didn't want to."

"No, I didn't." I rubbed a finger over my thumbnail. "Rebecca, I lived in a lot of places growing up. Small towns, big cities, and everything in between. I've already seen a lot of the country. I want to stay in one place. I want to belong somewhere. The way you and Violet and Roma do."

I looked around Violet's welcoming living room. "Violet grew up in this house. The two of you have been friends almost your entire lives. I don't know how many different places I've lived, and my whole childhood is in one cardboard box in a storage unit in Boston." I twisted my watch around my wrist. "I just want to belong somewhere."

"Your Andrew didn't understand that."

I looked over my shoulder, through the front window to the darkened street. "No, he didn't. He went on a two-week camping trip in Maine after I said no. He came back married."

"After two weeks?"

I nodded and tried to clear the lump in my throat. "Married. I went to work the morning after he came back, saw Everett's notice about the job here and applied." I held out my hands. "And here I am."

Rebecca studied my face. "You miss him, though."

"Sometimes. But it's over. Time only moves in one

direction: forward. So no matter how much I might want to change things sometimes, I can't."

Rebecca got a faraway look in her eyes. "There's something special about first love," she said. "But you're right, it's important to move forward. And your Andrew's loss has been our gain." She smiled at me. "I hope you're starting to feel you belong here."

Before I could answer, Roma poked her head in from the dining room. "Rebecca," she said. "What used to be on the corner opposite the market?"

"Anderson's," Rebecca said at once. "They sold fabric. He was a tailor."

Roma tapped the side of her head. "Anderson's. Of course. Thank you." She turned back to the album Violet was still looking at.

Rebecca looked at me. "Would you like to see what Mayville Heights looked like back in the good old days?"

"I would," I said. We walked over to join Violet and Roma. The framed black-and-white photograph was remarkably sharp and detailed. Rebecca walked me down the street in the old photo, pointing out each building and sharing stories about herself and Violet.

"You know, the downtown really doesn't look that much different," I said. "I would have recognized the hotel and all those little stores."

"That's because the buildings were built to last," Rebecca said.

"How about another cup of coffee?" Violet offered. "It's decaf."

"All right," Roma said. I nodded, as well. I probably drank too much coffee, but as vices went it wasn't that bad.

"How about another piece of blueberry tart?"

"A sliver," Roma said, holding up a thumb and forefinger about an inch apart.

"Kathleen?" Violet looked at me.

"Don't make me eat alone," Roma said. Something in her smile seemed forced.

"A tiny, tiny piece," I said.

Rebecca took the album from Violet. "Why don't you take that into the living room?" she said. "I'll be right in."

"Could I help?" Rebecca asked.

"Show Roma and Kathleen more of the old photographs. I can get the coffee."

We settled on the sofa on either side of Rebecca, who laid the album across her lap. "Look," she said, pointing to a picture of a somber-faced girl in a dark dress with a white collar and cuffs. "That's Violet, senior year of high school. You know the building that's the River Arts Center now? That's where we went to high school."

I leaned in closer to look. "She looks so serious."

"Look at this one," Roma said, putting a finger on a snapshot on the adjacent page. It was Violet in some kind of party dress with a little purse and a very unfortunate bubble hairdo.

"Interesting hair," Roma said, struggling not to laugh.

Rebecca did laugh, covering her mouth with one hand. "Oh, my," she said. "I'd forgotten about that. That was the first time I did Vi's hair."

"And it was almost the last," Violet said, coming in with the coffee tray.

I got up and took it from her, and set it on the coffee table.

"It wasn't that bad," Rebecca said. "Maybe a little too poufy."

"She back-combed my entire head and used a full can of hairspray on it."

"Well, I didn't want my handiwork to go flat."

"It was windy and raining the night of that party,"

Violet said as she poured. "The wind almost pulled the screen door off its hinges, but my hair didn't move."

"Then it was a good thing I used lots of spray." Rebecca smiled sweetly.

I had the feeling they'd had this conversation many times before.

I took the album off Rebecca's lap so she could reach her coffee. Roma had already started on her sliver of pie, which really wasn't a sliver at all. I flipped through the photographs. Violet looked so young. In most of the pictures she was smiling, even laughing in a few, and I wondered what she'd been like as a girl. My favorite shot was one of Violet and another young woman, arms around each other's shoulders, standing by the water, both of them with huge, happy smiles. "Rebecca, is this you?" I asked. She set down her cup and I turned the album toward her.

"Heavens, yes, it is. That was just before Violet left for Oberlin."

"That's the first picture I've seen of the two of you," I said.

She shrugged. "I don't really like having my picture taken," she said.

"You look very pretty in this one," I told her.

"Thank you," Rebecca said, sliding the album back onto her lap so I could pick up my pie. "That reminds me, do you have any pictures of your family? I'd love to see them sometime."

"I do," I said. "Remind me and I'll show you."

"Kathleen, how's the work coming at the library?" Violet asked, settling in a chair with her coffee.

"A little slower than I'd like," I said. "Larry Taylor has the wiring almost done in the new computer room. The circulation desk is finished, and I'm hoping the police will let us back into the meeting-room space in a day or two."

"Why have the police been at the library?" Roma asked. "Gregor Easton died at the Stratton."

I took a sip of coffee, wondering how much I should say. "Easton was at the library earlier in the evening and he may have come back again."

Roma started coughing. Rebecca reached around and patted her on the back.

"Do you need a glass of water?" Violet asked.

Roma held out a hand. She coughed a couple more times, then sucked in several breaths. "I'm all right," she gasped. She swallowed a mouthful of coffee and then took a few more deep breaths. "A blueberry went down the wrong way." She rolled her wrist over and checked her watch. "I really should get back to the clinic and check on the cat," she said. "Thank you, Violet. Everything was delicious."

She got to her feet and looked at me. "Kathleen, if I'm not rushing you, we could walk partway together." She didn't say *please* out loud, but I could see it on her face.

"You're not," I said. "I need to check on Owen and Hercules. Somebody"—I turned to look at Rebecca— "got Owen another catnip chicken. There are probably chicken parts all over my kitchen."

"Don't look at me," Rebecca said, keeping her head down over the album. "It was Ami."

Head bowed or not, I could see her smiling. I thanked Violet for dinner and for sharing her photographs. Roma and I said our good nights and headed out. The moon was almost full and the stars sparkled in a way they had never seemed to in the city.

Roma waited until we were out of sight of the house before she spoke. "Kathleen, could I ask you something?" she said.

"Of course," I said. "What is it?"

"You said Easton was at the library before he died."

"That's right," I said slowly, wondering where she was going.

"You're sure?"

"Uh-huh. The police have evidence. Why do you ask?"

We turned the corner and started up the hill. She let out a breath and stopped on the sidewalk. "Because I think Oren might be involved in Easton's death."

17

Wave Arms Like a Fan

"What do you mean, you think Oren might be involved?"

"The police talked to him this afternoon."

"The police talk to a lot of people," I said.

"This is the second time."

I was about to say they'd talked to me more than once when I remembered I was also a suspect of sorts.

"That's not the only thing," Roma said. "He wasn't at Fern's for meat loaf."

"You're going to have to explain," I said.

"Have you ever been to Fern's diner?" she asked. "It's a little place down near the marina."

"Like a fifties diner?"

Roma nodded. "That's Fern's. Every Tuesday night is meat loaf night. Meat loaf, mashed potatoes, green beans in the summer, carrots the rest of the time, brown gravy and apple pie."

"Sounds good."

"It is. I haven't missed a meat loaf Tuesday since I came back to Mayville. Oren probably hasn't missed one in twenty-five years." She kicked a rock on the ground and sent it skittering along the sidewalk.

"Oren wasn't there Tuesday night," I said.

"No." We started walking again. "And he wasn't at the theater when you got there the next morning, was he?"

"No, he wasn't."

"Kathleen, Oren didn't come home at all Tuesday night," Roma said, her voice low and troubled.

I brushed away a small cloud of midges fluttering just in front of my face. "How do you know that?" I asked.

"The Kings bought a horse for their daughter. They thought they were getting a deal when they heard the price. What they got was a sick animal. I was out at their place from about one until close to five a.m. The back of their property meets the back of Oren's." She tipped her head back to study the sky. "It was a full moon Monday night. I could see Oren's yard and house almost as clearly as if it were daytime. His truck wasn't there. He wasn't there."

"It doesn't mean Oren had anything to do with what happened to Gregor Easton." My shoulder ached, but I didn't want to rub it in front of Roma.

"If there was nothing off about Easton's death, the police wouldn't still be investigating. And it's not like they have a huge pool of suspects. Did you know that pretty much everyone in the choir was at a birthday party at Eric's Place that night?"

"I didn't."

"I know Marcus. He's good at what he does."

She was right. From what I'd seen Detective Gordon was thorough and persistent.

"Easton was at your library. Why does that matter if he died from natural causes? They're not going to keep looking at a case that wasn't criminal just so they won't look incompetent if *Access Hollywood* shows up."

She held out both her hands. "And they haven't."

"You think the police are investigating because there's something to investigate," I said.

"Kathleen, Oren is family. Our moms were cousins. I don't believe for a moment that he'd hurt anyone, but this looks bad."

I thought about Oren recognizing Gregor Easton's real name. And how beautifully he'd played the piano. Those things weren't coincidences. Oren knew Gregor Easton. How and why he was keeping it a secret, I didn't know. But I didn't believe he could have killed the man.

"Roma," I said. "I don't know what happened to Mr. Easton, but I don't believe Oren had anything to do with it." I held up a finger before she could interrupt. "I may have only been here a few months, but I know Oren well enough to know he wouldn't deliberately hurt Gregor Easton or anyone else, for that matter. He had no reason. And if there was some kind of accident at the library or the theater he'd get help, not leave someone to die."

Roma looked away and I waited until she looked back.

"Whatever reason Oren had for being gone all night, it had nothing to do with Easton's death. I know that."

Roma looked at me and I met her gaze steadily, because I did believe what I had said. Then she reached out and gave my arm a squeeze. "I'm glad Everett hired you, Kathleen," she said. "Have a safe walk home."

She turned left and I headed up the hill. I meant what I'd said. Oren didn't have it in him to hurt anyone, but he was tied up in this mess somehow. And so was I.

I let myself in the back door and stood in the darkness of the porch for a moment. I needed to talk to Oren before I did anything else. And this was the kind of conversation that had to be had in person—not that I was exactly sure what I was going to say. What would I do? Knock on the door and say, "Hi, Oren. I just came by to ask if you did anything to Gregor Easton"?

Well, maybe not that.

I'd left the light on over the stove in the kitchen. No cats. The laundry basket was on one of the chairs. I'd folded everything before I left, but I hadn't had time to put anything away. It wasn't that late. Maybe I'd go for a walk to clear my head. And if I happened to end up near Oren's place, well, that wouldn't be so bad. I found a pair of socks in the clean laundry so I could change from sandals to sneaks.

I wrapped up half a dozen brownies to take with me—in case I did happen to see Oren. If I was going to accuse him of hiding something the least I could do was give him a brownie. I got my messenger bag to carry the brownies so they didn't get too warm in my hand. Then I ran upstairs to change from my skirt to a pair of capris.

When I came back down Hercules was looking in the bag. I shook a finger at him. "Oh, no. No, no. We're not doing this again."

He put one paw inside the bag.

"No," I repeated more insistently.

He lifted his other front paw, studied the bottom of it for a moment, gave it a couple of quick licks and then got into the tote and sat down. I loomed over him.

"I'm going to Oren's. You can't come. Get out," I said. I knew he wasn't going to move. I tipped the bag forward, very carefully, intending to tip him out. He lay down and snagged the front mesh panel of the bag with his claws. I gave it a small shake. It didn't work.

I bent down. "Fine," I said through gritted teeth. "Stay in the bag. I'll take something else."

I put the brownies in a cloth grocery bag, grabbed

my keys and went out into the porch for my sneakers. Hercules came through the door behind me. Literally through the door. I rubbed the side of my head with the heel of my hand.

Out of the corner of my eye I saw the cat's ears twitch. I could put him back in the kitchen, but all he'd do was walk through the door again. It seemed that Owen and Hercules were determined to help me play detective, each in their own way. There was no way to make Herc stay in the house. And he knew it.

But I wasn't going to fold right away. I put on one shoe, slowly tied the laces and then did the same with the other shoe. Hercules didn't look at me. I didn't look at him. I straightened and brushed off my pants. "All right, you can come," I said. "Get in the bag."

This time he waited for me to open the kitchen door. Then he climbed in the messenger bag, lay down and looked at me, all innocent green eyes.

"Don't be smug," I said, closing the top zipper. I looked at him through the mesh. "And please be quiet."

I swung the bag over my shoulder, locked up and started up the hill. The closer I got to Oren's house the more foolish the idea of going to see him began to seem. Hercules scratched at the top of the bag just as Oren's house came in sight.

"Stop it," I hissed. That just made him dig harder at the nylon fabric.

I didn't know why I thought the cat would listen to me. He was a cat, not a dog that had been to obedience school, or a trained monkey in the circus. He was an independent, stubborn cat. Who was about to destroy my favorite bag.

I opened the zipper a couple of inches. Hercules immediately stuck a paw out. "No, no, no! Don't do that," I said.

He raked the inside of the bag with his other front paw. Great. Someone was going to drive by and see me talking to my purse at nine o'clock on a Saturday night in front of Oren's house.

"Fine," I whispered. "You can have a look around, but then you go back in the bag because we're going home. And I'm not drinking any more of Ruby's wine. It puts the 'stupid' in 'stupid ideas.'"

I pulled the zipper open a bit more. I knew mice and cockroaches could squeeze through incredibly small spaces. So can cats, I discovered. Hercules pushed through the small opening, coming out of the bag like water pouring to the ground. He took off across Oren's yard, disappearing into the darkness.

Crap on toast!

I scrambled across Oren's lawn and tripped over the bottom step of the verandah. I caught a glimpse of fur heading around the side of the porch. I felt for the railing and followed, hoping I was chasing Herc and not a nosy raccoon or a sidetracked skunk.

"Hercules," I called in a stage whisper, knowing I was wasting my breath.

Oren's house was a renovated farmhouse, like mine, with the same steeply pitched roof and bay window. His house had an addition on one side, set back from the front of the main house, with a covered verandah that ran along part of the main house, down the side and all the way across the front of the extension. Hercules paused by the wooden screen door that led into the extension.

"C'mon, puss," I called. He looked over his shoulder at me, his eyes huge and unblinking. Then he walked through the door and disappeared.

I sagged against the railing and said a word that well-bred librarians didn't generally say. Now what was I going to do? If Oren came home before Hercules came out, I was, to put it crassly, screwed. There was no way I could explain to Oren how Hercules had gotten into his house. There was no logical, reasonable explanation.

Not that I had a logical, reasonable explanation for why I was at Oren's house in the first place. Or why I'd brought my cat along. I was going to come off as very peculiar at best, and deranged at worst.

I looked around. No people. No cars. No lights. So far it looked like I hadn't been seen. I was very grateful that Oren didn't have motion-sensor lights.

I dropped to my knees by the door. My head hurt, my shoulder ached and Violet's blueberry tart was rolling in my stomach like the English Channel ferry in a rainstorm.

I called the cat again. Of course he didn't come. I lifted the strap of my bag over my shoulder and set the bag next to the railing. There was nothing to do but wait and cross my fingers that things didn't get any worse. I leaned back against the railing, knees pulled up to my chest, and watched the white wooden screen door.

I thought about Gregor Easton. What did I know so far? Easton had been in my library after hours, meeting someone who'd used my name to lure him there. Someone who had a key or access to a key. He'd had a gash on the side of his head. There was blood at the library. Easton had probably been hurt there, but was it deliberate or accidental?

Oren knew Easton. Oren hadn't been at the Stratton the morning I'd found the body and hadn't been at meat loaf night the night before. The most obvious inference was that Oren had something to do with Easton's death.

Tying Oren to Easton's death was the part that didn't

work for me. I thought about the beautiful sunburst Oren had created. So much care had gone into making that, and so much caring into the idea to create it in the first place.

It didn't matter how things looked. I knew how they felt—to me.

Just then I felt something else, the same thickening of the air I'd noticed at the library just before Hercules had come out of the storage area. I leaned forward, eyes on the bottom panel of the door. The screen and the thick wooden door behind it seemed to ripple and go out of focus just a little. I held my breath, hoping, hoping it was the cat and not an earthquake or some part of my brain short-circuiting.

One moment the surface of the door seemed almost fluid and the next there was Hercules. He walked across the verandah and climbed onto my lap. "Bad, bad kitty," I said. I might have been more believable if I hadn't had both arms wrapped around him.

"You have to stop doing that," I said. "What if Oren had come home? What if Oren had been in there? What if he had some huge, slobbery, pointy-toothed attack dog in there?"

Herc lifted his head and fixed his green eyes on me.

"Okay, I'm exaggerating a little," I said. "But there could have been a dog in there who thought it would be fun to play a game of catch with you as the ball."

He put a paw on my wrist and butted my hand with his head.

"So, what did you take this time?" I asked, holding out my hand, palm up. He spat out a crumpled ball of paper, damp with cat spit. Gingerly I pulled the edges apart and flattened the paper against my leg.

It seemed to be the top half of something. The page

was torn along one short edge. I held the sheet up close to my face, trying to read what was on the paper. It didn't make any sense. Someone had drawn a row of blocks—actually they looked more like little teeth. There seemed to be dots on some of the teeth and the dots were numbered, but some had more numbers than others.

There was another row of little boxes under the first with dots and numbers in a different pattern.

"What the heck is this?" I asked the cat. "Is it some kind of plan for something?"

Of all the things that were probably inside Oren's house, why had Hercules brought me this? It didn't look like any building plan I'd ever seen. In the dim light the handwriting looked like Oren's, but I couldn't be sure. "I don't get it." The cat's response was to climb down and sniff around the verandah.

I folded the paper and stuffed it in my pants pocket. "We have to go," I said. I unzipped the top of the messenger bag and tapped the bottom with a finger. "Hop in."

He stretched. He yawned. He took a couple of passes at his face with a paw. And then finally he walked over and climbed in the bag.

"Thank you," I said, before I closed the top.

I got to my feet, slid the bag over my shoulder and felt my way back along the porch. A moth—at least I hoped that was what it was—fluttered by my face. I waved it away. Hercules shifted against my hip.

I started down the walkway to the street and couldn't help letting out a sigh of relief. We'd made it. No one had seen us. I hadn't had to explain about Hercules or what I was doing crawling around Oren's deck in the dark on a Saturday night. We were free and clear.

A car came along the street and stopped in front of the house. The passenger's window lowered and Detective Gordon leaned over from the driver's side. "Good evening, Ms. Paulson," he said.

Free and clear? Maybe not.

18

Slap Face with Palm

Hercules stopped squirming. I put a hand around the bag as a warning for him to stay very still and very quiet. Walking around on a Saturday night with one's cat in one's bag didn't exactly make one look like a criminal, but it didn't exactly make one look all that stable, either. I put on what I hoped was an innocent-looking smile.

"Hello, Detective Gordon," I said, walking over to the side of his car.

"Is there anything I can help you with?" he asked.

"Thank you, no," I said. "I was out for a walk and stopped in to see Oren, but he isn't home." The brownies. I was still holding the cloth grocery bag with the brownies inside. "I wanted to drop some brownies off to Oren as a thank-you for fixing a leak at the library yesterday."

There—a perfectly good explanation for why I was standing in Oren's yard. I was in the clear after all.

"Get in," Detective Gordon said.

Or not. "Excuse me?" I said.

He leaned over a little farther and opened the passenger's door. "I'll drive you home. It's not a good idea to be walking around alone this late."

This late? I didn't want to do something as obvious as look at my watch, but by my calculation it wasn't more than nine o'clock. Plus, I had my big flashlight, my pepper spray, a cat, and six brownies.

"I'm fine, really," I said.

"I'd feel better if I saw you home safely." I couldn't decide if he was being charmingly old-fashioned or just a bit patronizing.

"I don't generally accept rides from strangers," I said. That made him smile.

"We're not exactly strangers, Ms. Paulson."

He was right. My feet were tired, not to mention my shoulder. And I had no idea how much longer Hercules would stay quiet, which could open a whole new can of worms, or at least a bag of cat. "You're right," I said.

I got into the car, setting Hercules between my feet. Detective Gordon turned in Oren's driveway and headed back along the street. "What are you doing out on a Saturday night?" I asked.

"Police business," he said.

"Gregor Easton."

He didn't answer and he kept his eyes on the road. But he did smile just a little.

It occurred to me that maybe the detective had been on his way to see Oren. Time to talk about something innocuous. "I didn't know you were a cat person, Detective," I said.

That got me a quizzical look. Then the light came on. "Roma drafted you to help her this afternoon," he said.

"She did."

"Did you have any luck catching Lucy?" He stopped at the corner, checked for traffic and then turned down Mountain Road.

"We got her," I said. "And you were right. Her leg is broken. Roma's scheduled surgery for tomorrow."

"That's good." He slowed to a stop behind a truck that was waiting to turn left. "I'd hate for Lucy to have to be . . ."

He didn't finish the sentence, but I knew what he was thinking. "Roma told me you were the one who found Desmond," I said, fighting the urge to lean down and check on Hercules.

"Yeah. He'd been in a fight with some other animal. He was by the edge of the road. I wasn't sure at first if it was some kind of animal or someone's coat that had been thrown out of a car."

"How on earth did you get him to Roma? How did you get him into your car?"

"Well, it wasn't easy." He slowed down, put on his turn signal and pulled into my driveway. "I didn't know he was feral." He turned sideways toward me in his seat. "I didn't know anything at all about feral cats. Desmond went crazy when I picked him up. He howled, he hissed, he scratched both of my hands. Luckily I was driving a department car with the divider between the front and back seats. I managed somehow to get him into the back."

He shook his head. "I threw a blanket over him, which seemed to help a little. Then I hightailed it for the clinic—lights and sirens blazing."

"You saved Desmond," I said, unbuckling the seat belt and reaching for my bag. "Because you rescued Desmond, Roma found out about the cats at Wisteria Hill. So in a way you saved all of them, too."

He fiddled with the collar of his shirt. "Roma is the one who saved the cats and she does the lion's share of the work."

"Even so . . ." This time I was the one not finishing a sentence.

I remembered the brownies again. They'd made it to Oren's and back pretty much intact. "Here," I said, handing him the foil-wrapped package. "And thank you for the ride home."

I got out of the car, holding Hercules against my body with one arm.

Detective Gordon leaned across the seat again. "Thank you for the brownies," he said.

I watched him back out, then walked around the house and let myself into the porch. As soon as I was inside I opened the messenger bag. Hercules was curled comfortably in the bottom. "We're home," I said.

He opened one eye.

"C'mon, I have some of those stinky crackers left." That got him out of the bag. "Don't think this means you're off the hook for what you did at Oren's," I said, shaking a finger at him.

I flipped on the kitchen light and Owen blinked at us from beside the sink. I laughed. "You heard me, didn't you?" I said, leaning down to pet him. "You heard me say 'stinky crackers.'"

He made a soft "murp" in the back of his throat.

I got a glass of milk and gave each cat a small pile of cheese-and-sardine crackers. Then I sat at the table and pulled out the piece of paper Hercules had found. The fact that Owen and Hercules seemed to be trying to help me figure out what had happened to Gregor Easton made no sense. No sense. On the other hand, neither did their other abilities. I decided, for now at least, to forget about logic and reason and just roll with what was happening.

I smoothed the piece of paper out flat on the table.

Now that I could clearly see the markings and numbers I hoped they'd make some kind of sense.

They didn't. And, realistically, what were the chances that Hercules would find the one clue that would help me make sense of how Oren was connected to Gregor Easton? Just because I talked to the cats like they understood what I was saying didn't mean they did. They were cats. Smart cats with some unbelievable skills, but cats nonetheless. At the moment one had cracker crumbs on his face and the other had a dust ball at the end of his tail.

Nothing made any sense. I was tired and frustrated and the only thing I wanted to do was sink into a tub full of bubbles and then into cool, crisp sheets.

So I did.

I woke up a bit later than usual on Sunday morning, after a night filled with bizarre dreams. In one of them Oren was playing the piano for an audience of cats.

I was in the kitchen in pajama bottoms and a T-shirt, cutting up fruit, when Rebecca tapped on the back door. She looked tired and pale without her usual deep-rose lipstick.

"Kathleen, I'm sorry. Did I wake you?" she asked.

"No," I said. "I was just about to make crepes. Is everything all right?"

"No," she said. "Well, yes." She rubbed the side of her face with her fingers. "I'm sorry. I'm not making a lot of sense. Ami is in the hospital. She's all right, but she's all alone. I hate to bother you, but would you be able to drive me there?" She held up her bandaged arm. "I can't drive—not safely—with this arm."

"Of course I'll drive you," I said. "You said Ami's all right, but what happened to her?" I asked.

"She had some kind of allergic reaction. Her throat

swelled and she couldn't breathe. She was at Eric's with some of the others from the festival. There was a doctor, a tourist, having dessert with his wife. What are the chances a doctor would . . ." She closed her eyes for a moment, then opened them again and gave a soft sigh. "But he was," she said in a stronger voice. "And Ami's all right."

"That's all that matters," I said.

"You're right," Rebecca said. "What matters is Ami is all right."

"Just give me a minute to pull some clothes on." I led her into the kitchen and pulled out a chair. "Have a seat. I'll only be a minute."

I grabbed the bowl of fruit from the counter, set a plate on top as a temporary cover and put the dish in the refrigerator. I touched Rebecca on the shoulder as I passed behind her. "Be right back," I said. "There's coffee, if you'd like a cup."

She covered my hand with her own for a moment. "Thank you," she said softly.

I gave her shoulder a squeeze and headed for the stairs. I pulled on shorts and a T-shirt, combed my hair and used a clip to keep my bangs back. Then I grabbed my purse and went back downstairs.

Rebecca was talking to someone. Owen. I couldn't make out what she was saying, but she was leaning forward in her chair, speaking quietly. Owen sat in front of her, head tipped to the side, listening intently.

"I'm ready," I said. "I'll be back soon," I told Owen.

The cats had already been fed and there was fresh water in their dishes. I switched off the coffeemaker, locked the door behind us and walked through the backyard with Rebecca to her little blue Toyota. She handed me the keys. I opened the passenger's door for her, then went around and unlocked the driver's side. It took me a moment to adjust the seat and mirrors.

"We're going to Riverview?" I asked Rebecca.

"Yes. Do you know where that is?"

"I do," I said. I backed out and headed down Hill Street, trying to figure out the most direct route to the hospital. On a Sunday morning in Mayville Heights there wasn't much traffic, so it really didn't matter which way I drove.

As we neared the hospital I braked to let a squirrel in the middle of the street bolt the rest of the way across, and gave Rebecca a smile.

She managed a smile back. She had been quiet, tense, the whole way. Finally she spoke. "I know I'm not Ami's grandmother, but I couldn't love her more if I were."

The squirrel made one last dash for the curb.

"How did you and Ami get to be so close?" I asked.

"I cut her hair." Out of the corner of my eye I saw her smile at the memory. "She was a little hellion. Her parents had died in a car accident when she was four. Her grandmother had died long before she was born, so Ami was being raised by her grandfather and a series of nannies."

"She was a little spoiled," I ventured.

Rebecca laughed at that. "She had hair like Mowgli from the *Jungle Book* and she was saucy and rude. I told her I'd cut her hair when she learned some manners."

"And did she?"

"She went home and cut her own hair with a pair of kitchen shears she swiped from the pantry."

I grinned. "Not good."

"No, it wasn't. The nanny brought her back to get me to repair the damage. She was just as rude and just as stubborn as she had been the first visit. But I liked the child. She reminded me of someone . . . someone I used to know." She cleared her throat. "I told her if she was going to cut her own hair she should at least learn how to do it properly. Saturday morning she was sitting by the door of the shop when I arrived to open up. A few weeks later she ran away from home. I found her wrapped up in a sheet she'd pulled off someone's clothesline, asleep on a lawn chair."

I pulled into the hospital driveway and found a parking spot to the right of the entrance.

"Thank you so much, Kathleen," Rebecca said.

"I'm coming in with you."

"You don't need to do that."

"Don't make me get out my kitchen shears to make a point," I said with mock sternness. "Do you want that on your conscience?"

Rebecca smiled. "All right, you win."

We found Ami sitting up in bed. Her hair was lank, her skin was pale and she looked about twelve years old. She bit her lip and swallowed hard when she caught sight of Rebecca.

Rebecca wrapped her arms around Ami and kissed the top of her head. "Are you all right?" she asked. She leaned back out of the hug, pushed the hair back off Ami's face and studied it.

Ami nodded. "I couldn't . . . breathe," she said.

I noticed a couple of long scrapes on her throat, as though she'd clawed at it.

Rebecca laid a hand on Ami's cheek. "But you're all right now and we're going to find out what you're allergic to and how to keep you safe." She gave Ami another hug. "Everything's all right," she said.

Ami laid her head on Rebecca's shoulder. "I just want to go home," she said.

Rebecca gently patted her back. "We're going to take you home and I'm going to spoil you for the rest of the day."

Ami looked over at me. "Hi, Kathleen," she said.

"Hi," I said. "I'm glad you're all right."

"Thank you for bringing Rebbie," she said. "I didn't know who else to call. I didn't think about her not being able to drive."

"Don't worry about it," I said.

"Sweetie, where are your clothes?" Rebecca asked, looking around the room.

"I think they might be in that closet," Ami said, pointing at a narrow cupboard by the window.

Rebecca looked inside and pulled out a clear plastic bag. Ami's things were inside, the end of the bag tied in a loose knot.

"Let me get that," I said. I undid the knot and handed the bag back to her. She shook out Ami's clothes and laid them on the bed.

"Can you get dressed by yourself?" she asked.

Ami nodded.

"Okay. I'm going to find a nurse and see if there are any special instructions you need to follow."

"I think there's a referral to an allergist," Ami said. "I'm going to have to be tested even though the doctor—the one here, not the one at Eric's—is pretty sure it was the poppy seeds."

Rebecca closed her eyes for a moment. "Poppy seeds," she whispered. She swallowed and opened her eyes. "I'll be right back," she said.

"I'll wait outside," I said to Ami. "Yell if you need help."

By the time Ami was dressed, Rebecca was back with a list of allergists and the rest of Ami's paperwork. I drove them to Ami's small apartment, down the street from the Stratton.

"Kathleen, would you take the car home for me?" Rebecca asked.

"Of course," I said. "But how will you get home?"

"I can walk," she said. "I do it all the time."

"You don't have to stay, Rebbie," Ami said from the backseat, but her face didn't match her words.

Rebecca and I exchanged looks.

"Sorry, sweetie. You're stuck with me," she said. "At least for the next couple of days."

I saw Ami's shoulders sag with relief.

"Thank you for everything, Kathleen," Rebecca said.

"Anytime, Rebecca," I said. "I mean it. Call me if Ami needs anything or if you'd like me to come and get you."

She nodded, undid her seat belt and got out of the car.

Ami leaned over the seat. "Thank you," she said. "I'm so glad you moved in behind Rebbie."

"Me, too, Ami," I said. "Take care of yourself."

I drove Rebecca's car back to her house, backing it into the driveway so it could be easily driven out the next time. Rebecca had left her sweater behind on the seat and it had fallen onto the floor mat. I picked it up. There was a smudge of dirt on the bottom edge. I decided to take the sweater with me and wash it for Rebecca.

I locked the car, stuck the keys in my purse and walked through the backyard to my house. Hercules was in the porch, watching out the window. He jumped down off the bench, looked past me, then at me and meowed.

"What is it?" I said. "If you're looking for Rebecca, she's with Ami and Ami's fine." Herc followed me into the kitchen. Owen was sitting just inside the door. "Rebecca's with Ami and Ami's all right," I said.

I tossed Rebecca's sweater over the back of a chair. "I need coffee," I said to no one in particular.

Once the coffeemaker was doing its thing I turned toward the fridge. Maybe I'd have French toast and fruit instead of crepes. Owen was standing on his back legs, front paws on the seat of the chair where I'd dropped Rebecca's sweater. He was chewing on one sleeve.

"Owen! Stop that!" I shouted. Startled, he dropped to all fours on the floor and looked at me with the same stupid expression he got when he was chewing on one of his catnip chickens. "What is the matter with you?" I snapped. "That's Rebecca's sweater."

I picked up the cardigan, folded it and laid it on the chair back. Then I went to the refrigerator for the fruit I'd been cutting up when Rebecca had knocked on the door. When I turned around again Owen was in mid-jump, trying to snag Rebecca's sweater with a paw. "Hey! Stop it!" I yelled, snatching the sweater before the cat could get it.

Owen hung his head. Hercules appeared in the living room doorway. I bunched up the sweater with one hand and held it against me as I bent down to Owen. "What on earth is wrong with you?" I asked, lowering my voice to normal volume.

Owen looked up at me and then thrust his head into the tangle of Rebecca's sweater. Before I could push him away he pulled his head back and shook it. If I hadn't known better I would have sworn there was a Fred the Funky Chicken hidden in the sleeve.

I looked at Owen, who was doing his best not to look at me. Maybe I wasn't exactly wrong. I reached down and scratched the top of his head. "It's okay. I'm not mad at you," I said.

I stood up, shook out the sweater and held the right

arm close to my face. It smelled faintly of catnip. I bent down to Hercules, holding out the sleeve to him. He sniffed, made a face and pulled back his head—the same reaction he had to Owen's collection of catnip chickens. Rebecca had promised she wouldn't buy Owen any more chickens. *The poultice must have had catnip in it,* I realized. I didn't know catnip was a remedy for arthritis. No wonder Owen was acting so weird.

I went downstairs, filled the sink next to the washer with warm water and a bit of soap and left the sweater soaking.

I was just finishing the last bite of my French toast when the phone rang. I padded into the living room in my sock feet, figuring it was either my mother or Rebecca. It was neither.

"Hi, Kathleen." Lise yawned through the phone at me. "Guess what I found out."

19

Single Lotus Kick

"Hi, Lise," I said. "Is this about Gregor Easton?"

"Oh, yes, it is," she said, and there was a smug gleefulness in her voice. Then she yawned again.

"Have you been to bed yet?" I asked.

Lise's husband was a jazz guitarist who played regularly in clubs all over Boston and up and down the East Coast. He didn't keep exactly regular hours, and on the weekend neither did Lise.

"I'm lying across the bed right now," Lise said.

"So what did you find out?" I asked. "I got your e-mail." I pictured her sprawled across her queen-sized bed with all the pillows piled under her head.

"Well, as I told you in the e-mail, Easton was born Douglas Gregory Williams. The pulled-himself-up-from-humble-beginnings story?"

"A fake?" I had to change position because one of my feet was falling asleep.

"Uh-huh. Just like the name. He did his first degree at a small university in Florida. And get this: It was a teaching degree."

"Easton was going to be a teacher?"

"Apparently," Lise said. "Hang on a second; I'm losing

a pillow." There were some muffled bumps and then she was back. "There's a year and a half unaccounted for, as far as I can tell, after he got that degree. Maybe he was teaching, for all I know. Anyway, after that he enrolled in the graduate music program at Oberlin Conservatory. He shaved a couple of years off his age at that point, too."

"Wait a second," I said. "Easton went to Oberlin Conservatory?"

"Yep." When Lise got excited her educated, cultured way of speaking disappeared.

Violet had gone to Oberlin. My heart started to race. "But I thought his graduate degree was from the University of Cincinnati."

"It is. Easton went to Oberlin when he was still Douglas Gregory Williams—and he was only there for a year. He didn't graduate."

"Wow." I pulled my legs up underneath me. "Do you know why he left?"

"Does a bear have a hairy butt?" she chortled. "Yes, I know."

A goofy Lise reminded me of the eighteen-year-old girl from northern Maine I'd met in college.

"So?" I prompted.

"Scandal," she crowed. "Sex, drugs and rock and roll."

"What?"

"Hang on a sec," she said. "Yes, babe," I heard her say. "I'd love a cup." Then she was back again. "Okay, so there weren't any drugs that I heard about, and it was classical music, not rock and roll, but the sex part definitely happened."

"Do I want to hear this, Lise?" I asked, wishing I had a big cup of coffee myself.

She laughed. "Don't worry. I don't have any gory details."

"What do you have?" I heard her take a slurp of coffee before she answered.

"Two things. First of all, Easton was struggling in his composition classes, and then suddenly he got very, very good."

"He was cheating?"

"That's the general consensus among people I talked to."

I stretched both arms over my head. "He could have been homesick or just needed time to adjust to the program."

"Maybe. But no one seems to think that was it. Apparently he didn't go from good to better; he went from mediocre to great." I heard more coffee-slurping sounds.

"So was he kicked out for cheating?" I asked.

"No," Lise said. "There was a fair amount of talk and a lot of suspicion, but no proof."

"So, what's the sex part?"

Hercules wandered over. I stretched my hand down to pet him.

"Easton took some pictures of another student in the program—a female student. Now, by today's standards they're pretty tame, but then . . ."

"I get it," I said.

"And there was some suggestion that he'd pressured the young woman."

"Is that why he left Oberlin?" Herc was purring.

"Indirectly. The young woman came from a wealthy family. Money seems to have made the entire thing and Easton go away."

"Paid off or run off?" I asked.

"That's the question, isn't it?" Lise said, yawning loudly in my ear. "I have to go to bed. But there's one more thing. The young woman, the one Easton took the pictures of? I have her number. Do you want it?"

"Yes," I said, scrambling out of the chair. "Let me grab a pencil." I wrote down the woman's name, Phoebe Michaels, and her number, thanked Lise profusely, reminding her that I owed her, and said good-bye.

Hercules had been waiting patiently for me. I picked him up and went into the kitchen. Lise had pretty much confirmed Ruby's assessment of Easton's character.

I was curious about Violet, and did some fast calculations. She could have been at Oberlin at the same time as Easton. Why hadn't she said anything? She had to have recognized Easton. Could she have killed him? What reason would she have? It made about as much sense as Oren being involved.

"So far my choices are Oren or Violet," I said to Hercules. "I don't like either one."

There was a knock at the door. I set Hercules down and went to see who it was.

Abigail stood on my back stoop, holding a cardboard box. "Did I catch you at a bad time?" she asked.

"No," I said. "I was just getting a cup of coffee. Come in. Can I get you a cup?"

"Thanks, Kathleen, but I can't stay. I just wanted to show you these books." She followed me into the kitchen and set the box on the table. "I was sorting more things for the yard sale yesterday." She opened the flaps of the box. "I found these and I didn't want to leave them at the library so I brought them home."

I picked up the top volume, a copy of *Alice's Adventures in Wonderland* in excellent condition.

"That's a first edition," Abigail said.

I almost dropped the book. "Are you serious? Do you know what this could be worth?"

She nodded. "I do now. I spent some time online last night, researching prices." She gestured to the box. "There's several thousand dollars' worth of books in just that box. I didn't feel right about leaving them at the library. I hope that's okay."

"It's very okay," I said. "Thank you. The board will have to have all the books valued, but this is going to be a big boost to the book-buying budget."

"I'm so glad," Abigail said.

"Where do you think they came from?" I picked up *Alice* again, then wondered if I should be handling the book.

"I suppose they could have been part of the library's collection, but I'm guessing they were donated by someone who didn't know what they had."

I pointed to the side of the box where it looked like a chicken had been practicing hieroglyphics with a Sharpie. "Your secret code?" I asked.

Abigail smiled. "I didn't want anyone to know what was in the box and I didn't want to mix up the books with the others for the sale. It seems kind of silly now."

"I don't think so," I said. An idea was beginning to tickle the back of my mind. "I have a meeting with Everett on Monday," I said. "I'll show him these and he can arrange to have them appraised and sold."

"If I find anything else, I'll let you know," she promised.

I walked her to the back door. "Thanks," I said. "I have a wish list of kid's books I've been itching to order, and now it looks like I'll be able to."

Abigail smiled. "See you tomorrow," she said.

Hercules, who had disappeared when Abigail knocked, came back to the kitchen. "You may be a genius," I told him. "Your brother, too."

He ducked his head. It may have been modesty or, more likely, he'd noticed a couple of stinky-cracker crumbs on the floor.

I pointed at him. "Don't move." The piece of paper Hercules had taken from Oren's was on my dresser. So was the scrap Owen had swiped out of Rebecca's recycling bin. I grabbed both of them.

Hercules was waiting by the table. I showed him the piece of paper he'd found last night. "You see this?" I asked. "I think it's code. Only instead of being letters and words I think it's music." Hercules studied the paper as if he was trying to decide if he agreed with me.

"See this?" I held out the sheet music Owen had pilfered the other day. "Gregor Easton wrote that." I pointed to the composer's name in the top corner of the paper. "At least he's supposed to have written it, but look at the first line of music, and then look at the first line of the other page. The pattern's the same."

Herc actually looked from one sheet of paper to the other. I sat down, laying both bits of paper on the table. My mind was throwing out ideas faster than I could sort them into sense.

"Lise said Easton was suspected of cheating. His music went from nothing to spectacular almost overnight." I tapped my nails on the tabletop. "Oren didn't finish university because of some kind of breakdown. What if he was at Oberlin, too? What if Easton's music was really Oren's?"

There was a sour taste in the back of my throat. If Easton had stolen Oren's music I'd just come up with a motive for him to want the conductor dead. I got up and had a glass of water instead of more coffee. Phoebe Michaels's phone number was still sitting on the counter. She'd been there at Oberlin with Easton—actually

Williams—and Violet. Maybe she could give me some answers.

I looked at the clock. It wasn't too early to call anymore. I picked up the number. "What do I say to her?" I asked Hercules. He was busy washing his face and had no suggestions.

Then I thought of my dad. "When all else fails, Katie, just tell the truth," he liked to say. Before I could talk myself out of it I went into the living room, picked up the receiver and punched in the number.

Phoebe Michaels answered on the fourth ring.

"Dr. Michaels, my name is Kathleen Paulson," I said. "I'm sorry to bother you on a Sunday morning, but I'm hoping you'll talk to me about Gregor Easton. You knew him as Douglas Williams."

"You're Dr. Tremayne's friend," she said.

Thank you, Lise, I thought. "Yes, I am. You know that Mr. Easton is dead?"

"Yes," Dr. Michaels said. "Did you kill him? That doesn't mean I won't talk to you. I'd just like to know."

"No, I didn't kill him," I said. "In fact, the police haven't said how he died yet."

"But you don't think he died of natural causes." Her voice was low and husky.

I sat down on the footstool. "I don't. I'm the librarian here in Mayville Heights, Minnesota. Mr. Easton was in my library the night he died, and I'm the one who found his body at the Stratton Theater the next morning."

"Ah, so you're a suspect," she said.

"Yes, I guess I am. And it doesn't help that I've only been here a few months."

"So how can I help you, Ms. Paulson?"

"First, please call me Kathleen," I said.

"All right, Kathleen—if you'll call me Phoebe. I'm

only Dr. Michaels to my students and pretentious colleagues."

I smiled, liking her more the more she talked. "You were in the music program at Oberlin Conservatory with Gregor Easton, when he was known as Douglas Williams."

"I was."

"What was he like?"

"Handsome, charming, amoral, manipulative and not very talented."

"There were rumors he was cheating somehow when it came to his compositions."

"Oh, I think that was more than a rumor. I think it was the truth."

"Why?" I asked, stretching both my legs out in front of me.

"He had no ability, no talent as a composer. Then suddenly he got incredibly good. He claimed he'd just been suffering from performance anxiety."

"You didn't believe him?"

I heard a snort of derisive laughter.

"No, I didn't," she said emphatically. "Doug— Easton—was confident to the point of arrogance. The music he started handing in was complex, sensitive and inspired. All the things he wasn't. I don't know where it came from, but I've never believed he wrote it."

"Easton left after a year," I said, trying to work up to asking her about the pictures. I didn't need to.

"Kathleen, I'm sure Dr. Tremayne told you about the pictures."

"She did. I didn't want to embarrass you."

She laughed. "Oh, that ship sailed a long time ago." Her voice grew serious again. "Yes, he took photographs of me. Nothing that would be a big deal now."

"But not then."

"No," she said. "Then it seemed like the end of the world. I was eighteen. I'd been sheltered by my parents from everything. He was older. He seemed so sophisticated, so worldly, compared to the boys I knew. They seemed like, well, boys. I was an easy mark."

"Did he pressure you to pose for the pictures?"

"'You would if you loved me,'" she said. "How many women have fallen for that line? He promised the pictures would be art. They were just shots of me in my underwear, wrapped in some gauzy black fabric that had probably been a window curtain."

"But no nudity?"

"No. Just bare shoulders or a curve of cleavage. But it was how things seemed that was the problem, not how they really were."

"I'm sorry. I don't understand," I said, changing my position on the footstool.

"He did my makeup—red lips, black eyeliner, false eyelashes. I didn't exactly look like some inexperienced young woman from a good family."

"What happened after?"

"He dropped me as soon as he had the pictures. I cried. I begged. He laughed. I was terrified he'd show them to everyone I knew."

I tried to imagine how humiliated she must have felt. "I'm so sorry that happened to you, Phoebe," I said. "It must have been horrible."

"At the time it was. But I was very lucky. I had a mother I could talk to and a father with money. I went home for ten days. When I went back Easton was gone."

"Your father paid him off."

Her voice turned thoughtful. "You know, I don't

know for certain. I just assumed he did. We never spoke about it. I thought at the time that my father had gotten the photographs from Easton and destroyed them."

"He didn't?"

"No. One day the photos and negatives just showed up in my mailbox in the proverbial plain brown envelope."

"And you don't have any idea who sent them?"

"I don't think I was the first young woman Easton took photographs of. Or the last. I always felt it was one of the women from our Tuesday seminar class."

"Why?"

"Those were the people Easton spent all his time with."

"Was there a young woman named Violet in that group?" I asked.

"No."

"You're certain?"

"I am. I still have a photo of all of us. Ironically, it was Easton who took it. There was no Violet in the class." She listed off the names from memory.

So either I was wrong about when Violet had been at Oberlin or she hadn't known Easton. I felt relieved, but it was a long time ago and I wanted to be sure.

"Phoebe, do you think you could find that photograph?"

"I think so," she said. "But it'll take some time. I'm a bit of a pack rat."

"That's all right," I said.

"Give me your e-mail address. If I find the picture I'll scan it and send it to you."

"One last question," I said. "Oren Kenyon. Was he in the seminar class?" *Please say no,* I thought, crossing my fingers.

"Oren Kenyon? Would he have been maybe sixteen or seventeen?"

"Yes."

"He was. But I think he was auditing the class, not taking it for credit."

I let out the breath I hadn't realized I was holding. "Thank you so much for talking to me," I said. "I won't keep you any longer."

"You're welcome, Kathleen," she said. "When this is finally settled, when you finally figure out what happened, please call me and let me know how it ends."

"I'll do that," I promised. We said good-bye and hung up.

I went back to the kitchen, where the papers were still on the table. It always came back to Oren, no matter which way I turned. The more evidence that piled up against Oren, the more resistant I got to the idea that he'd had something to do with Gregor Easton's death.

"I have to talk to him," I said to the empty kitchen. I shut off the coffeemaker. Again. I went upstairs, brushed my hair and put on some lipstick.

I stared at my reflection in the mirror. Was I crazy? Was going to talk to Oren a mistake? But I needed to find out if he was involved in Gregor Easton's death in some way.

Was this like one of those old melodramatic, women-in-jeopardy movies? Was I just like the innocent young heroine who, when she hears a noise in the cellar late at night, with a violent serial killer on the loose, tosses her hair, licks her lips and goes down into the basement instead of getting the heck out of there? My hair was too short to toss and I didn't want to lick off the lipstick I'd just applied. Oren was not the bad guy in some old Hollywood B movie.

I got my keys. Both cats were sitting on the bench in the porch. I stopped to pet them. "I have to go see Oren," I told them. "I'll be back soon." I locked the door behind me. It would at least keep Owen from roaming around.

The clouds overhead were thinning, being blown away to wisps of nothing over the lake. It was another beautiful day. I realized I was beginning to think of Mayville as home.

I could see Oren's truck in the driveway as I approached his house. Moving closer, I caught sight of him on the verandah. He was painting something. It looked like a wooden trough; then I realized it was a window box. Oren looked up and waved his paintbrush in greeting.

I took a deep breath, wiped my sweaty palms on the bottom of my T-shirt and walked down the driveway toward him.

"Good morning, Kathleen," he said.

"Good morning." I pointed at his work. "A window box?"

He nodded. "For Eric at the café. The bottom rotted out of the old one."

The paint was a deep robin's-egg blue. "I like the color."

"That would be Susan's idea."

Exchanging social pleasantries was just putting off what I'd come to do. I cleared my throat. "Oren, could I talk to you about Gregor Easton?" I asked.

He studied the paintbrush for a moment before looking at me. "Yes," he said. "I just need to put the paint away and wash the brush."

He put a couple more strokes of paint on the end of

the flower box, then put the lid on the can and stood up. "I'll only be a minute," he said.

I nodded.

"Why don't you come in, Kathleen?" he said.

"All right." I stepped inside the extension, which was obviously Oren's workshop, and my mouth literally gaped open. All I could manage was a faint "Oh."

The space was completely open, floor to ceiling. High windows on the back wall flooded the room with light. More windows on the end of the room overlooked a long workbench. On the other side there was a counter with a sink, and cupboards underneath. There weren't nearly as many tools as I would have expected. Everything was neat, clean and perfectly organized.

But what dominated the room, almost forcing you to look, were the sculptures. An enormous metal bird, an eagle, I realized, as I moved closer, with a wingspan of at least six feet, was suspended in flight from the ceiling beams at the back half of the room.

I could visualize the feathers, the bird's beak, its powerful chest muscles, even though the sculpture was nothing more than a metal framework. Somehow I could see the bird. Somehow I could see it flying.

Below, reaching probably eight feet into the air, was a bear, one paw raised above its head. Again, somehow I could see fur and claws and power in the curves of metal.

But it was the eagle that drew me. I stood below it, head thrown back, and just stared. Behind me I heard Oren turn off the water at the sink and in a moment he came to stand beside me. "Oren, this is incredible," I said.

"My father," he said.

We moved to the huge bear, which was even more imposing up close. I reached out a hand to touch it and then pulled it back. "It's okay," Oren said. "You can't hurt anything."

The metal was rough under my fingers. "Your father was incredibly talented," I said. I realized these were the sculptures Rebecca and Roma had been talking about.

Oren nodded. "Yes, he was."

I turned slowly to look at the other sculptures. Over by one of the smaller, abstract pieces stood a beautiful . . . piano? I wasn't sure. I walked over to it. "This isn't a piano, is it?" I said to Oren.

"No."

"A harpsichord?"

He smiled. "That's right."

"You built this."

He ducked his head. "I did."

"You're very talented, as well," I said. I pushed my hands into my pockets, afraid I'd touch something I shouldn't.

Oren hauled a hand back over his hair. "Thank you," he said softly. He cleared his throat. "I have coffee. Would you like a cup?"

I nodded. "Yes, I would."

The coffeemaker was on the counter by the sink. Oren pulled over a couple of stools, then poured a cup for each of us. There was a small carton of milk and a dish of sugar cubes on a tray by the coffeemaker. After we'd both doctored our coffee, he folded one hand around his mug and looked at me. "You want to talk about Mr. Easton," he said.

"You knew him when he was Douglas Williams."

He nodded, took a drink from his mug and set it on

the counter again. "The other day in your office, I tried to convince myself you hadn't noticed that I'd recognized his real name."

"You were both at Oberlin at the same time."

He looked past me, nodding slowly again.

I fished in my pocket and pulled out the sheet of paper Owen had brought me, unfolding it on the counter between us. "That's your music." I flattened the paper with my hand. "Gregor Easton stole it."

For a long moment Oren didn't move, didn't speak. Then finally he said, "Yes."

The truth hung there between us. I wanted to reach out and somehow wave it away. "Why didn't you say something?"

Oren looked past my left shoulder at the sculpture suspended from the rafters. "Kathleen, my father was incredibly talented," he began.

I turned for another glimpse of the sculptures myself. "Yes, he was."

"He was an artist. But all anyone saw him as was a carpenter." Oren studied his own hands for a moment. "He was a good carpenter, but he wanted to be an artist."

I nodded, unsure of where the conversation was going, but reluctant to stop Oren while he was talking.

He looked at me now. "I could play the piano when I was four. I was composing music when I was six. I created my own method of notation because I couldn't read music back then."

The piece of paper Hercules had found. I was right. It was a kind of code.

Oren picked up his mug and took a long drink. "I could—I can—make music with almost any instrument: piano, guitar, bass, mandolin. I can play that harpsichord." He set the coffee back on the counter.

"A musical prodigy. That's what they told my parents I was. Gifted. If I look at a piece of music just once, I can remember it and play it. Years later I can play it." He wiped his mouth with one hand. "I was sixteen when they sent me to Oberlin. I'd long since outgrown all the music teachers in this area, probably in the state. I was auditing a seminar class Easton was teaching as a grad student. I dropped a piece of my music one day. I knew how to write music by then, but I was so used to notating my way that I'd kept on doing it."

"What happened?" I asked, although I was pretty sure I knew.

"I explained how the notation worked. He offered to help transcribe what I'd written into conventional notation. There was too much music for me to do it by myself. By then I had stacks of compositions, but no one else could play them."

I set my cup on the counter. "He took your music. Why didn't you say something? Your notation proved you'd written everything. The university would have expelled him."

Oren wiped his hands on his pants. "I don't know if this will make sense to you, Kathleen, but I didn't want to end up like my father."

"I'm sorry," I said. "I don't understand."

"No one knew I was composing music. To me, all I was doing was writing down what I heard in my head so it would go away. It was bad enough people were already beginning to see me as some kind of musical wonder. If they found out I was writing my own music, as well . . ." He didn't finish the thought.

"My father wanted me to have the chance he never had—to be an artist. The thing was, I wanted what he had."

I realized then what he was trying to tell me. "You didn't want to be a musician." I looked around at the tools and the work space. "You wanted to be a carpenter."

Oren nodded. "So many people thought I had a gift. I thought it was a curse." He played with his coffee cup, turning it in slow circles on the counter. "The funny thing is, he helped me."

"Easton?"

"I know it sounds strange. Doesn't it? I had a breakdown. He told my parents I wasn't nearly as talented as everyone thought."

"Oren, you know that's not true. From what I've heard Easton was the one who lacked talent."

He leaned toward me. "I didn't care," he said. "His saying I didn't have much talent let me have the life I wanted to have." He pushed the mug away across the counter. "It was years before I realized Doug Williams had become Gregor Easton. I was in a music store in Minneapolis and I heard my own music. Before that, I had no idea. And when I thought about it, I decided where was the harm? I didn't want that life and he did."

"Something changed," I said.

Oren slid off his stool and walked over to the harpsichord. He ran his fingers lightly over the keys. "I was working at the theater the second day of practice after Easton got here. He was playing that piece you heard me playing the other day." He picked out a melody on the keyboard. "It wasn't . . . right. It didn't sound the way it was supposed to sound." He pulled his hands away from the keys. "I knew how that music was supposed to sound. When everyone was gone I sat down at the piano.

I hadn't played for many, many years. But someone was still in the theater."

"Easton."

"Yes." Oren sat on the harpsichord bench. "He wasn't a good person, Kathleen. He hadn't come to help out the festival. He was looking for more music."

"More of your music." I leaned back against the counter.

"He told me the music should be given the audience it deserved." He stared at the wide wooden floorboards. "The Stratton has had money problems for years. I told Easton I would give him the rest of my music and he could claim it as his own, but he had to give half of everything he made with it to the theater. He said we could work something out, but he'd have to see the music first to decide how many changes he'd need to make."

Finally he looked up at me. "I'm not sixteen anymore. I knew he was lying and I told him so. I told him I was going to tell the whole world that it was my music, not his."

"And?"

"And he laughed at me. Said it was my word against his, and who would believe a mental case like me?"

I wanted to smack Easton myself. "Lots of people would believe you, Oren," I said. "All they'd have to do is hear you play."

He smiled. "Thank you for saying that," he said. "But I had—have—proof. I have all my original notation, all the work as the music evolved. The papers are in a safe-deposit box in St. Paul. At least they were."

"You saved everything?"

"I guess maybe I cared more about the music than I thought."

My mind began to race ahead. "That's why you missed meat loaf night. That's why you weren't at the Stratton the next morning. You went for the proof."

Oren walked over to where I was sitting. He stood in front of me, hands jammed in his pockets. "I thought with the proof I could convince him to take the deal I'd offered. I'm sorry I wasn't at the theater that morning. I'm sorry you found Easton's body."

"You didn't kill him, Oren. You don't have anything to be sorry about." I stretched my arm across my chest to try to ease the knot in my shoulder, which had stiffened up while I was sitting.

"Your shoulder?" Oren asked.

I nodded. "It's still a bit stiff," I said. "Oren, have you told Detective Gordon where you were?"

He nodded.

"Did you tell him who Easton used to be? Did you tell him you knew each other?"

"I didn't," he said softly. "I like my life, Kathleen. I don't want to lose what I have."

I slid off my stool. "Maybe it won't come to that. Maybe if you give people a chance they'll surprise you." I waited until he looked at me. "I think you need to tell Detective Gordon who Easton used to be."

"Do you really think it has something to do with his death?"

"I do," I said. "Oren, he met someone the night he died." I flashed on the wound on the side of Easton's head. "Someone was with him at the Stratton. Someone he knew. Someone he'd let his guard down around. Virtually the entire choir was at a birthday party at Eric's. He knew someone else here besides you."

Oren stared out the window for a moment. "Have you read *The Go-Between*?"

I nodded. "'The past is a foreign country.'"

"I didn't think I'd ever go back," Oren said. "But maybe it's time."

I took a deep breath. "I think for Gregor Easton, the past was getting a little too close to home."

20

Step Back Ride the Tiger

I thought it was Rebecca knocking on my door first thing Monday morning, but it was Detective Gordon standing on my back stoop, holding a jar of something in front of his chest. I wasn't sure if it was a shield or a peace offering.

"Good morning, Ms. Paulson," he said, smiling at me.

"Good morning, Detective Gordon," I said. "Are you here on police business or have you come for breakfast?"

He had the good grace to blush a little. "Police business," he said. "May I come in?"

"Of course." I stepped back so he could come into the porch, and wondered if people ever said no when he asked to come in.

I led the way to the kitchen and turned around, back to the table and crossed my arms. "How can I help you, Detective Gordon?" I asked. I was pretty sure this visit had something to do with Oren's visit to the police station the day before, but I wasn't going to spot him any gimmes.

"First of all, this is for you." He handed me a jar of jam. It was strawberry rhubarb. "I thought you might have changed your mind."

The jam was a deep crimson in the jar, tart from the rhubarb, I imagined, and sweet from the berries. "Umm, thank you for this," I said, finally remembering my manners.

"You're welcome. Thank you for encouraging Oren Kenyon to come talk to us."

"He told you that?"

"He did." He shifted awkwardly from one foot to the other. "What he told us about Easton—Douglas Williams—saved us some time, so I appreciate having the information."

"Would you like a cup of coffee?"

"I don't want to put you to any trouble."

"Detective, you've probably noticed how much I like a good cup of coffee. In fact, I like a not-so-good cup of coffee, too. It's no trouble."

"Then yes," he said. I got a cup from the cupboard and poured coffee for him, topping up my own cup at the same time. I set his on the table and pushed out one of the chairs as an invitation to sit down. Then I grabbed plates for both of us and set them on the table, along with a couple of knives and some butter.

"You don't have to give me breakfast, Ms. Paulson," the detective said. "Coffee's fine."

I put four multigrain rolls in a little breadbasket and set it on the table, too. "I know I don't have to feed you, Detective," I said, "but you do seem to keep showing up at breakfast time. And since we are sharing a meal again, could you please call me Kathleen?" I picked up the jam. The cover was tight on the mason jar.

He smiled. "I guess I'm just a morning person, Kathleen. I had a paper route when I was seven. What about you?"

I twisted the lid of the jar as hard as I could, trying not

to make a face at the effort. "Me?" I said. "My parents are actors. A lot of the time they'd be going to bed when everyone else was getting up. I think being an early bird was an act of rebellion."

I was beginning to think the lid had been welded on. I braced myself against the counter and twisted again, trying to smile and not grunt.

Detective Gordon cleared his throat. "Uh, Kathleen, would you find it sexist if I offered to open that for you?"

I could feel drops of sweat on my neck from the effort, and there was no way I could get the stupid top off the jar. I was almost out of breath. Wordlessly I handed the bottle to him and he uncapped it without any effort at all. How had he done that? My mouth probably hung open a little bit.

"I'm sure you loosened it," he said, handing me the jar.

"No, I didn't," I said, laughing. I put the jam on the table between us and sat down. "So." I reached for a roll. "Oren isn't a suspect in Easton's death."

"He never was. There's surveillance footage of him at the bank, as well as on several highway cameras."

"What about me?" I asked as I buttered my bread and added a thick layer of jam.

He took a drink of his coffee before answering. "You weren't a suspect. You were a person of interest."

"You thought I was having an affair with Easton."

He held up his thumb. "He had a note from you in his pocket." He added the index finger. "You had ordered breakfast to be sent to his hotel room." The middle finger popped up. "You showed up very early at the theater." And finally the ring finger. "And you both spent the previous year in Boston, where you could have easily met Easton through your job or your parents." There was something condescending in the smile he gave me as he picked up his mug.

I held up my own thumb, which had a dab of jam on the end. "I didn't write the note to Easton." I added my index finger. "I sent breakfast as an apology, not as an illicit invitation. And, by the way, it was never delivered." I added my middle finger, which stuck out at a bit of a weird angle. "I was at the theater to find Oren, not Mr. Easton. And finally"—I stuck my ring finger in the air with the other three—"Boston is full of people, most of whom I don't know."

Instead of a condescending smile I gave him the raised eyebrow. Then I nudged the rolls in his direction and took a bite of my own. I couldn't help making a little grunt of pleasure. The jam was sweet, with just enough tartness from the rhubarb. It was thick with fruit and good, good, good.

I wiped a drip of fruit off the side of my mouth and smiled across the table. "That's delicious," I said. "Thank you."

He bit into his own bun. "Mmm, this is good," he mumbled.

I stood up to get the coffeepot. "Detective, what happened to Gregor Easton? How did he die?" I filled both of our cups.

He licked a blob of jam from his finger. "Please call me Marcus."

"Okay. How did he die, Marcus?"

"It was an epidural hematoma."

"So a head injury?" I said, sitting down again.

"Yes. The blow to the side of Mr. Easton's head caused bleeding in his brain."

"That could take time."

"It's likely Mr. Easton didn't know how serious the

head injury was. And it didn't help that he took aspirin, probably for the headache. It's an anticoagulant."

I added sugar to my coffee and stirred. "So he could have been walking around, talking, acting normally."

"He probably seemed fine. For a while."

I watched as he slathered butter and jam over the other half of his roll. "He would have been all right when he left the library. Or at least he likely thought he was."

He nodded. "It's possible."

"Then you don't know that someone killed him." I smacked the table lightly with one hand. "You don't know that someone even tried to kill him. It could have been an accident. Easton could have hit his head on something at the library. He could have fallen or bumped into something. The renovations have been going on for a long time. For that matter, he could have hit his head before he even got to the library."

"I don't think so," the detective said, picking up his cup again. "Mr. Easton thought he was meeting you at the library." He touched the side of his head. "I don't think he was the type of man to show up with a head injury."

"Maybe he thought it would get him a little sympathy."

He raised his eyebrows at me. "I don't think Mr. Easton was looking for sympathy from you."

I had to admit he was probably right. "Even so," I said, "you don't know what happened at the library."

He leaned back in his chair and folded one arm over his chest. "I know someone used your name to lure Mr. Easton to a meeting at the library. I know Mr. Easton was injured inside the library and a few hours later he was dead. I also know whoever that person was, he hasn't come forward." He gave a slight shrug. "I don't see any other way to look at that evidence." He grabbed his cup, drained it and then stood up. "Thank you for the coffee and breakfast. Again."

I got to my feet. "Thank you for the jar of jam." I walked him to the door.

He turned, one hand on the screen. "I almost forgot. We're finished at the library. The space is yours again." He gave me his professional-policeman smile. "Have a nice day, Kathleen."

I went back into the kitchen. A gray, furry head was looking around one side of the living room door. A black one was peeking around the other. "You can come in. He's gone," I said.

Owen went for a drink while Hercules came to sit at my feet. "Murp," he said, rubbing his face against my ankle.

I broke off a tiny corner of roll, buttered it and gave it to him. That made Owen come scooting over. I did the same for him. "You two eat too much people food," I said. They both gave me their best *don't be ridiculous* looks.

The phone rang then. I went into the living room to answer it.

"Hi, Katydid." My mother's voice came warmly through the phone and I felt the familiar pinch of loneliness that always accompanied her calls.

"Hi, Mom," I said.

"How's everything in Minnesota?" she asked.

"Good." *Except for the murder I'm still tied up in, a contractor who doesn't show up when he's supposed to and a couple of klepto cats with magical powers.* "How's Boston?"

"Rainy at the moment. I called to tell you your father booked a commercial."

"Hey, good for Dad," I said, moving the phone so I could sit down. "Is it for the bank? He said he was thinking of auditioning for that because they were planning a series of ads."

"No. It's not the bank, but the director is a former student. He asked John to audition."

My parents' former students tended to be a little eclectic, and why wasn't she saying what the ad was for? "It's for some kind of erectile-dysfunction product, isn't it? Is Dad going to be sitting half naked in a bathtub on a mountaintop?"

My mother snorted. "Of course not. You know how easily he sunburns."

"What is it, then? Enlarged prostate? Hemorrhoid cream? Spray hair in a can?" My father may have talked about auditioning for bank commercials, and he certainly had the trustworthy, dependable look, with his height, his silver hair and classic profile, but he always ended up in the more colorful projects.

"Very melodramatic, Kathleen," my mother said, her voice slightly reprimanding. "He's going to be a flea. That's all."

I held the receiver away from my ear for a moment and stared at it. "A flea?" I said, putting the phone back to my face.

"It's for a commercial for a new flea-control product. The director wanted your father because he's casting against type."

"There's a type for a flea?"

She ignored me. "He wanted a classically trained actor. He wanted John's voice, his presence."

"To play a flea?" I said, enunciating each word to make my point.

"A very, very well-paid flea, Katydid," Mom said.

"Well, there is that," I said with a laugh. "Is Dad there?"

"He went for bagels."

"Tell him I said congratulations."

"I will," she said. "Any more news about Gregor Easton? It's a sign his career was waning. His death didn't even make it to the front page of the arts section."

"There's not really much news," I said, stretching my legs onto the footstool. "It turns out he changed his name."

"Really? Well, actors change their names all the time. Why not musicians? No one is going to pick Lula Mae Crumholtz for the next Bond girl. And Gregor Easton is going to sell more classical music than Buford Hornswaggle." She paused. "Easton's name wasn't Buford Hornswaggle, was it?"

I laughed. "No, it wasn't. He was born Douglas Gregory Williams. I think that would be a great name for a conductor."

"Sweetie, maybe he was trying to get away from something. Maybe he had a family he was embarrassed about. Or maybe he just didn't like his name. You went through that."

"No, I didn't."

"Yes, you did. When you were seven."

"That doesn't count," I said indignantly.

"Yes, it does. You put a lot of work into changing your name. You wrote up an official name change. Actually you wrote six of them. You melted a crayon to make a seal and almost set fire to the shower curtain. You delivered one document to your dad and me, one to your teacher and the rest to the neighbors."

I closed my eyes and pressed a hand to my forehead.

"Princess Aurelia Rosebud Nightingale," I said with a sigh.

"You do remember."

"I do. Joey Higgins refused to call me by my new name."

"And you bloodied his nose."

"I had to stay after school and write lines, which took a long time because all I knew how to do was print."

Mom was laughing now. "You argued with the vice principal that writing lines was cruel and unusual punishment under the constitution, because the school hadn't taught you how to write yet."

"Hey, it got me out of detention half an hour early."

"Poor Mr. Campbell let you go because he was afraid his head was going to explode," she chortled.

I remembered Mr. Campbell, a tiny, wiry man with a rodentlike face and thinning hair who reminded me of a Stretch Armstrong toy—his sleeves and pant legs were always just a bit too short. I remembered how surprised and impressed I'd been years later when nebbishy Mr. Campbell ran into a burning building to save the teenage son of his old high school girlfriend.

"I have to go," Mom said.

"Okay. Tell Dad I'll call him tonight."

"I will. Take care of yourself. I'll hold a good thought for your music festival. Talk to you soon." She blew a kiss through the phone and hung up.

I replaced the receiver and lay back with my head on the seat of the chair. My father was going to play a flea in a series of television commercials. An apparently highbrow flea. Was it too late to change my name back to Princess Aurelia Rosebud Nightingale?

21

Shoot the Tiger

I decided to stop at Maggie's studio on the way in to the library in the morning. I was feeling a bit uncertain about my meeting with Everett. He did have the option of ending my contract—after all, the renovations to the library weren't going smoothly and I'd gotten tied up in a murder.

Maggie's studio was on the top floor of the River Arts Center. Climbing the stairs always reminded me of high school, which made sense, given that the brick building once was a high school. Maggie was leaning over her worktable, in a white tank top and baggy blue cotton pants, chewing on a pencil.

"Maggie," I said.

She looked up with the same guilty expression Owen got when I caught him doing something he shouldn't be doing, like stealing things from Rebecca's recycling bin, for instance.

"What happened to 'no more chewing pencils'?" I asked, crossing the open studio space to stand on the other side of the table.

"This project is what happened to 'no more chewing pencils.'"

Maggie chewed pencils the way a beaver chewed trees. At least she used to. It used to be that every pencil she had was pockmarked with teeth imprints from the point to the metal end that held the eraser. Even she admitted it was gross and more than a little unsanitary and not particularly good for her teeth. So she'd given up pencils cold turkey, experimenting with substitutes like gnawing on a carrot stick.

"How about some banana bread instead?" I asked, holding up a paper bag containing a couple of slices of the loaf I'd made the night before.

"You don't have any caffeine on you, by any chance. Do you?" she asked with a sigh.

I brought my other hand from behind my back. "Not for you, but I do have a large chai from Eric's." I handed the cup across the table to her.

"How did you know I needed this?" She took a long drink through the sippy-cup lid.

I'd bought myself a large dark-roast coffee. I took a drink and set the cup on the table. "Because when I stopped at Eric's he said you'd been in first thing. I figured you'd be ready for another cup by now."

"You figured right. Thank you." She unfolded the top of the paper bag and peered inside. "I love banana bread." She broke off a bite. "So what was bugging you last night? You weren't making banana bread just for the fun of it, were you?"

"No."

"So?"

"So I have a meeting tonight with Everett about the library renovation."

"You know he's going to back you."

I scraped at a blob of dried paint on the table. "He could just end my contract."

She shook her head. "Not going to happen. Next problem."

"My father is going to be a flea," I said.

Maggie almost choked on the banana bread. "He's going to be a flea or he has fleas?"

"Ha, ha, very funny," I said. "My father is going to play a flea in a TV commercial that will probably be seen all over the country."

"Oh, c'mon, it's not that bad."

"It was my sophomore year when he did the cereal commercial where he was the dried-out, dancing, singing raisin."

She opened her mouth and I held out my hand. "Do not sing that song if you ever want to eat another one of my brownies. Ever."

She wisely popped another piece of banana bread in her mouth instead.

"Everyone was singing that song. Five of my friends dressed up as the shriveled raisin for Halloween. We did Secret Santa in the dorm. Guess what I got for my present."

"You're not in college anymore, Toto," she said.

"Let's change the subject. What are you working on?" I set my forearms on the table and leaned over to get a better look, albeit an upside-down look, at her current project.

"It's a collage for Roma for the clinic. I'm using photos of the Wisteria Hill cats. And I'm hand coloring them. I was just going through the last batch of paper I made, looking for backgrounds, but there's still something off about the layout." She leaned back and studied her work spread out on a large sheet of Masonite. Then she shook her head and took another pull from her tea. "Oh, I'm assuming you heard about Ami."

I nodded. "I drove Rebecca to the hospital to pick Ami up."

"Eric feels awful."

"It's not his fault," I said, straightening up to pick up my coffee. "Ami didn't even know she had the allergy."

"I've heard of being allergic to seafood and peanuts, but never poppy seeds."

Suddenly I remembered Everett sitting at my kitchen table, turning down my offer of a muffin. "I have," I said slowly. "Everett's allergic to poppy seeds."

"That makes sense," Maggie said, dropping a chunk of banana bread in her mouth.

"It does?"

She held up a finger until she'd finished chewing and swallowed. "Well, yeah, since Everett is Ami's grandfather."

"What?"

"Yeah. You didn't know?"

"No. Rebecca never said anything."

Maggie knocked crumbs off her shirt. "Ami had some kind of fight with her grandfather, maybe seven or eight months ago. According to the town grapevine they haven't spoken since then."

"That's sad," I said.

"It is," Maggie agreed. "Ami's the only family Everett has." She looked at me across the worktable and a small smile turned up the corners of her mouth.

"Stop smirking," I said. "I get it. My dad's going to play a flea on TV. So what?"

She made a show of brushing off her hands. "My work on this planet is pretty much done," she said. She folded the paper bag into a small, neat rectangle and handed it to me. "How's your shoulder?"

I raised and lowered my elbow like a bird's wing. "It's

pretty good. The bruise is about eight different colors and it's really stiff first thing, but other than that I'm okay."

Maggie opened her mouth and closed it again. "What?" I said.

"In less than a week you were almost electrocuted and then hit with that roll of plastic?"

"Bad timing and a certain careless contractor." I drained the last of my coffee.

She fiddled with a paintbrush. "Kathleen, are you sure?"

"What do you mean?"

"I mean, are you sure they were accidents?"

"Oh, c'mon," I said. "You think someone was trying to hurt me on purpose? You sound like Susan. Who? Will? Eddie?" I shook my head.

"Hurt you. Or scare you. At first I thought maybe Will was trying to sabotage the renovations, but now I'm wondering if he's trying to sabotage you. Look at what's been happening. I don't believe in coincidences."

"Well, if someone is trying to get rid of me they should have said so. Left a note, a voice mail, a tape that would self-destruct after I listened to it. Maybe hung a sign from the staging. All these stupid accidents have done is make me think Everett hired the wrong person for the job."

Maggie stared at the table. I could see her mind working. "That's it, Kathleen," she said, looking up.

"What's it?"

"These last couple of accidents aren't the first problems you've had at the library. Remember the mice in your office?"

"Vividly."

"The only area in the entire building with a rodent

problem. And they showed up overnight." She shuddered. "It was like the road company of *Willard* in
there.

"And the burn you got from the radiator?" She tapped
her fingers on the table. "I don't know why I didn't see it
before. It's Will. He's trying to get rid of you."

"He's trying to get rid of me? Why? Is he part of
some conspiracy group? 'Let's all work together to stop
the spread of reading'?"

Maggie propped an elbow on the table and leaned
her chin on her hand. "I don't know. But remember
when you said it was almost as if he had a schedule for
the times he goes incommunicado? Maybe he does.
Maybe he's doing something at those times."

I suddenly wished I had a lot more coffee. "So what is
he doing and what does it have to do with me?"

"I'm not sure. Maybe it has something to do with
what happened to Gregor Easton at the library. We
need to find out where he goes when he leaves and you
can't reach him."

"And how are we going to do that?"

"Follow him."

"Follow him? How? By using one of the book carts as
a skateboard? I don't have a car, remember? And your
bug isn't exactly discreet."

"Getting a vehicle isn't a problem."

"Okay," I said slowly. "So, what do I do? Put on my
trench and call you from my shoe phone the next time
Will shows up at the library?"

"You're not taking this seriously, Kath," Maggie said.

"You're right. I'm not. Why would Will want to hurt
me? I've given him more chances than he should have
ever gotten. And as for where he goes when he's not
answering his phone, he's probably hanging around the

contractor's desk at the building-supply store, drinking coffee."

Maggie put her hands on her hips. "So let's find out for sure. When do you expect him?"

"He won't ignore my messages forever. At least he hasn't so far. So he'll probably show up today—I'm guessing after lunch. I usually don't see Will in the morning."

"Fine. When he walks in the door, call me."

"And?"

"And I'll pick you up. We'll follow him and find out where he's going."

I slid down off the stool. "I have to get to the library."

"Thanks for the tea, Kath," Maggie said. "And the banana bread."

"You're welcome," I said. "Talk to you later."

"Keep your shoe phone handy," she called after me.

I didn't even dignify that with a rude gesture.

Will Redfern stuck his head around my office door without knocking at about two o'clock. "Hello, Kathleen," he said. "Do you know what happened to my staging? Eddie said the boys had it set up."

"Did you get my messages?" I asked.

"Messages? When?" Then he immediately held up a hand and said, "Nah. Damn cell phone isn't working right again." He shrugged. "Sorry. Were they important?"

I stood up but stayed behind my desk. "Eddie and the boys set up your staging and then just disappeared."

"Coffee break," Will said with his toothy smile. "It's a union rule."

"They didn't come back, Will," I said. "That's a long coffee break."

"Well, you have to understand, Kathleen, that this isn't the only job I have. Emergencies happen. Adjustments have to be made."

The smirk stayed stuck to his face.

"I understand that problems come up with any renovation," I said. "But it seems that when they happen here I can't find you."

"Was there some kind of emergency here?" He gave off insincerity the way a skunk gives off scent.

"Someone left a roll of plastic vapor barrier at the top of the staging. It fell and just missed my head. When I looked for you, you were gone."

"I'm so sorry," he said. "Are you all right?"

"I'm fine," I said, placing both hands flat on my desk for support. "But somebody could have been seriously hurt."

"I'll talk to Eddie. I'm sorry about that." He leaned against the doorframe like he had all the time in the world.

"That's why the staging was taken down. Everett was concerned someone else could be hurt."

"You called Everett over a roll of vapor barrier? No offense, but I think you overreacted, Kathleen."

"I didn't call Everett about the plastic." That was true. I'd called Everett about Will. "He called here to check on the renovations. When he heard what happened he made arrangements to have your staging taken down. I'm surprised he didn't leave you a message." I raised one hand and smiled. "Oh, wait a minute. Your phone. You wouldn't have gotten a message." Now who was oozing insincerity?

"That reminds me, Will. The staging is stacked in the landing bay at the back."

I'll give Will his due. He recovered fast.

"This is going to throw a wrench into today's work schedule, Kathleen. I'm sorry."

I fought the urge to look for a wrench to throw at his head. "It's all right. I expected it would, Will," I said with an evenness I didn't feel.

"I'll try to get Eddie back here today. Could be a problem, though."

"I knew you might say that."

"Okay. Well, I gotta get some tools out of the storage room, and I better check the staging to make sure it's all there." He looked at his watch. "I can't make any promises about Eddie. I'll see what I can do."

As soon as he started for the storage room I grabbed the phone and dialed Maggie. "The eagle has landed," I whispered into the phone. "The ghost walks at midnight." Okay, it was still hard to take Maggie's cloak-and-dagger stuff seriously.

"Kathleen?" she said. "What are you talking about?"

"Will is here at the library," I said in my normal voice.

"Parking lot. Five minutes. Brown truck." She dropped her voice to a whisper and hung up.

I shut off my computer, locked my office and walked down to the checkout desk. Abigail was on the phone and Susan was checking out two women. I waited until she finished.

"Hey, Kathleen," she said. "Did Will find you?"

"Yes, he did," I said. "He needs some tools from the storage room. Will you make sure that the door is locked when he's finished, please?"

"Sure thing." she said, pushing her glasses up her nose. She had two straws stuck in the hair piled on top of her head.

"I have an appointment. I won't be long."

"Okay." She scribbled a note to herself on one of the blue library pads. "How's your shoulder?" she asked, as I turned toward the door.

"A lot better," I said. "I think I'm going to go to Roma from now on."

Susan laughed and I gave her a little wave good-bye. I stepped outside, hoping I'd given Maggie enough time to make it over.

A dilapidated pickup was parked in the far corner of the lot. It looked like it was being held together mostly with dirt. Could that be Maggie's brown truck? I walked across to it. Mags was slumped in the driver's seat. The passenger's window was open. "Hi," I said.

She glared at me. "Get in," she whispered.

I glanced around the lot. No sign of Will. His truck was parked on the street.

I opened the passenger's door. It groaned like I was trying to rip it off the truck body instead of just getting inside. I climbed in. "I'm not hiding on the floor mat with my head squashed under the dashboard," I said.

"You don't have to get down on the floor, but you could at least duck down your big, giant head," she said.

I slid down until I was sitting on my spine.

Maggie watched the street from her window. Roma drove into the lot. That made me sink a little lower out of sight. I didn't want to have to explain to Roma why I was hiding out in a truck that was stuck together with hope, grime and duct tape.

"There he is," Maggie said.

I took the chance of sitting up enough to see. Will was getting into his truck, talking on his cell phone.

"Let's go, Starsky," I said.

She made a face and turned the key in the ignition. Nothing happened. She gritted her teeth and tried again. Nothing. Thumping the steering wheel didn't help, either.

"C'mon, you piece of scrap metal," she muttered.

Will had started his truck. Maggie looked out the windshield. She opened the driver's door. "C'mon, Kath," she said. "Run."

I ran after her. "This isn't going to work," I huffed, already embarrassingly out of breath. "I think he's going to notice us running behind his truck."

She reached back to grab my arm and dragged me over to Roma's SUV, pushing me toward the passenger's door. Maggie climbed in the back and I got in the front seat. Roma looked at us, more bemused than surprised.

"Roma, you have to follow Will Redfern," Maggie said. She pointed. "That way." Roma snapped on her seat belt, started the car and pulled out of the lot. Will was at the end of the street at the stop sign.

"There," Maggie said.

Roma nodded. "I see him."

Will kept going straight along Old Main Street. Roma settled in behind him, far enough back that I hoped he wouldn't notice. She looked in the rearview mirror and gave me a quick sideways glance. "Hello, Kathleen. Hello, Maggie," she said. "Lovely afternoon for a drive, isn't it?"

"I can explain," Maggie said, leaning farther forward in the seat than she probably should have.

"I'm sure you can," Roma said.

Maggie touched her shoulder. "He's turning," she said.

"I see him," Roma said. "It looks like Will has one of those trucks with a turn signal."

I bit my tongue so I wouldn't laugh. Roma merged smoothly onto the highway, leaving one car between Will and us. I had no idea where we were going, but it wasn't to the building-supply store.

Maggie sat back in her seat. Roma glanced at me again. "You were going to explain," she prompted.

"Mags." I did my best sweeping, Vanna White gesture. Maggie summed it all up very quickly for Roma.

"Kathleen, I had no idea you'd been injured so many times during the renovations," she said.

"I didn't realize it either, until Maggie pointed it out," I said. "But I'm finding it hard to believe Will made all those things happen on purpose. Why would he do something like that?" *And if Will really is capable of violence...*

"That's what we're going to find out," Maggie chimed in from the backseat.

"Wherever Will's going, he's in a hurry," Roma said, glancing at the speedometer. She pulled out to pass the car between Will and us. Will was almost out of sight, over the next hill.

"You're good at this," Maggie said approvingly.

"This is not my first rodeo," Roma said with a smile.

"You make a habit of following people?" I asked.

"No. But I did a lot of car rallying in college."

Another couple of miles up the road Will suddenly turned off, seemingly into the trees.

"Where did he go?" Maggie asked.

Roma checked the rearview mirror. "There's no one behind us. I'm slowing down. Watch for a driveway or a turnoff."

I twisted sideways, but it was Maggie who spotted the road.

"There it is," she said. "See the gap in the trees?"

"I see it," Roma said. "I'll turn up there and we'll double back."

She turned around on a service road, drove back to

the turnoff and pulled onto the shoulder, just past the gravel road that went back into the woods. "If we're going any farther it'll have to be on foot."

"Let's go," Maggie said, undoing her seat belt.

"It's probably a job site," I said. "The only thing we're going to find down this road is Eddie scratching his armpit."

Maggie paused, already half out of the backseat. "Kath, if all we find is Eddie scratching his armpit or anything—anything—else, I'll take you to Tubby's and buy you the largest container of frozen yogurt they have."

She wasn't going to give this up, I could see. "Okay," I said.

We all got out. Maggie led us down the road, sticking close to the grassy edge by the trees. Roma and I followed, dodging low branches.

"You're going to share that yogurt, right, Kathleen?" Roma said behind me.

"I'm thinking no," I said.

"I'm thinking it's a long walk back to the library," Roma countered.

"You like strawberry?" I asked, without turning around.

"I love strawberry. How nice of you to ask."

Maggie abruptly stopped in front of me. "Shush," she whispered.

"What is it?" I said.

Ahead the trail opened into a cleared area. Will's truck was parked on the left. Up a slight rise a small building was being framed—four walls on a slab, like a boxy, wooden skeleton.

"I don't see anything," I said in Maggie's ear.

"Over there," she said softly.

She reached back with her hand and pushed my head a little to the right. And then I saw them. Will was standing in front of the framed cabin, kissing a blond woman almost his height.

Roma leaned out around me, then pulled back and looked at Maggie and me. "That's not Eddie," she said. "That's Ingrid. Why is Ingrid playing tonsil hockey with Will Redfern?"

22

Step Forward and Punch

"Ingrid?" I asked.

Maggie waved Roma back behind us. "That's not Ingrid, is it?" she asked.

"Yes, it is," Roma said. "Her hair's blonder, but it's Ingrid."

Maggie leaned forward again to look. "You're right," she said slowly. "It is Ingrid."

"Ingrid?" I asked again. "Is that the same Ingrid who was head librarian before me?" Will had his arms around the woman—Ingrid—and their faces were close together.

"Let's get out of here," Maggie said. She turned and gave me a little push.

We followed Roma back to the main road and got in the SUV. Roma started the car, eased off the shoulder and started back toward town. "Well, I didn't see that coming," she said.

"Me, either," Maggie agreed.

"I'm lost," I said. "Explain, please."

"Yes, that's Ingrid who was the librarian before you got here," Roma said. "And, no, she wasn't fired, if that's what you're thinking."

It had been what I was thinking. "Doesn't Will have a wife?" I asked.

Roma nodded. "Uh-huh."

"So what is he doing with the former librarian?"

Maggie raised her eyebrows and gave me a look.

"Okay, I know what he's doing, but what does it have to do with the library or me?"

"I don't have a clue," Maggie admitted. "But it's way too big a coincidence that Will is involved with the woman who used to have your job, and you've been having problems at the library."

"But if Ingrid wasn't fired why would Will have a problem with me? I could maybe see it if he thought I was the reason Ingrid lost her job." I was trying to be the voice of reason. I looked at Roma. "Roma, are you sure she wasn't fired?"

She nodded without taking her eyes from the road. "I'm positive. Ingrid gave her resignation to the board right before the renovation plans were finalized. They tried to convince her to stay at least until the major work was done."

"She obviously said no."

"She said she had personal reasons for leaving."

"I heard that, too," Maggie said.

"That's why Everett was so pleased to find you," Roma said.

"Do you think her personal reasons had something to do with Will?" I asked.

"I don't see how they could," Maggie said. "It's not like the two of them ran off to Tahiti together."

"Maybe she's sorry she resigned," Roma said. "Maybe Will figured if Kathleen got hurt, Everett would ask Ingrid to come back."

"Mags, this is crazy." I rubbed the top of my shoulder, which seemed to ache more if I stayed in one position too long. "I don't know that Will had anything to do with what happened to me. Those accidents could all just have been accidents."

"They could be," she agreed. "But everything that's happened has happened because of something stupid Will or his guys did." She tugged at her seat belt, pulling it a little tighter across her shoulder. "C'mon, Kath, think about it. The radiator they forgot to properly disconnect. The roll of plastic that fell. I'm not a contractor, but I know you don't need vapor barrier to fasten a plaster medallion to the ceiling."

"Kathleen, how did Will react when he found out about your accidents?" Roma asked.

I shrugged. "He apologized, but it seemed a bit insincere to me. He always manages to find a way to point out that I don't understand what's involved in a major renovation and I don't know the building."

"Has he said anything about insurance or liability?"

"No."

Roma turned the car onto Old Main Street. "I agree with Maggie," she said. "Why isn't Will worried about his liability in all of this? Maybe it's just he's so caught up in this affair he seems to be having. Whatever it is, someone's going to get hurt, a lot worse than you've already been. If they haven't already."

"What do you mean, 'if they haven't already'?" Maggie asked.

"Something happened to Gregor Easton at the library," Roma said.

"Uh-huh."

"How do we know that something wasn't another accident meant for Kathleen?"

"You think Will did something to Easton? *Will?*" I said.

"I don't know," Roma said. "Maybe he and Ingrid were together in the library for some reason, and Easton walked in on them. Who knows? I'm just saying be careful, that's all."

"I will," I said. "I have a meeting tonight with Everett. He knows some of what's been going on."

"I think you should tell him the rest," Roma said.

"I plan to."

She slowed and pulled into the library lot. "Kathleen, Maggie." She put the SUV in park and looked at each of us in turn. "This has been fascinating to say the least, but . . . get out of my car."

I leaned my head against the headrest and laughed. "Roma, I'm sorry," I said. "We kind of pulled you into the middle of this and you've been a very good sport."

"Yes, you did, and, yes, I have," she said. "Now get out of my car." She smiled to soften the words. "I have patients to see. The four-legged kind that bite when I keep them waiting."

Maggie and I both got out of the SUV. "Thank you, Roma," Maggie said.

Roma pointed across the lot at the old brown truck. "You have to pump the gas twice to get it started."

"Are you sure?" Maggie asked, shading her eyes as she looked at the rusty half ton.

"That's Ruby's truck, isn't it?" Roma said.

"Uh-huh." Mags nodded.

"I'm sure," Roma said. "It used to be mine. Neutral's kind of mushy, too." She put the SUV in gear and drove off.

Maggie walked me over to the steps. "I told you Will was up to something," she said.

"Just because he's having an affair—assuming he is having an affair—doesn't mean he's been trying to get rid of me. Or that he did something to Gregor Easton," I said.

"What?" she snorted. "You think that kiss was a substitute for a hearty handshake?"

"Okay," I said. "Probably not."

"All I'm saying is, be vigilant." I could see the concern on her face.

"I will. I promise."

"I've gotta go," she said. "Call me later."

"I will," I said. "Are you going to try the truck again?"

She nodded. "Cross your fingers."

I stood on the step and watched her get into the truck. It started on the first turn of the key. She drove out of the lot with both hands on the top of the steering wheel and a look of intense concentration on her face.

I went up the rest of the stairs and into the library. Lita called just before four to let me know Everett expected to be at my house about eight thirty. I left Mary in charge and headed home at about five o'clock.

Hercules was in the backyard on the lawn chair. Now that I knew what he could do, it wasn't as disconcerting to find him somewhere unexpected. He jumped down and walked beside me to the back door.

"How was your day?" I asked.

"Merow," he said, and he may have shrugged; I wasn't sure.

"Maggie, Roma and I were playing *Charlie's Angels*," I said as I unlocked the door. Hercules paused on the second step. "It's a long story," I said.

Owen was sprawled on the bench in the porch. He jumped up when he saw us and a whisper of yellow feather drifted to the floor.

"I'm not saying a word," I said, heading for the kitchen.

The cats kept me company while I changed and made spaghetti for dinner. I told them all about Will and the former librarian. "Maggie thinks Will's up to something," I said. Owen gave my leg a swat with his paw. "You always agree with Maggie," I told him. "You're not exactly unbiased."

That got me a cranky kitty glare. I set my dishes in the sink. I still had lots of time before my meeting with Everett. I decided to make cinnamon rolls. I wanted to thank Roma for going along with Maggie's "Let's stalk Will Redfern" idea.

While I rolled out the dough I couldn't help wondering what Everett was going to do and how Will would react. Whether or not he was up to something, he was going to be angry.

When the cinnamon rolls were in the oven I went down to the basement for a new vacuum bag so I could clean up before Everett arrived. That was when I noticed Rebecca's sweater still soaking in my sink. "Crap on toast!" I said. I'd forgotten about it.

Luckily it was cotton, not wool. I rinsed it in clean water and rolled it in a towel. Then I lugged my folding rack upstairs and spread the cardigan out to dry.

I could smell the rolls. I'd forgotten to set the timer. I jerked open the oven door. They hadn't burned, but they were extra crispy. And I'd spaced them too close together. The rolls slid off the baking sheet onto the rack like a big cinnamon paving stone.

Herc and Owen had disappeared. I pulled out the vacuum, taking out my frustration by aggressively chasing every speck of dirt on the kitchen floor, even muscling out the stove and fridge.

The cats peeked in once from the living room, watched

me for a moment and exchanged knowing glances. After I finished striking terror into the hearts of dust bunnies everywhere, I went out to the porch to check Rebecca's sweater, hoping it hadn't gotten small enough to be a winter coat for Owen.

Will Redfern was standing just inside the porch door.

I jumped, sucking in a breath. "Good heavens, Will," I said, pressing a hand against my breastbone. "You scared me. I didn't hear you knock."

"You were vacuuming," he said. "And I didn't knock, anyway."

My heart started thumping in both ears like a drummer keeping time in stereo. I wrapped an arm across my chest. "What can I do for you, Will?" I asked. I tried not to think about what Maggie suspected. I tried not to think about how much taller, heavier and stronger Will was. I didn't do a very good job of it.

"Go back to Boston," he said.

"Look," I said. "I know we haven't always gotten along during the renovations—"

He cut me off. "You don't belong here. Ingrid should be the librarian." He made a dismissive gesture with one hand. "I know you know who Ingrid is. I know you and your exercise buddies followed me today."

So much for being the new *Charlie's Angels.* "I thought Ingrid resigned," I said. *Just keep him talking,* I told myself. *Keep him talking until Everett shows up.*

Will clenched his teeth. "That was a mistake. You need to just go back where you came from, because you don't belong here, anyway. Then Everett will have to ask Ingrid to step in and everything will be just fine." His voice was getting louder.

"I'm sorry," I said. "I didn't realize Ingrid wanted her job back."

"She will when she sees how much everyone needs her." He kept flexing and squeezing his left hand.

"I don't think Ingrid would want you to do this," I said, deliberately keeping my voice low and steady. I couldn't get around him, I realized. Could I beat him to the kitchen? I didn't think so. The best I could do was keep him talking.

"You don't know Ingrid, so there's no way you can know what she'd want."

I held up a placating hand. "You're right. But I saw the two of you together and she seemed crazy about you." *You, on the other hand,* I thought, *just seem crazy.*

The muscles along his jaw tightened. "Stop trying to screw with me, Kathleen. You're stalling. You think if you keep on talking someone will show up."

Will was more on the ball than I'd thought. "Not happening." He jerked his head toward Rebecca's. "The old gal isn't home, and your artist friend is out having dinner."

"I'm not stalling, Will," I said. "I don't know what you want me to do."

He leaned toward me, so suddenly I automatically took a step backward. "I want you to go away," he spat. "You, Everett, that conductor guy—you all keep interfering in what I'm doing."

"Conductor? You mean Gregor Easton?" I stammered.

"He almost ruined everything," Will said. "I had to do a little work on that wall outlet in the computer room and I couldn't exactly do that when the library was open. Now, could I?"

My legs were shaking. All those accidents. They hadn't been accidents. Maggie and Roma were right.

"You see what happens when you end up somewhere

you aren't supposed to be, Kathleen?" He clapped his hands together right in front of my face and I almost came out of my skin. "You end up dead. That's what happened to that pretentious old fart."

I pressed a hand to my mouth. Will killed Easton? *Will?* Because he'd showed up at the library at the wrong time? It didn't make any sense.

Will held up his hand and waved his fingers the way a child might. "Bye-bye, Kathleen. Time to go now."

I took a shaky breath and felt behind me for the doorframe. Nothing. I wasn't close enough. "I can't just go. Everett will ask questions. You know how he is."

Will swiped a hand over his face and looked around as though the answers were somehow on the walls of the porch.

I took a step back and this time my hand made contact with the side of the doorframe. Maybe I could distract him. Maybe I could bolt, run through the house and out the front door.

"You're gonna write a letter," Will said suddenly. He took several steps toward me. His eyes were bloodshot, his skin was pasty and he needed a shave. He looked like hell. I would have felt sorry for him if he weren't scaring the crap out of me. He was too close now for me to cut and run and make it. "Let's go," he said. "Letter. Find something to write with."

"I have a pen and some paper inside." Will grabbed my arm and half dragged, half marched me into the kitchen. I pulled a small pad I used for making grocery lists and a pen out of one of the drawers. He shoved me down into a chair.

"Write," he ordered.

My mouth was too dry to swallow. "What do you want me to write?" I asked.

Will rubbed his face again. He was breathing heavily. "Put down that you're going back to Boston. You don't . . . You don't like Minnesota." His strong fingers dug into my injured shoulder.

I ground my teeth together against the stab of pain.

"Make it sound real," Will said.

I wrote slowly and neatly, hoping to buy a bit more time.

Will's fingers continued to bite into my skin. He leaned over my shoulder. "Speed it up!" he hissed.

He'd been drinking. I could smell it. I finished the letter and placed my hands flat on the table.

Will read the words and seemed satisfied with what was on the page. I pressed the ends of my fingers against the painted wooden tabletop to keep my hands from shaking.

"That'll do," he said. He grabbed my upper arm. "Now you're gonna pack."

"All right," I said. "But first I have to call Roma and ask her to take my cats."

He yanked me around to face him. The pain sliced down my back and my stomach lurched. He jabbed a finger in my face. "No phone!" he snapped.

I made myself take a couple of steadying breaths. "No one will believe I just left the cats here."

"They're not going to be here," he said. "I heard you say they came from out at the old house. I'll just dump them back out there."

"You can't do that," I said. "Owen and Hercules can't take care of themselves in the wild."

"They're cats. They can hunt." He shrugged. "And if they can't, well, life is hard."

I felt a knot of anger burning in my stomach. It wasn't unlike the feeling of taking a drink of Ruby's homemade wine. Will wasn't going to hurt my cats. He wasn't going to get near them.

"So's this, Will," I shouted, kicking him as hard as I could in the knee. Pain shot through my foot and up my shinbone. I lunged for his face, but he was faster. He grabbed my wrist, twisting the skin.

"You're gonna regret that," he yelled. His skin was mottled now. His eyes were two angry slits. He hauled my arm up behind my back.

My bruised shoulder screamed and my knees started to buckle. I tried to stay upright so I could kick him again, but he kept pressure on my arm and the world began to go dark from the edges in. For a second I thought I was hallucinating the flash of gray fur.

But I wasn't. Owen appeared in midair, teeth bared, ears flattened against his head. He landed, yowling, on Will's head and dug in his claws.

Will screamed, let go of my arm and swiped at his head. I fell against the counter.

Owen launched himself onto the table, arched his back and yowled again, all his fur standing on end.

Blood dripped down the edge of Will's forehead. His lips pulled away from his teeth like a rabid dog's. He pulled back his arm to punch me. I shrank even farther against the cupboards, my good arm, my good hand grabbing for something to hang on to. I touched the ruined rolls, welded together like a cinnamon-scented chunk of rock. Without even thinking about it I grabbed them and swung for Will's head with all the strength terror gave me.

I connected with the left side of his face. His mouth fell open. The color drained from his face as his eyes rolled back in his head and he dropped to the floor.

For a moment the only sound was my ragged breathing. "It's okay," I wheezed to Owen. He looked over the edge of the table at Will sprawled on the floor. "We have to get out of here," I said.

I grabbed the cat, sidestepped around Will and backed rapidly out of the kitchen, into the porch, and against the very strong, very normal chest of Harry Taylor.

"Harry, thank heaven," I gasped. He caught me by the arm. I winced and he dropped his hand.

"Kathleen, are you all right?" he asked.

"No. Yes." I took a breath. "Will Redfern is on my kitchen floor," I said, thinking that if I didn't sit down soon I was going to be on the floor, too.

"Why's Will on your kitchen floor?" Harry asked, leading me over to the bench.

"I hit him," I said. I sat down and set Owen beside me. My legs were shaking. Hercules was sitting on the floor by the door.

I thought about what Will had been planning to do with the cats. And what he might have done to Gregor Easton. It made me want to hit him again, this time with something harder than a batch of failed cinnamon rolls. On the other hand, I wasn't sure there were a lot of things harder than those rolls.

"Stay here, Kathleen," Harry said. "I'm just going to take a look at Will."

I nodded. As soon as Harry got up Hercules jumped up on the bench. He put his front paws on my lap and studied my face. "I'm all right," I said. He laid his chin on my leg. Owen climbed all the way onto my lap on the other side and placed his paws on my chest. I stroked his fur. "I can't believe you did that," I said. "You saved me from Will." He bumped my shoulder with his head.

"Tomorrow I'm going to buy you the biggest, yellowest Fred the Funky Chicken that the Grainery has." Owen started to purr.

Harry came out of the kitchen, his face serious. "Police are on their way," he said.

I looked past him, heart suddenly pounding again. "Is Will . . . ?"

"I tied him to the table leg with my belt," Harry said. He wiped a hand across his forehead. "Will's been drinking."

"I know," I said.

"What did you hit him with?"

"Owen jumped on . . . on Will's head, and I hit him with a batch of rolls."

"Remind me to say no next time you ask if I'd like coffee and a muffin," Harry said. He held out his hand. A drywall knife with a retractable blade lay on his palm. "Will had this in his pocket. What was he doing here?"

I wrapped my aching arm around my body. "He wanted me to leave. He was . . . involved with Ingrid."

"Ingrid? The old librarian?"

I nodded. "He got the idea if I was gone, she could come back to the library and they'd have some kind of happy ending."

Harry shook his head. "Damned idiot," he muttered.

"Harry, how . . . what . . . What are you doing here?" I asked.

"That cat of yours. Hercules?" He tipped his head toward Herc, who lifted his head at the sound of his name. "I was working over at Rebecca's. Suddenly there he was, just a few feet in front of the mower. Wouldn't move, either. He was howling like a banshee. I thought something was wrong with the cat, not you."

I bent over and kissed the top of Herc's head. "You

went for help," I said. He gave me his *it's not a big deal* look. I didn't want to think about what could have happened if Owen wasn't able to disappear and Hercules couldn't walk through walls.

"Not bad for a couple of cats," Harry said.

"You have no idea," I said.

23

Push Forward

A patrol car and Marcus Gordon pulled in my drive-way one behind the other. Right behind them was Roma, with Maggie riding shotgun. Harry met the police officers at the door and took them into the kitchen.

Marcus stood in front of me. "Are you all right, Kathleen?" he asked.

"I am," I said. The fear and shakiness were being replaced by anger now.

"Why was Mr. Redfern here?" he asked.

"It's my fault," Maggie said from the door. "Kathleen, I'm so sorry." She looked on the verge of tears.

I shook my head. "It's not your fault, Mags. You were right about Will. None of the accidents was an accident. He was trying to get me to go back to Boston. And I think he might have confessed to killing Gregor Easton." I leaned forward, wincing at the pain in my shoulder.

"You're hurt," Roma said, easing past Maggie.

"I'll call for an ambulance." Marcus reached into his pocket for his phone.

I shook my head vigorously.

"No," I said. "I'd rather have Roma. Please."

"It's not like we haven't done this before," Roma said.

The detective sighed. "Go ahead."

Roma bent in front of me and carefully checked me over. She pulled the neck of my shirt to one side and made a face when she saw my shoulder. Then she felt her way down my arm. My wrist was already swelling and changing color.

"Are you going to have to shoot me?" I joked.

"No, but I'm thinking a good dose of cod-liver oil couldn't hurt."

I sucked in a breath and bit my tongue as she felt her way around my wrist.

"I'd like to get some ice on both that wrist and that shoulder," she said.

"I've got ice packs in the freezer."

"May I get them?" Roma said to Marcus.

"I'll get them," he said. "I'll be right back."

Roma sat back on her heels. "I don't suppose there's any chance you'd agree to go to the emergency room for an X-ray?"

"Nope," I said.

She looked at Maggie. "I told Kathleen that this is why I became a vet," she said. "Two-legged patients talk back too much." She looked at me again. "What do you think, Maggie? Any chance we could wedge her into that dog cage I have in the car and get her to the hospital?"

"You should know that like your four-legged patients, I bite."

Roma grinned. "I knew I wasn't going to win this one, but I do want you to go to the clinic tomorrow."

"All right," I said.

"I'm just going to see what's holding up those cold packs," Roma said, getting to her feet. She went into the kitchen.

Maggie leaned over to hug me. "You're shivering," she said. She reached for Rebecca's sweater.

"That's not dry," I said.

Roma came back then with two cold packs, followed by Marcus. She put one on my wrist; then she eased me back against the rear of the bench and set the other on top of my shoulder.

"She's cold," Maggie said, looking pointedly at the police officer.

He looked around the porch and then realized Mags wanted him to surrender his sport coat.

"I'm fine," I said.

Neither of them was listening to me. He shrugged out of his jacket and handed it to Maggie. She draped it around me. It was much warmer. Hercules kept his head in my lap and Owen stayed stretched out on my chest.

Marcus folded his arms. "Okay," he said. "Tell me what happened."

So I did, beginning with stepping into the porch and finding Will.

"Way to go, Fuzz Face," Maggie whispered to Owen when I got to the part about Owen landing on Will's head.

"You hit him with a pan?" Marcus asked when I explained how I'd hit Will with the cinnamon rolls.

"No, I hit him with the actual rolls," I said.

He rubbed a hand down the side of his face. "I'm sorry," he said. "It's kind of hard to believe you could knock someone out with overcooked bread."

"Well, I did," I said, stiffly.

Just then Harry came out of the kitchen. "Excuse me," he said to Marcus. "Do you need anything more from me?"

He shook his head. "No. You can leave."

Harry looked at me. "Kathleen, is there anything else I can do for you?"

For the first time all evening I wasn't sure what to say. I swallowed a couple of times. "I don't know how to thank you, Harry," I finally managed.

He ducked his head, clearly embarrassed. "I'm glad I was close," he said. "If there's anything you need, you know how to find me." He gave me a smile and was gone.

I finished explaining what had happened.

Hercules got a fist-pump salute when Maggie heard how he'd gotten Harry's attention.

"Tell me about these accidents at the library," Marcus said.

"You know about the problem with the outlet," I said. I explained about the roll of plastic falling from the staging, how I'd almost been badly burned with the radiator, and I told him about the mice in my office. I couldn't help yawning by the time I got to the last details. I was cold and tired, and the last of the adrenaline rush was gone.

"That's enough for tonight," he said.

I held up a hand to stop him. "There's something else you should know," I said. "Will saw Easton at the library the night he died. I think Easton saw Will doing something to the wiring. I think he might have . . . shut Easton up."

"What?" Maggie exclaimed.

"Will told you that?" I couldn't read the expression on Marcus's face.

"He did," I said.

"Okay. I'll check it out. I'll be in touch tomorrow." He opened his mouth as if he wanted to say something more, but didn't.

"Thank you for coming so quickly," I said, handing back his jacket.

"That's my job." He hesitated in the doorway. "You shouldn't have any more problems tonight, but if you do"—he pulled a card out of his pocket, wrote something on the back and took one step back into the porch to hand it to me—"that's my cell number. If you need anything, please use it." He lifted a hand in good-bye and was gone.

"He likes you," Maggie said.

"Of course he does," I said, giving her the eyebrow, because that was all the sarcasm I could muster.

"Do you think Will killed Easton?" Roma asked.

"It's starting to look that way."

Maggie shook her head. "Because he was in the wrong place at the wrong time? I wouldn't have guessed that." She reached for Rebecca's sweater. "Are you still cold?" she asked.

"That's not dry," I said. "And remember it's Rebecca's."

"What are you doing with Rebecca's sweater?" she asked.

"She forgot it yesterday when I took her to pick up Ami. I washed it because Owen chewed on the sleeve. In his defense, it smelled like catnip."

"Catnip?"

"I think it was in her poultice."

Maggie shrugged. "I suppose it could have been. It's just usually used for cuts and that kind of thing, at least as far as I know."

She held out a hand. "I'm staying all night," she said.

I didn't argue. I didn't want to be by myself and I knew Mags would fuss over me, which, truth be told, I could use a little of. Maggie looked at the cats. "Okay, hop down, guys. We're moving into the living room."

I got to my feet and the ice pack slid off my back onto the bench. Roma rescued it. "I have to clean up the kitchen first," I said.

"Of course you don't," Roma said.

I ended up on the sofa in the living room. Roma cleaned up the kitchen while Maggie made me hot chocolate and peanut butter toast. I didn't care how warm it was outside. It made me feel better to wrap my hands around the warm mug. She even made peanut butter toast for the cats, cutting it up into tiny bites and serving it on a plate, one for each cat.

"I can't keep this ice pack on my shoulder," I told Maggie as it slid down my back for the third time.

She pulled the lavender scarf from around her neck. "Lean forward," she said. She draped the scarf across my body like Miss America's sash, slid the cold pack in place and tied the ends of fabric at my collarbone. "How's that?"

I moved gingerly from side to side, but the scarf and the ice pack stayed put.

"Better. Thank you." The beaded ends of the material tickled my chin. I pressed them down out of the way. The fabric was incredibly soft. "Did Ami make this for you?" I asked.

"She did. I told her how much I liked the one she made for Rebecca and the next day she came back with this one for me." She smoothed down one stray bead. "Now, stay put while I make you some more cocoa."

She headed back to the kitchen, trailed by Owen and Hercules, sniffing around for more toast for themselves.

I leaned back against the cushions and thought about Will Redfern. I could almost feel sorry for him. Then I remembered Gregor Easton's body slumped over the piano at the Stratton. I remembered that drywall knife

Will had in his pocket and how he'd planned to dump the cats out at Wisteria Hill, and the feeling pretty much passed.

Maggie spent the rest of the evening catering to the cats and me. "If they hack up something I'm getting you the mop," I warned her when I caught her sneaking each of them more peanut butter.

She just laughed. She'd called Everett, postponing our meeting, so we spent the evening watching silly sitcoms on TV. A couple of times I noticed a police car cruise by the house. *Marcus Gordon's doing,* I guessed. Sometimes he made it hard to dislike him.

I soaked for a long time in the bathtub and figured I'd be unconscious once my head hit the pillow, but I couldn't sleep. My shoulder ached. My wrist hurt and my mind wouldn't slow down, let alone shut off. Finally I eased out of bed, settled more or less comfortably in a chair by the window and opened my laptop.

And there it was. The e-mail from Phoebe Michaels with the photo of Gregor Easton's seminar class from Oberlin, on the grass outside a lecture hall. Phoebe had listed all the names in her e-mail, working clockwise around the circle.

I found the face right away. And another that surprised me. I had to check the names twice.

Maggie's scarf was over the arm of the chair. I ran my hand over the soft fabric, putting together the pieces of what I knew. Tab A into slot A. I knew the how. I was pretty sure I knew the why. And I knew the who. I knew who had killed Gregor Easton. And it wasn't Will Redfern.

24

Cross Hands

In the morning I called Susan and asked if she could open the library and take my morning shift. She already knew about my encounter with Will.

"You're really okay?" she asked.

"I really am."

"Good," she said. "Take your time coming in."

It was harder to convince Maggie to go home.

"I'm all right," I said, thinking how many times I'd said that in the last week. "Mags, Will is in jail for assault. There's a police car driving by every time I look out the window, and I have Owen and Hercules." I hugged her with my good arm. "And if it'll make you feel better I'll make more cinnamon rolls."

She left after we agreed she'd bring food from Eric's and we'd have supper before the special episode of *Gotta Dance*.

I sat at the table with my coffee, both cats at my feet. I told them what I'd figured out. They listened or at least pretended to. I thought maybe saying it out loud might make my reasoning fall apart. But it all still made sense.

I washed the dishes, and spent a lot of time fiddling with my hair. I was stalling.

I hesitated before I stepped into the porch, flashing back to seeing Will standing there. The cats were waiting by the door. I took a couple of deep breaths and a couple more. Hercules meowed at me. I was going to hyperventilate if I didn't stop with the deep breaths. I squared my shoulders and stepped into my gardening clogs.

"Let's go," I said, heading outside with Herc and Owen at my heels. Over in Rebecca's yard, Rebecca, Violet and Roma were sitting in the gazebo, having coffee. I started across the grass. It wasn't how I'd planned to do this, but maybe it would be better.

Rebecca caught sight of me and waved. Roma stood up. As I came up the gazebo steps she moved around the table to meet me.

"How's your arm?" she asked.

"Sore," I admitted. I knew she wouldn't believe me if I told her I was fine.

"May I?"

I held out my arm. I was wearing a long-sleeved cotton shirt. Roma pushed back the unbuttoned cuff and examined my bruised wrist. The swelling had gone down a little and the bruises now formed a pattern from where Will's fingers had been on my arm.

"What about the shoulder?" Roma said.

I made a face. "It's okay," I said. "It hurts, but I think it looks worse than it feels." I held up my other hand. "And, yes, I'm going to the clinic."

She smiled. "Good." She gestured to the table. "Sit down. Take my chair. I'll get another one."

"Thanks," I said.

"Roma, would you get Kathleen a cup from the kitchen, please?" Rebecca called after her.

"I will," Roma said.

Rebecca turned to me. "We heard about Will. Did he hurt you?"

"Just some bruises," I said. "I managed to hit him with . . . something, and then Harry showed up."

"I'm glad to see you're all right," Violet said. "Is it true Will wanted to scare you into leaving town?"

I nodded. "He was involved with the previous librarian."

"Ingrid?" Rebecca said.

"Yes. He wanted Ingrid to get her job back."

Violet took a sip from her coffee and set the cup on the table. "But she wasn't fired. She resigned."

"That didn't matter to Will. He thought if he could get me to leave, Everett would ask Ingrid to return to her old job."

"Ingrid's leaving for Canada—Montreal—at the end of the month," Violet said.

Roma returned with a chair for her and a cup for me. Rebecca reached across the table for the pot and poured me some coffee. "Maybe that's why Will was getting desperate," she said. "Ingrid is a very nice woman, but she's not the type to make a man—"

"—fall into the deep end?" Roma finished.

"Yes," Violet said.

"Love and loyalty will drive people to do things you'd never expect them to do," I said, wrapping my hands around my mug so the others wouldn't see them shaking.

"That's true," Rebecca agreed.

"That's why Gregor Easton died," I said.

Violet looked at me. "I beg your pardon, Kathleen?" she said.

"Love and loyalty. That's what killed Easton." I looked at Violet. "Your loyalty to Rebecca." I turned to look at the older woman. "And your love for Ami."

Rebecca folded her hands in her lap. "Yes," she said.

Roma and Violet both started to talk. Rebecca looked at both of them. "Stop," she said. "It's time to tell the truth." She seemed so calm. "How did you figure it out?"

I turned to Violet. "Gregor Easton was Douglas Gregory Williams," I said. "You were in his class at Oberlin."

She said nothing.

"I found a charm, a silver musical note, on the floor at the Stratton. It was yours."

"It may have been," she said.

"I thought it was a musical note hanging from a silver circle, but it was hanging from an O, for Oberlin."

"I did lose my note charm," she said. "Somewhere."

I continued as though she hadn't spoken. "The problem was the only person I could connect to Easton and Oberlin was Oren. I talked to Phoebe Michaels and there was no other connection. It seemed like a dead end. Then she said she thought she had a photo of the group. She sent a copy of it to me yesterday. Along with the names of everyone in the picture."

For the moment I focused all my attention on Violet. "I should have made the connection the first time Phoebe told me the names of the women in the class—maybe I would have, if I'd seen them written out. Your house is called Llŷn House. It's Welsh, just like your name."

A touch of a smile appeared on Violet's face. "Yes, it is. That's not exactly a secret."

"It's not exactly common knowledge, either," I said. "Violet is your middle name. Your first name is Gynwafar."

I pulled a folded piece of paper from my pocket and smoothed it flat on the table. "There you are," I said, pointing to a young and smiling Violet. She leaned forward to study the image.

"Were we ever that young?" she said softly.

I moved my finger one face to the right and turned to Rebecca. "And there you are. Gwyn's friend, Phoebe told me."

"Yes, that's me," Rebecca said.

"You met Easton when you were visiting Violet."

"He seemed so sophisticated, so charming," she said. "He wasn't."

"I know what he did," I said. "When you came home on Tuesday and found out that Easton was here—a last-minute replacement for Zinia Young—and that he'd been favoring Ami, you were afraid he'd take advantage of her somehow. The way he took advantage of you. I know how much you love her. You couldn't let that happen."

Rebecca was incredibly composed. "No, I couldn't," she agreed.

"You got Easton to meet you by pretending to be me. You overheard me tell Maggie what had happened at the library with Owen."

Rebecca put both hands on the edge of the table. "I'm so sorry about that. You're young and pretty. I knew in his arrogance he'd come for you. He'd never have shown up for an old lady."

Roma looked like she'd been hit in the head herself. "That's where you were coming from?" she whispered.

Rebecca nodded. "I'm sorry. I couldn't tell you the truth."

"How did you get into the building?" I asked.

"I'm on the library centennial committee," she said. "We have an office at city hall. Like all the committee members I have access to it. There's a set of keys there."

"Rebecca didn't do anything to that man," Violet said.

Rebecca smiled across the table at her best friend. "It's all right, Vi," she said. "I need to do this." She poured more coffee for herself and added a little to my cup.

"I knew what I had to do, so I got the key, and then I left the note at the hotel."

"No one saw you there. How did you manage that?"

"I'm an old woman," she said. "To young people we're just like furniture. One old lady looks like the next." She tipped her head back and studied Old Harry's handiwork above her head.

"He didn't remember me," she said. "I never forgot him, but I had to tell him who I was."

My hands were trembling just a little again. "He took pictures of you."

She looked at me then. "They'd mean nothing today. I wasn't naked, just bare shoulders and back, but in those days . . ."

I remembered what Phoebe Michaels had said. "Nice girls didn't pose for pictures like that."

"No matter how innocent the photographs were." Rebecca shook her head. "He said I was beautiful. And I was very foolish."

"What happened at the library?" I prompted.

"He laughed." She traced her finger around the rim of her cup.

"Easton was a pig," Violet said, and her face twisted for a moment with anger.

"He told me no one would care about some old photographs," Rebecca said. "He said I wanted to pose for him. He called me a tease." She looked directly at me.

"I'm not that naive girl from Mayville Heights anymore. I told him all I needed was a little suspicion that he was a dirty old man, not proof. I told him I was willing to bet there were other women out there he'd tricked into posing for him over the years, and worse. I said maybe someone else would speak up if I started." She rubbed her hand over her bandaged wrist.

"He came after you," I said. My shoulder was aching and I had to shift in the wooden chair. "That poultice isn't for arthritis, is it?"

"He grabbed my arm and his ring cut my wrist."

The other blood at the library.

"I pushed him and I ran," she said, her voice barely above a whisper. "I didn't know he'd hit his head."

"You met Roma somewhere on the way home."

"I was on my way up the hill. I'd had an emergency—a dog choking on a chicken bone," Roma said. "Ever give a German shepherd the Heimlich?"

"You wrapped Rebecca's wrist."

"Yes."

"Catnip, for its antiseptic properties." I folded my arm across my chest, sliding my hand under the cuff of my shirt.

"That's right. She's allergic to neomycin and I didn't want to take a chance with anything else."

"She didn't tell you how she got hurt."

Roma still looked a little lost. "She said she'd tripped on the sidewalk. She was embarrassed."

"You realized you'd dropped your scarf somewhere," I said to Rebecca.

"Yes, I did."

"You didn't find it because Violet had beaten you to it."

Violet smiled, but there was no warmth in it. I fished
in my pocket again and held out the bead from Rebecca's scarf. "This was at the library."

Rebecca took the glass ball from my hand and rolled
it between her fingers.

"Where was the scarf?" I asked Violet.

She shrugged but said nothing.

"You found Easton at the theater."

"Yes."

As usual she was calm and collected, her posture
perfect. I was surprised she'd admit to having been with
Easton.

"He'd always practiced late at night, so no one would
find out how much work it was for him to learn a new
piece. I knew he'd be there. A leopard doesn't change
its spots. I went to tell him to leave. Then I went home.
That's all."

My mouth was so dry. I took a sip of my now-cold coffee. "He didn't remember you, either, did he?" I asked.

She laughed. As with her smile, there was no trace
of warmth or humor in the sound. "No more than he
remembered Rebecca."

"He'd hit his head at the library when he grabbed
Rebecca and she pulled away. I'm guessing he lost his
balance and fell against the disassembled staging."

Violet gave an elegant shrug. "I don't really know
how he hit his head. He seemed fine."

Rebecca blanched. "I didn't mean to hurt him," she
said.

"You didn't," I said. "He grabbed you. You pushed
him away. You were protecting yourself. He was twice
your size."

"Kathleen's right," Roma said. "What happened isn't
your fault."

I turned back to Violet. "You cleaned up his head."

She nodded imperceptibly. "There's a first-aid kit backstage. I may have helped him a little."

"And you gave him aspirin."

She studied her nails for a moment. "He was complaining of a headache. He may have taken something."

"You gave him aspirin?" Roma said, clearly shocked. "He had a head injury. He was probably bleeding into his brain."

"Vi, what did you do?" Rebecca asked.

Violet smiled over the table at her. A genuine smile. "Only what I should have done a long time ago."

"I don't understand," Rebecca said.

"I knew who—what—Easton was the first day I walked into his class. I should have protected you from him. Instead I ruined your life."

Rebecca stood up and walked around the table to Violet's chair. "You didn't ruin my life. Why do you think that?"

"You went after Easton because of Ami," Violet said. She reached up and took Rebecca's hands in her own. "You love her as if she were your own granddaughter. If it hadn't been for him, for me, she would have been."

Tears filled Rebecca's eyes. "No, no, no, Violet," she said. "I lost Everett because I was afraid to tell him the truth. Because I didn't trust that he loved me as much as he said he did."

Rebecca and Everett?

She squeezed Violet's hands, then let go of them and turned to me. "Kathleen, I'm so sorry for getting you involved in this and then not speaking up. I hope you can forgive me."

"I can and I have," I said.

She paused, searching for just the right words. "I saw

those pictures, you know. Someone sent them in the mail. They weren't so terrible. I should have told Everett. I was scared that I wasn't good enough for him. My mother cleaned other people's houses. I thought that mattered."

"It didn't."

We all turned at the words. Everett was standing on the gazebo steps. His eyes were locked on Rebecca. I'd forgotten that Maggie had rescheduled our meeting for this morning.

"That man was the reason you ended things with me? Over a few pictures of your bare shoulder?"

"It was a long time ago," Rebecca said, blinking away her tears.

"And you risked everything to protect Ami."

"I'm all right," she said. "And I love Ami. For herself. I would do anything for her."

She swallowed and pulled the sleeve of her blouse down over her bandaged arm. "There's something I haven't told anyone," she said. "When I was away last week, it was really so I could see a doctor. A specialist."

Violet paled and pressed her lips together. Roma leaned forward in her chair.

"I was getting a second opinion. I have a growth on my leg. I was afraid . . . I thought maybe I wouldn't have another chance to stop Easton and protect Ami."

"I wouldn't let that happen," Everett said. The way he looked at her gave me a lump in my throat.

Rebecca turned her attention to Violet again. "Tell me you didn't do anything to that man," she said.

"I didn't do anything wrong, Rebecca," Violet said. "Things worked out the way they were supposed to."

I leaned over to Roma. "Do you have your cell phone?" I asked.

She nodded.

"Would you call Marcus and ask him to come out here?"

She hesitated.

"Call him, please, Roma," Rebecca said. "No more secrets." Her eyes never left Everett's face. It was like a scene from a romantic old movie.

Roma stood up, pulled out her cell and walked over to the railing. Behind me Violet got out of her chair and moved over to the far side of the gazebo, and I followed. Everett and Rebecca moved toward each other.

"You sent the pictures to Rebecca and to Phoebe Michaels," I said. "Rebecca was your best friend, the sister you never had. As for Phoebe, she'd been very sheltered. I think you felt sorry for her." Rebecca had told me Violet was deeply loyal to the people she cared about. I didn't think Rebecca realized how deep that loyalty ran.

I pictured Violet as a lonely only child, without parents as a young woman and widowed shortly after that. Rebecca was, in many ways, the only constant, the only family in her life. I'd do anything for Sara and Ethan. Was it so far-fetched for Violet to feel the same way about Rebecca?

"I guess there's no harm in telling you," she said. "Yes, I did."

"How did you get them?"

"I got them. Does it matter how?"

"I think you made it your business to find out where Williams—who had become Gregor Easton—had gone after he left Oberlin. I think you're a very patient woman. You waited months, maybe a year. You tracked him down and you seduced him." I was guessing, but her expression told me I was right.

It made my skin crawl to think about what a young

Violet had probably done to gain Easton's trust and swipe those photographs. "I think you let him take pictures of you, a lot more explicit than the ones he took of Rebecca and Phoebe, so you could win his confidence." I remembered the photos I'd seen at her house. "You were interested in photography, too." Their common interest had likely disarmed any suspicions Easton had about Violet.

Her shoulders stiffened and her chin went up slightly. Other than that there was nothing else to indicate my guess had been right. Still, I was certain it was.

"That's a fascinating story, Kathleen," she said. "But that's all it is."

I put both hands on the railing. "I think you did give Easton aspirin, and I think you did it deliberately."

"I already told you, he said he had a headache."

"And you gave him aspirin for that headache." I gripped the railing tightly. "Aspirin wouldn't have been in that first-aid kit. I'm guessing you had some in your purse. My mother takes a low-dose aspirin every day, and I bet you do, too."

"Lots of people my age take an aspirin a day," she said, evenly. "Maybe Mr. Easton did."

"How many did you give him?" I asked, turning to look at her then, keeping one hand on the railing.

"I'm not a doctor, Kathleen. I didn't give him anything. If he did take something for his headache, who's to say how many pills that might have been? He was a man given to excess." She continued to look out over the backyard.

"You didn't really tell him who you were, did you?" I said. "Otherwise he never would have trusted you."

"You don't think he should have trusted me, Kathleen?" she asked.

I rubbed my hand back and forth over the rough wooden railing. "I think you convinced Easton not to go to the hospital. You probably told him he didn't need a doctor and he'd look like a clumsy old fool. He was arrogant. It would have been easy to use that against him. I think you gave him aspirin and I think you stayed at the Stratton until he was unconscious. Once you knew it was too late to save him, you left. You took Rebecca's scarf from him, but your chain caught on something and the charm came off. Ironic that charm was the one that came off."

She turned to face me. "I can tell you've spent a lot of time with books, Kathleen," she said with the cool smile I'd seen before. "As I said, you've created a fascinating story. The only person who knows what happened is me."

She smoothed the front of her shirt. "Of course, I'll be happy to tell the police my story."

"You left a man to die," I said. "I don't care what he did. You left him there to die."

She took a step closer to me. "No, Kathleen. I didn't." Hate sharpened her voice. "Yes, I gave him aspirin. Yes, I convinced him not to go to the hospital. But I didn't leave him to die." Something in her face, in her smile, made my stomach clench. "I made sure he was dead before I left," she hissed.

She turned to look at Everett and Rebecca and her expression changed. She looked . . . pleased. "Look at them," she said.

My hands were shaking.

"See? The Big Bad Wolf is dead. And everyone's going to live happily ever after." She turned back to me. "I'm sorry, Kathleen. No one is going to believe your little story. I grew up here. I'm a respected member of the community. You've been here a few months. No one is going to believe you over me."

I reached into the pocket of my shirt with my shaking fingers and pulled out the tiny voice-activated digital recorder. "I think they will," I said.

25

Conclusion

Owen looked up from under the table, where he was chewing on a yellow catnip chicken.

I bent down to peek at him. "I don't want to come home and find that you're into the stinky crackers and watching *The Rocky Horror Picture Show*," I warned.

He rolled over and went back to chewing. Herc came in from the living room, sat at my feet and looked expectantly at me. I bent to scratch his head.

"I can't pick you up," I said. "I don't want to get cat hair on my dress."

He made an annoyed grumble and stalked into the porch.

I got my purse, locked up and headed for the Stratton and the last concert of the Wild Rose Summer Music Festival.

The concert was sold out. That was because composer, conductor and brilliant pianist Michel Demarque had stepped in as guest clinician.

I wasn't sure what she was talking about when Lita had called to thank me and pass on the festival committee's thanks to my mother—my mother—for convincing Demarque to step in. Baffled, I'd called Boston.

"You know Michel Demarque?" I'd asked.

"Yes," she'd said. "So do you."

"I do?"

"You remember Uncle Mickey."

I'd had to search my memory. Vermont. A Stephen Sondheim musical. A blond Hugh Jackman look-alike who slow danced with my mom while my father seethed with jealousy.

"Uncle Mickey is Michel Demarque?" I said.

"Yes."

"Oh. Well, thank you," I said. "You didn't have to do this."

"If it matters to you, Katydid, it matters to me," she said.

An usher showed me to my seat in the theater. Oren had finished working at the Stratton just days before the first performance. The building looked wonderful. At Everett's request Oren was supervising the rest of the library renovations.

I looked at the empty seat beside me. Where was Maggie? I spotted Everett and Rebecca on the other side of the theater. Rebecca hadn't been charged with anything connected to Gregor Easton's death. As a member of the centennial committee, she had a right to be in the library and she'd clearly been defending herself from Easton when he'd injured his head. No one believed she'd planned to hurt the man when she'd sent him the note asking him to meet her, even though she'd been pretending to be me. Violet, however, had been arrested. Everyone expected she'd take a deal to avoid a trial. It was clear she had some serious psychological problems, and I hoped she'd get the help she needed.

The overhead lights flashed—five minutes until the concert began. Where the heck was Maggie?

"Excuse me," a voice said from the aisle. I looked up to see Marcus Gordon standing there. He pointed to the empty seat. "I think that's my seat," he said.

I shook my head. "No, that's Maggie's seat," I said. "She'll be here any minute."

"No, I think it's mine," he said, holding out his ticket. He was right.

I stood up to let him pass. *I'm going to kill Maggie,* I decided. It wasn't enough that Matt Lauer had won the coveted *Gotta Dance* crystal trophy over the divine Kevin Sorbo; now she was trying to set me up with Marcus.

Yes, he looked very nice in an open-neck blue shirt and tan jacket. And he smelled yummy. But he wasn't my type. Not. At. All.

"How's your arm?" he whispered, bending his head close to mine.

When I'd finally gotten to the clinic, I'd discovered my wrist was broken. Now I had a cast from my fingers halfway to my elbow. "The cast comes off in a couple of weeks," I said. "And at least it doesn't hurt."

"I'm glad to hear it," he said.

He had a nice smile. Not that it made any difference to me. He wasn't my type. He didn't have a library card, I'd noticed. The man had never borrowed a single library book, as far as I could tell.

"Rumor has it you had a lot to do with the festival getting this conductor," he whispered in my ear as the lights went down.

"I really didn't do anything," I whispered back. Which was true. I hadn't.

"What other superpowers do you have?" he said

softly. I could see his grin, even in the dark. "Can you walk through walls or magically disappear?"

The curtain rose and Uncle Mickey lifted his baton. I looked at the detective, put my finger to my lips and just smiled.

ABOUT THE AUTHOR

Sofie Kelly is an author and mixed-media artist who lives on the East Coast with her husband and daughter. In her spare time she practices Wu-style tai chi and likes to prowl around thrift stores. And she admits to having a small crush on Matt Lauer.

Also Available

Leann Sweeney

The Cat, the Quilt and the Corpse
A Cats in Trouble Mystery

Jill's quiet life is shattered when her house is
broken into and her Abyssinian, Syrah, goes
missing. Jill's convinced her kitty's been
catnapped. But when her cat-crime-solving
leads her to a dead body, suddenly all paws
are pointing to Jill.

Soon, Jill discovers that Syrah isn't the only
purebred who's been stolen. Now she has to
find these furry felines before they all become
the prey of a cold-blooded killer—and she
gets nabbed for a crime she didn't commit.

**"A welcome new voice in
mystery fiction."** —Jeff Abbott,
bestselling author of *Collision*

Available from

Kate Carlisle

If Books Could Kill
A Bibliophile Mystery

Book restoration expert Brooklyn Wainwright is attending
the world-renowned Book Fair when her ex Kyle shows
up with a bombshell. He has an original copy of a
scandalous text that could change history—and
humiliate the beloved British monarchy.

When Kyle turns up dead, the police are convinced
Brooklyn is the culprit. But with an entire convention of
suspects, Brooklyn's conducting her own investigation to
find out if the motive for murder was a 200-year-old
secret—or something much more personal.

**Available wherever books are sold or
at penguin.com**